S0-AXJ-656

"CHESBRO HAS A COUP . . . A TOTALLY BELIEV-ABLE HERO AND A VIOLENT SUSPENSE STORY WITH A HUMANE PERSPECTIVE."

—*Booklist*

MONGO WALKS THE SHADY SIDE OF MANHAT-TAN'S STREETS TO INVESTIGATE THE DEATH OF ARCHITECT VICTOR RAFFERTY AND SUDDENLY MAKES A MACABRE TURN INTO THE DARKEST CORNERS OF THE HUMAN MIND. . . .

Shadow of a Broken Man

"A DELIGHTFUL HERO IN A GREAT SERIES OF SUSPENSE THRILLERS."

—*Playboy*

"CAN YOU MIX A DWARF, ESP, AND THE UNITED NATIONS AND COME UP WITH A SUCCESSFUL MYS-TERY NOVEL? GEORGE CHESBRO DOES. . . . THE RESULT IS NOT JUST GOOD—IT'S TERRIFIC!"

—Paul Erdman, author of
The Panic of '89

"MIXING THRILLER TACTICS WITH ESP AND CHURNING UP A STORM THAT INCLUDES A HEAVILY SADOMASOCHISTIC SCENE, CHESBRO ENTERTAINS."

—*Publishers Weekly*

The Mongo Mysteries

Shadow of a Broken Man
City of Whispering Stone
An Affair of Sorcerers
The Beasts of Valhalla
Two Songs This Archangel Sings

QUANTITY SALES

Most Dell Books are available at special quantity discounts when purchased in bulk by corporations, organizations, and special-interest groups. Custom imprinting or excerpting can also be done to fit special needs. For details write: Dell Publishing Co., Inc., 666 Fifth Avenue, New York, NY 10103. Attn.: Special Sales Dept.

INDIVIDUAL SALES

Are there any Dell Books you want but cannot find in your local stores? If so, you can order them directly from us. You can get any Dell book in print. Simply include the book's title, author, and ISBN number, if you have it, along with a check or money order (no cash can be accepted) for the full retail price plus $1.50 to cover shipping and handling. Mail to: Dell Readers Service, P.O. Box 5057, Des Plaines, IL 60017.

Shadow
of a
Broken Man

GEORGE C. CHESBRO

A DELL BOOK

Published by
Dell Publishing Co., Inc.
1 Dag Hammarskjold Plaza
New York, New York 10017

Copyright © 1977 by George C. Chesbro

All rights reserved. No part of this book may be reproduced or
transmitted in any form or by any means, electronic or mechani-
cal, including photocopying, recording, or by any information
storage and retrieval system, without the written permission of the
Publisher, except where permitted by law. For information address:
William Morris Agency, New York, New York.

Dell ® TM 681510, Dell Publishing Co., Inc.

ISBN: 0-440-17761-8

Reprinted by arrangement with the author

Printed in the United States of America

December 1987

10 9 8 7 6 5 4 3 2 1

KRI

For my parents,
George W. and Maxine Chesbro,
and for Ori

1

In another five minutes I'd have been gone. It was five fifteen on a Thursday afternoon at the end of the merry month of May; which meant I was tired of lectures, tired of grading papers, and especially tired of students. In addition to carrying a full teaching load, I'd spent the last three months on a case that hadn't turned out well; which meant too many bodies, a lot of filth, and a few innocent people whose lives had been permanently twisted out of shape. I was ready for a long vacation.

The man who clumped through the open door of my office was big and wore his muscles well. He obviously spent a lot of time out of doors; the sun had bleached his hair and seared a permanent tan into skin the color of cordovan leather. He was dressed in workman's clothes; laced boots, green cotton shirt and pants. Pencils, pens, and a piece of paper that looked like a business form stuck out of his shirt pocket. His blue artist's eyes, sensitive and quick-moving, belied his hayseed appearance; he looked like the kind of man you wouldn't mind buying a used car from. I put his age at around forty.

He glanced at the peeling nameplate on my desk, then at me. He did that twice; the implication seemed to be that I was sitting in someone else's chair.

"I'm looking for Dr. Robert Frederickson." His voice

was a rich, rumbling baritone that was used to giving orders in large, open places, probably over the roar and cough of heavy machinery.

I considered sending him over to the next building, then sneaking down the back stairs. Instead, I admitted to being Frederickson and asked what I could do for him. I expected him to turn around and walk out. Shadows, gray ripples of doubt and discomfort, suddenly appeared and moved just beneath the surface of his pale eyes. The shadows were familiar to me; I'd watched them cloud people's eyes all my life. Dwarfs who aren't safely ensconced in some circus sideshow tend to embarrass people.

He surprised me. "Frank Manning tells me you're a licensed private investigator."

"That's right."

"Frank also says you're good." His tone was distant, the sound of an afterthought.

I nodded my head in a halfhearted invitation to sit down, and he disappointed me by accepting it. Whatever he had on his mind, it looked as if he wanted to go with the dwarf sitting in front of him. I'd already decided that I was going to find a delicate way of brushing him off, as opposed to the blunter numbers in my repertoire. Frank Manning was Dean of the College of Architecture at the university. He also happened to be a good friend of mine; I didn't want to offend him by proxy.

"How can I help you, Mr.—?"

"Foster," he said, quickly leaning forward in his chair and extending his hand. The chair groaned. "Mike Foster. Sorry."

The hand I shook was matted with calluses. "I assume you want to hire a private investigator, Mr. Foster—"

"Mike."

"Okay, Mike. Why do you need a detective?"

He hesitated a moment. "I'd like you to investigate a man who's supposed to be dead."

"Sounds intriguing," I said in my most neutral tone of voice.

"Have you ever heard of Victor Rafferty?"

Indeed I had, and I was begining to see the connection with Frank Manning. Anyone who appreciated beauty in functional design had to be familiar with the work of Victor Rafferty. Rafferty had been as exceptional—and controversial—in his field as Picasso had been in his; like Picasso, Rafferty would have been at home talking shop with Michelangelo and Leonardo. His architectural genius was represented by structures in every major city of the world.

Rafferty had, in effect, died twice. About five years earlier, he'd been involved in an automobile accident that had killed all the occupants of the other car. It had taken three firemen half a day to pry Rafferty out of the crushed-metal puzzlework. He'd been pronounced dead at the scene, but someone had detected a sign of life just as they were about to plastic-bag him. They rushed him off to a hospital and he survived, thanks to what were modestly referred to as a series of medical miracles and a steel plate to replace the portion of his skull that had been pulverized.

The effort had been largely wasted. Five or six months later he'd fallen off a catwalk into an open smelting furnace in a metallurgical laboratory he maintained in New York City. That kind of dead is permanent, I told Foster.

The big man squirmed like a witness who's been tripped up on cross-examination. "You're very well informed."

"I'm a building freak," I said with a half-smile.

"Of course he couldn't have survived that," Foster said, swallowing hard. "But they never found any trace of his body."

"There wouldn't be any body to recover—not after it dropped into a vat of molten steel. Wasn't there someone who actually saw him go in?"

"The only witness was a watchman at the laboratory. It was a Sunday."

9

"What's your connection with Rafferty, Mike?"

His hands were resting on the edge of my desk. The giant fingers of the right hand found the fingers of the left, interlocked, and squeezed; a knuckle popped. I was glad I wasn't in the middle.

"I'm married to his widow," he said quietly. "I mean, I *hope* she was really a widow. Maybe I'm not so sure anymore."

I studied his face. Foster didn't look like the type to be jealous of a dead man, even if that man had been light-years ahead of him intellectually, and more than a few light-hours socially.

Foster seemed to be reading my thoughts; he reached into his back pocket and took out a thin, glossy magazine. I caught a glimpse of the title as he unfolded it: MODERN ARCHITECTURE. He flipped it open to a marked page and laid it on the desk in front of me. There was a full-page photograph of a building; on the facing page was the beginning of what looked like a long, scholarly article. It was an impressive building, simple yet amazingly complex to the practiced eye; it had a grandeur that, even on the flat page, thrilled and swept up the viewer.

The caption identified the building as the Nately Museum. The architectural credits went to a Richard Patern of the firm of Fielding, Fielding and Gross.

I glanced up and found Foster watching me, or looking through me; I wasn't sure which. "My wife hasn't been the same since she saw that picture," he said, tension creeping into his voice. "She's convinced it's Rafferty's."

"She thinks he built it?"

"She says he planned it. Elizabeth knows every line of that building; she told me all about it just from looking at the photo. I read the article and she's right. She says the building is Victor's."

"How can she be *that* sure?"

10

"Apparently he discussed it with her a number of times, showed her some of the preliminary sketches. That was seven or eight years ago."

"Maybe he showed the sketches to someone else."

Foster shook his head; a lock of hair fell across his eyes and he brushed it away impatiently. "Rafferty never discussed or showed his preliminary work to anyone, except Elizabeth. Of course he had his own firm and assistants, but when he was working on one of his own projects he never shared the idea until it was ready for final blueprinting. In fact, he kept all his papers in a locked file."

"Is that what your wife told you?"

"Yes, and it's what I know from my own experience."

"What experience is that?"

"I'm a builder. I knew Victor Rafferty casually. That's about as well as anyone knew him, except for Elizabeth." He paused and held out his hands; his veins sprang up and writhed like snakes trying to escape from their fleshy prison. "That's where my brains are. Rafferty liked my work and I was prime contractor on a number of his buildings. After his death Elizabeth became executrix of his estate, which meant she was supervising a lot of his unfinished projects. We met and . . . we fell in love." He suddenly, self-consciously, placed his hands in his lap. "The point is that I know there's no way Rafferty would have told anyone about that building until the final drafting was ready to be done, and Elizabeth says he never got beyond the preliminary sketches he showed her. All his personal effects like that were locked in a safe after his death. I checked, and they're still there."

"Well, maybe somebody else simply got the same idea."

Foster shook his head again. "That isn't likely," he said emphatically. "Other people just don't get Victor Rafferty's ideas. Still, according to Elizabeth, that museum is almost exactly the way Rafferty planned it."

I spoke slowly. "Do you think this Patern could be Rafferty?"

"I really don't know, but I strongly doubt it. I've never met Patern, but I've worked on a few of his buildings. Mostly shopping centers; nothing to compare with Rafferty's work—until this. Besides, I don't see how Rafferty, if he is alive, could operate under an assumed name. He's too famous. *Was* too famous," he added uncertainly. He fumbled in his pocket and came up with a snapshot which he shoved across the desk to me. "This is what he looked like."

I was reluctant to look at the photograph. I knew what Rafferty had looked like, and I didn't want Foster to assume I was going to take the case. But I picked up the photograph anyway.

It had been taken at a beach and was overexposed; Rafferty seemed to be floating in a puddle of light. He looked as if he wanted to be someplace else; his smile was forced and didn't touch the black, hawklike eyes that were his dominant feature. The widow's peak in his black hair was crested in the wind like the waves in the camera-frozen sea behind him. His body was thin and pale. The few black dots that were bathers in the surf behind him only made him seem more alone, trapped in an alien environment. I found the picture depressing.

"That picture was taken before the accident," Foster said. "Of course, he looked different afterward; pretty wasted."

"He looks pretty wasted here," I said, shoving the photograph back toward him.

"Rafferty was a very cerebral person. He lived in his mind, never took very good care of his body. Why don't you keep the picture?"

I left it in the no-man's land of the desk between us. Victor Rafferty wouldn't be the first man to fake a death in order to escape certain problems, such as a wife he didn't want. On the other hand, men who do such things don't usually have as much to give up as Rafferty had. "Can you think of any reason why Rafferty would *want* to operate under a false name, assuming he is alive?"

"I don't know," Foster said after a long pause.

It seemed to me that the question bothered him and he wasn't sure; I made a mental note to come back to the point. There was an aura about Foster suggesting that more than the Nately Museum was disturbing him; it wasn't *what* he said as much as the way he said it. Perhaps he was jealous of a dead man after all. "You're still left with a witness who claims he saw Rafferty fall into that open furnace."

"Yes," Foster said.

"Then what you're really interested in is the Nately Museum. Did Patern steal Rafferty's idea, and if so, how? Is that right?"

"Well, not exactly," Foster said haltingly. "I . . . think I'd like you to look into more than just that."

"You *think*?"

"I *know*," Foster said more forcefully.

"Like what?"

"I don't know for sure." Foster rocked nervously in his chair, then suddenly seemed to reach some kind of decision. He abruptly leaned forward, his massive hands bracketing Rafferty's picture as if to prevent the escape of some dark secret that might be lurking there.

"Rafferty's haunting our marriage in a way I don't understand," he continued. "I'm not jealous of his memory, if that's what you're thinking. Victor had more brains than I do, and he sure as hell was more famous. But I've got my own strengths, and I don't envy any man. I know Elizabeth loves me, and I don't ask for anything more. In fact, I don't think Victor and Elizabeth were happy together—at least, not in the last few years of their marriage. Victor was too *much* of a genius, if you know what I mean. He lived in his own world and didn't share much of it with anybody,

13

not even Elizabeth. Elizabeth's a red-blooded woman; she needed—needs—a whole man, a real man."

He paused, reddened. "I'm sorry. That was a stupid thing to say. I didn't mean it the way it sounded."

I wasn't sure whether he was apologizing to me or for me; it didn't make any difference. "I understand what you're saying," I replied evenly. "Go on."

"I'm sure there's something important concerning Victor that I don't know about. It's tearing Elizabeth apart; she tries to hide it, but she's been beside herself ever since she saw that photograph of the museum."

"Why don't you just ask your wife if there's something else bothering her?"

"Because I *know*. I know my wife. I *did* ask her and she denied there was anything; but just my asking upset her terribly. I never mentioned it again and she hasn't volunteered any information, but I'm convinced that something happened to Victor in the months between his car smashup and the accident in the foundry lab. Whatever it is, I think it's driving my wife out of her mind." He paused, continued more quietly: "Elizabeth's very nervous. She doesn't know I'm doing this, and one condition of your taking the case is that you don't talk to her about it."

"I haven't said I'd take the case, Mike."

He flushed. "I . . . I thought—"

"In one week I'm going to be sunning in Acapulco."

Foster looked at his hands as though they'd betrayed him. "Maybe you could recommend somebody to me." His voice had thickened with disappointment. "I made up my mind to look into this thing, and I'm going to do it; but I don't want to get taken by some smart-ass joker. I know finding a good private detective isn't as easy as they make it look in the movies."

I enjoyed my first good belly laugh in four months. "The only place you're likely to find a dwarf private detective is in real life, hiding in a university."

Foster smiled almost shyly. I seemed to have taken some kind of pressure off him. "Frank says you're a criminologist."

"True. You'd be amazed how limited the demand is for dwarf private detectives; I don't eat much, but I still have to eat."

"Now you're pulling my leg. I looked up some of your press clippings after Frank mentioned you. You're pretty famous yourself."

I grinned. "That's because I get weird cases, Mike."

That amused him. "Frank also says you're a circus star."

"*Former* circus star," I corrected him. A wink. "I gave up the circus; too common for a dwarf."

Foster waited until he was sure there was a joke to get, then laughed. The laugh quickly turned sour, and he dropped his eyes. "I've known Manning for a few years. He's not like a lot of these ivory-tower architects who don't know a nut from a bolt and couldn't care less. Anyway, when he recommended you I thought I was really in luck."

It suddenly occurred to me that I had received my Ph.D. and left the circus at about the same time that Rafferty was—maybe—getting himself killed for the second time. Maybe it was some kind of omen.

In honor of omens, I gave it some thought. The background checking Foster wanted could boil down to nothing more than a lot of reading: if not in bed, then in a cool, secluded library. Considering the length of my legs, I could always use a little extra walking-around money in Acapulco.

"Let's see what I can come up with in a week, if anything," I said. "That's it if you want me. If I think it's worth more digging, I'll turn it over to somebody else. Or I can give you a name now. It's up to you. My rate is a hundred ten a day, plus expenses."

"That seems pretty steep," Foster said.

In fact, it was fifteen dollars cheaper than my usual rate, and twenty-five cheaper than he'd pay for a big agency.

He was getting my friend-of-a-friend rate. But I didn't say anything. I'd begun to regret the offer almost as soon as I'd made it; I really didn't feel like working.

Foster made his decision. "You'll agree not to talk to my wife?"

"As long as I'm working under the other conditions I outlined."

He nodded, fumbled in his pockets. "I'm sorry. I thought I'd brought my checkbook along. I guess I didn't."

"Well, you send me a check for one day's pay as a retainer. While you're at it, you might send along a good snapshot of Rafferty, taken *after* the accident."

"Will do. Thanks, Frederickson."

"Don't thank me yet. Has it occurred to you that you could discover some things you don't really want to know?"

He thought about it, shook his head. "I want to save my marriage. I don't believe the truth ever hurt anybody who didn't deserve to get hurt."

I suppressed the temptation to tell him how wrong he was. "You must have asked Frank Manning about the building. What did he say?"

"He didn't say anything. He told me it was professional ethics not to comment on another man's work."

2

Dr. Franklin Manning kept professor's hours—highly erratic. I was lucky: it was after six, but I found the tall, gawky-limbed man in his loft-sized office, playing in his sandbox. He would stack a series of multicolored blocks into different configurations, study each for a few moments, then knock down the blocks and start over again. Great buildings rose and fell before my eyes.

Well past seventy, Manning was still Professor of Design, a world authority on all aspects of architecture—far too valuable for the university to retire. He loved blue suits; they were all he owned. For all his brilliance and knowledge of color, he could never quite seem to find ties that matched.

I asked him whether he thought Victor Rafferty had designed the Nately Museum.

"I don't think I want to comment on that, Mongo," he said after a long pause.

"C'mon, Frank," I prodded with a grin. "The least you can do after sending some business my way is to answer a few questions."

"I'm an old man, Mongo, with an old man's distaste for lawsuits. Some people consider me an expert on these matters; I could say something that someone else might take serious exception to."

"There's not going to be any lawsuit here, Frank; at least, none revolving around any conversation we have. I'd like to hear what you have to say strictly for my own information. I understand it's only an opinion about something nobody can be sure of."

"The Nately Museum is Victor Rafferty's work," he said drily.

The absolute certainty in his voice took me completely by surprise. "Have you seen Rafferty's sketches?"

"What sketches?" he asked absently.

"Foster's wife told him Rafferty made preliminary drawings of a building like the Nately Museum."

He destroyed a monument, started to build another. "Nobody ever saw Victor Rafferty's sketches, not until after the building was already up. He'd even prepare the major portions of the blueprints himself. He had to; most of the time it was the only way he could make the builders see how the structure was actually going to be put together."

"Then how can you be so damn sure, Frank?"

"I don't need a sketch with Rafferty's name on it to know that the Nately Museum is basically his work." He spoke slowly as he put an oblong blue block on top of a square red one, then stood back to study the effect. "The building has Rafferty's stylistic fingerprints all over it. The Nately Museum is a Victor Rafferty creation inasmuch as it is a Rafferty *concept*; it has his signature. There are a thousand details in the building that lead me to that conclusion. If you had a week, I'd go over all of them with you."

"How long did it take to build the museum?"

He thought for a few moments. "About a year and a half." He paused, then added: "Word got around fast that something special was going up. The building has won just about every major architectural award."

"Frank, do you think Rafferty's alive?"

18

He looked at me as if I was a very slow student who had accidentally stumbled into a graduate course and would have to be gently eased out. "Rafferty's dead, Mongo. Died in . . . '69, I think." His eyes went out of focus for a moment as he looked at a memory. "Yes. It was August of '69. I attended the funeral."

"Is there *any* possibility that Patern could be Victor Rafferty?"

"Not the slightest." His tone was emphatic. "I knew Rafferty, and I know Patern. Richard was one of my students." There was a curious note of disapproval, even scorn, in his voice.

"You don't like Patern?"

His silver eyebrows arched. "Now, Mongo, I never said any such thing. Richard is a gifted, brilliant architect. He's also, well . . . *abrasive*. He can be grating at times."

"The point is that you don't think Patern could have come up with a building like that on his own, if I'm reading you right."

"Anything's possible," he said evasively. "It's *possible* that the idea for the Nately Museum originated with Richard. In *my* opinion, the structure is a Victor Rafferty concept."

"Then Patern must have stolen the idea somehow."

Frank put up his hands as if to ward off an impending attack. "*Whoa*, my friend. I don't want to slander anyone. I said that Richard was an aggressive, ambitious young man; I didn't say he was a thief. As far as I know, he's completely honest—and proud. He wouldn't have to steal another man's ideas."

"But the fact remains that he's now the shining star of his architectural firm."

"Sure," Frank said easily. "The Nately Museum is a beautiful building."

"With a design that you believe came from a dead man. How can that be unless Patern stole the idea?"

"You're the detective, Mongo." He shrugged. "I'm sorry if what I have to say seems contradictory."

It was getting pretty tedious marching around in verbal circles; I decided to try a new tack. "You've told me something about Patern. What about Rafferty?"

"A man apart," he said slowly, as if choosing each word with great care. "I knew him quite well; and yet I didn't know him; I'm not sure anybody did." He breathed deeply and flashed a broad grin. "I trust that's sufficiently confusing. He was a giant; like many giants, he was inaccessible."

"You must be able to tell me something else about him."

Frank shrugged again and thrust his hands into his pockets. "As an architect he was without peer. As a person, well, that's something else again. He would occasionally come to see me to discuss some professional matters. . . ." He paused, chuckled. "We'd usually end up here, at this table. We'd play like boys for hours, challenging each other to come up with new designs and concepts. Rafferty was good to be with at those times. But I'm rambling." He took one hand out of his pocket and rubbed the bridge of his nose. "Victor had an incredible ability to concentrate, to filter out all distractions. But he could be extremely impatient—even cruel—if he felt his time was being wasted. You see, he simply didn't *care* about most other aspects of living. I'm sure his health was atrocious even before the accident. *Horrible* diet; he had an absolute passion for those cheap fast-food-chain hamburgers."

"How'd he get along with his wife, Frank?"

He made a gesture of distaste. "I don't know anything about Rafferty's personal life, Mongo. I only met his wife once or twice at some official functions. As you know, she's married to Mike Foster now. Seems like a nice woman." His gaze shifted slightly. "I'm not sure any normal woman could have been happy married to Victor; he was married to his work, and totally independent."

"Did he work after his first accident?"

20

"Not as far as I know. He was too weak from a series of operations. Most of his time was spent recuperating."

"What about Mike Foster?" I asked. "How do you know *him*?"

"As a matter of fact, he was introduced to me by Rafferty, who considered Mike one of the best contractors around. I use Mike for an annual lecture to first-year design students. Very successfully, I might add. He serves to remind the dreamers that there are men who actually have to *build* the structures they think up."

I thanked Frank and said I'd find my own way to the door. By the time I reached it he was already absorbed in his acrylic towers in the sandbox.

The obvious thing to do, of course, was to celebrate the imminent end of school. But I'd already done that; three times, beginning in March. Besides, I didn't feel right; the case didn't feel right. I couldn't forget the quiet desperation in Foster's voice. I went home and found a fly struggling in a pool of water in the bottom of the sink. Feeling like an absolute idiot, I gently lifted the fly out of the water and put it on the sink counter to dry. It died anyway. I kept thinking about omens.

That night I slept badly. I finally gave up the struggle with my subconscious and waited for dawn with the latest Ross Macdonald caper; Lew Archer was still tracking lost children—masterfully, propelled by words that shone as bright and hard as diamonds and left a warm glow in the mind.

I finished the book and went down to my favorite diner for a big breakfast. The *Times* and the crossword took me to nine. I walked to Park and Fifty-ninth, where Patern's architectural firm was headquartered.

Richard Patern's sudden success had earned him a large suite of offices deep in the inner sanctum of Fielding, Fielding and Gross. The blonde with the hard green eyes and

Mary Quant makeup who sat at the desk in the walnut-and-chrome outer office was there to protect the young genius from distractions like dwarf private detectives.

She listened to my story about being the representative of an eccentric billionaire who wanted to erect a circus monument. Either too amused or too much of a lady to call me a liar, she penciled me in for a four-o'clock appointment.

It was a nice day, and I kept walking—this time to the Forty-second Street library, where I settled down in the periodical reference room with a smuggled container of coffee. With a person as famous as Rafferty, I figured the logical place to begin was at the end. His obituary, in *New York Times* small print, was a page and a half long. I paid special attention to the report on his death; it gave the name and address of the watchman who had supposedly seen Rafferty fall into the furnace at the metallurgical lab. According to the report, Rafferty's wife had refused to talk with newsmen. I wondered why. A desire to grieve in privacy? Or fear?

I studied the photos of the woman who was now Mike Foster's wife. The difference in the appearance of the woman in the photographs taken before and after Rafferty's death was striking. In the earlier photos she was beautiful, carefree, conscious of the camera and seemingly not at all averse to the attention her husband abhorred.

All that had changed in the later photos. She looked—to use Foster's expression—haunted. There were dark rings under her eyes and a wild, almost desperate, air that had transformed her vibrant beauty into something plastic and hollow. It struck me that there seemed to be far more fear than grief in the stiff mask of her face.

There was an accompanying, detailed report on Rafferty's first "death." The car accident had made headlines; Rafferty's recovery made even bigger ones. It was apparently considered by medical men to be the most amazing medical

22

rally since Lazarus, and most of the credit went to a New York–based neurosurgeon named Arthur Morton.

Morton's picture showed a large, thick-bodied man who might have been a decent athlete fifty pounds before. He was standing in front of a wall papered with framed diplomas, looking extremely pleased with himself.

An intriguing aside near the end of the article mentioned Morton's death. I checked the appropriate cross-index and came up with his obituary.

I skipped the Grosse Pointe and Harvard Medical School background. There were two things about the account of his death that immediately caught my attention. The report said that Morton had been murdered in his Park Avenue office by an intruder—at approximately three-thirty in the morning, a decidedly unlikely hour for a Park Avenue physician to be in his office. I also found it curious that Arthur Morton had been killed less than two weeks before Victor Rafferty's final, presumably fatal, accident.

The fact that the two men who had been paired to produce one of history's greatest medical miracles had died violent deaths a few days apart seemed like an interesting coincidence.

Scanning through succeeding issues, I couldn't find any mention of the murderer's being caught, but I noted down some of the details in my pocket notebook. Next I started checking through all the issues of the *Times* published in the six months between Rafferty's car accident and his death —a laborious task made easier by the library's microfilm records. I had no idea what I was looking for, but the added fact of Arthur Morton's murder made me curious enough to make the effort.

Aside from the series of follow-up reports on Rafferty's recovery, there wasn't much about him up until the time of the final accident—except for one item that I almost missed and that then seemed to leap out from the page.

It was a photograph, and the only caption was a large

question mark. A short paragraph below noted that the picture had been taken outside Victor Rafferty's home, but that reporters had been kept behind police lines and forbidden to question any of the men present.

When I magnified the photo under the viewer, I could make out two men lying on a flagstone walk leading up to a large Tudor house. One of the men was trying to rise, a hand to his head, and seemed to be in pain. The other lay in the kind of final, splay-limbed position I'd come to associate with death.

Rafferty's wife was standing just outside the house, almost hidden in the shadows of the huge willows that dotted the lawn. Her hand was clamped over her mouth, and in the silence of the library I imagined I could almost hear her screaming.

There were four men standing around the two who had fallen. Three of the four had the burly, no-nonsense look of plainclothes detectives or government agents. The fourth man was of a different breed. The picture had been taken with a telephoto lens and was slightly blurred under magnification, but I could see that the man's head was completely bald. He seemed to be in charge of whatever was going on, because his face was pointed toward the camera and he was gesturing angrily in the direction of the photographer.

The heavyset men were dressed in light, sweat-stained summer suits; Mrs. Rafferty wore a sleeveless frock; the bald-headed man was wearing what appeared to be a heavy winter overcoat, complete with fur collar. I frowned and rechecked the dateline in the newspaper; it read Friday, August 15: two days before the accident in the metallurgy lab. I photocopied the picture and left the library.

I still had some time to kill before my appointment with Patern, so on a hunch I went back uptown to my university office. There was an envelope from Mike Foster that had been delivered by messenger. Inside was a check for an unexpected five hundred dollars that brought visions of sunny Acapulco beaches to my mind. The accompanying head-and-shoulders shot of Victor Rafferty, taken after the accident, brought the temperature back down; it showed, in good detail, that the right side of his skull had been shaved, as if for an operation. A thin, furry matting of hair was just beginning to grow in over an ugly, puckered mass of scar tissue; a network of scars ran like rivers of ugliness down the right side of his face, over the area of his temple, through his eyebrow, and down his right cheek. The unscarred flesh on his high forehead looked almost transparent, like cheap tissue paper. His thin lips seemed locked in a painful grimace. The black, sensitive eyes were very bright, almost feverish. There was a brooding quality about the face; the torment in those smoldering eyes seemed fueled by more than just physical pain.

I let the photograph slip from my fingers onto the top of my desk, as though the fire in those eyes might burn me. Then I hurried back out into the day.

3

It was time for my meeting with Richard Patern, and I wasn't looking forward to it; I'd lied to get the appointment, and I was hard-pressed to think of a reason why Patern should want to talk to me once he discovered my real interests. I made it a point to be on time.

After a swift, whining ride in a Muzak-filled elevator, I found myself in familiar territory at the main reception desk of Fielding, Fielding and Gross. I was somewhat surprised when the receptionist waved me on into the interior network of corridors, and even more surprised to find a man I assumed was the resident genius waiting for me outside his office in his shirt sleeves. He grinned when he saw his secretary staring at me as if I had no clothes on.

Richard Patern was a man in his early thirties who projected the image of an athlete-scholar. He'd kept in shape, and was obviously proud of his body; he had broad shoulders, a trim waist, and the tight, somewhat awkward gait of a former football player or wrestler. His deep tan nicely complemented bright, intelligent hazel eyes. To round off the image, he wore a twenty-five-dollar razor haircut and a two-hundred-fifty-dollar Brooks Brothers suit. He looked good and he knew it.

Patern stepped forward and extended a tapered, sinewy

hand. "Mongo the Magnificent," he intoned like an announcer. I shook his hand. Gripping me firmly by the elbow, he presented me to his secretary, who was still staring at me wide-eyed. "This is one of the greatest circus performers of all time. Incredible gymnast and tumbler; absolutely able to defy gravity."

"So you told me," the woman said breathily. Her green eyes blinked like traffic lights. "Hello again, Dr. Frederickson."

Patern ushered me into an office decorated in browns and golds, with vast areas of tinted glass that afforded a dizzying view of Manhattan. Outside, a helicopter flapped silently toward its aerie somewhere along the East River.

The walls of the office that weren't glass were decorated exclusively with antique, lacquered circus posters which looked very old and valuable. Frank Manning, preoccupied with his sandbox, had neglected to mention the fact that Patern was a circus buff. It could make things difficult.

"Would you like some coffee, Dr. Frederickson?"

I nodded. Patern buzzed his secretary, who appeared within seconds with cups and a pot of coffee on a tray.

"Let's see," Patern said, stirring his coffee. His gaze slowly rose to the ceiling, then snapped back to my face as his memory circuits revved up. "You were a headliner with the Statler Brothers Circus. Genius I.Q.; used your time and money to study for a Ph.D. in criminology. You retired from the circus, and you work uptown at the university." He paused, apparently inviting me to respond. I declined with a smile. He asked, "Do you know Frank Manning?"

"I do," I said a little stiffly. "Frank" Manning sounded a little strained and familiar coming from Patern. I indicated his office with a sweep of my hand, tried to keep my voice neutral. "You've come a long way in a short time, Mr. Patern."

He didn't seem to hear me. "Let's see," he said distantly,

"I think I saw a piece on you in *Newsweek* . . . something about you also being a private detective. Is that right?"

I nodded, beginning to feel uncomfortable.

"Well, I'm really delighted to meet you," he said with apparent sincerity. "My secretary tells me you want to talk to me about a building."

"A particular building, Mr. Patern. I'd like to ask you some questions about the Nately Museum."

His smile remained, but the hazel eyes above it grew hard and cold. "That sounds like detective talk, not client talk."

"It *is* detective talk." With my personal dossier in Patern's head, there didn't seem much point in trying to maintain the potential-client masquerade. "I'd appreciate your giving me some information."

He gave it some thought, then said, "I don't mean to be rude, but I just can't see why the Nately Museum should concern a private detective."

"Why don't you let me be the judge of that? You may be doing yourself a favor in the long run. There are some people who don't believe the idea for the museum was yours."

"What people?" he snapped.

"I'm told there's a similarity between the Nately Museum and some of Victor Rafferty's work. The people who mention it definitely don't mean it as a compliment to you."

A look of genuine surprise and concern swept over his face. "What's this Rafferty business?" he said impatiently. "Rafferty's been dead four, five years."

Something in the architect's voice suggested that I hadn't been the first to make the comparison to his face. I asked him about it, and he made a quick, nervous gesture with his hands.

"A guy at the dedication ceremony mentioned it," he said tightly.

"Do you remember the man's name?"

Patern absently rubbed a knuckle in one eye while he thought about it, then shook his head. "No. I remember he was well dressed, had a full beard, and walked with a limp. Look, is this really important?"

It struck me that it was to him; otherwise he'd already have asked me to leave. "It could be, Mr. Patern. Is there anything else you remember about this man?"

"I think he had two first names. I mean, his last name was a first name. He wanted to know where I got the idea for the museum. I told him I thought it was a stupid question."

"*I* don't want to sound stupid," I said, clearing my throat, "but where *did* you get the idea for the museum?"

"It sounds like somebody may be preparing a legal action against me," he said tightly. "Accusing me of stealing somebody else's idea is a ridiculous charge, and it's ridiculous for you to expect me to help somebody who might be out to embarrass me."

"Nobody's trying to embarrass you. My investigation doesn't involve a lawsuit."

He studied me intently for a few moments; when he spoke, it was very softly. "Then you won't mind telling me who hired you."

"I can't tell you that, Mr. Patern."

He smiled crookedly. "You mean you won't."

I didn't say anything, and his voice suddenly turned ugly. "You're helping somebody poke their nose in my business. You want me to give you information, and you won't even tell me who wants it, and why. You can get out, Frederickson."

I could see his point, but held my ground. "What is it that you have to hide, Mr. Patern?"

He half-rose out of his chair, then slowly sat down again. When he spoke his voice was controlled, but a blue vein throbbed in his forehead. "I don't have anything to hide, and I find it insulting for you to imply that I do. Look, I don't *need* to copy another man's work; I'm too good an architect. Besides, I have my preliminary sketches to prove that the Nately Museum is my work."

"It's not your sketches I'm interested in; it's the basic concept for the museum. Where did that come from?"

He hesitated for only a split second, but it was enough to convince me I was onto something. "That's none of your business," he said with controlled anger.

I tried pushing another button to open a door and reveal what had been hidden behind the hesitation. "What about the 'Rafferty angles' in the building?"

"You'll find 'Rafferty angles' in any one of hundreds of buildings constructed in the past fifteen years," he said easily. He seemed comfortable with the question. "They're the only means you can use to get that special lighter-than-air effect. They're no secret."

"I don't know about that, Mr. Patern," I said, watching his face. "I do know this: the design for the building that became the Nately Museum was one of Victor Rafferty's pet projects, right down to the last line."

His eyes clouded. "How do you know that?"

"You'll just have to take my word for it. Now, would you like to tell me about the Nately Museum?"

"My God," he whispered. He blinked rapidly and turned his face away. "I . . . don't understand. It never occurred to me that I might be stealing someone else's idea."

"I believe you, Mr. Patern. You could help your case by telling me how that building came about."

"I don't know where the idea came from," he said quietly, after a long pause. "More precisely, I don't know *who* it came from." He shook his head and leaned forward in his chair; it brought him back into the room with me. "I saw a sketch; a very rough pencil drawing."

"Do you have this sketch?" I asked quickly.

"No. It wasn't something that you'd keep. Here—"

He took a pencil and scratch pad out of his desk and

quickly drew some lines. It was a crude drawing of a building that could be recognized as the Nately Museum. It was difficult to see how such a simple sketch could have been transformed into a structure that, according to Foster, was a virtual line-by-line replica of Rafferty's project.

"This is all there was?"

He nodded. "It's close. It was only a scrap of paper, but it just seemed to open up so many possibilities ... like watching a paper airplane soar can lead to the development of a new type of wing. I don't call that stealing."

Neither did I, assuming Patern was telling the truth. "What about all the details in the building?"

He shrugged helplessly, as though he despaired of making me understand. "I studied Rafferty's work for years, like thousands of other architectural students. After a time, I suppose, you begin to absorb certain principles of style and design. The design for that building, even in the sketch that I showed you, is so *organic* that one thing necessarily leads to the next. Once you understand the concept, it almost completes itself."

"Did you mention this to the man with the beard?"

"No. I was busy, flying high. We didn't have what you'd call a conversation. To me, he was just a stranger."

"Where did you find this drawing?"

"I was taking part in a two-day seminar at the U.N. on housing problems in underdeveloped countries. I remember coming ... into a room for a meeting. I was early. Another session had just finished when I sat down and found this paper in front of me."

"Was it the only paper on the table?" I asked quietly. I sensed that remembering—and telling me—the story had cost him something.

He sighed. "No. The room was a mess; there was a tight schedule between sessions and the janitorial staff only had a few minutes to clean up. Anyway, that drawing was like a Rorschach blot; I sat there staring at it, and all of a sudden

I knew what the whole building would look like. At the time I just chalked it up to my fertile imagination. Now I can see—"

"When did this seminar take place, Mr. Patern?" My question brought him back to the present.

"A couple of years ago; in the fall, I think. Once I had the idea, the planning and construction went very quickly."

I believed him: Patern's description of the creative process roughly jibed with the stories I'd heard other artists tell. My concern had shifted to the identity of the person who had left the paper behind. "Do you have any idea who was at the meeting just before yours?"

"God, there were probably more than a couple of hundred people there. Rolfe Thaag was speaking, and you know how *he* attracts a crowd. I have a program in my files somewhere. If you'd like, I'll give you a copy."

"I'd like," I answered wryly.

Patern rummaged around in a filing cabinet and emerged with an official-looking program, which he took out for his secretary to copy.

"Incidentally," he said as he came back into the office, "I did ask around afterward to see who might have left that sketch there. Nobody claimed it."

I wasn't surprised. "Rafferty's obituary mentioned that he did a lot of work for the U.N.," I said.

Patern nodded as his secretary came back into the office with two copies of the program. The names of the participants were listed on the last three pages, in small print; it would take me years to check out every person on the list. By now, they'd be scattered all over the globe. I thanked Patern for his time, pocketed the program copies, and rose to leave.

"The sketch," Patern said, his voice strained. "Do you think Victor Rafferty made it?"

"*Somebody* made it." I had an urge to leave him with something. "But the building is yours. Don't worry about it. I doubt there are more than five architects in the world who could have accomplished what you did from only that sketch."

He smiled and leaned back in his chair like a man whose troubles were over. I had the feeling mine were just beginning.

4

It was time to shake the local branch of the family tree and
see what might fall out. I caught a cab, which wallowed
slowly crosstown through the rush-hour traffic. As I sat in
the nearly motionless cab, somewhat out of joint from my
talk with Patern, my own past suddenly reared up from
behind an idle thought and leered at me.

The time I'd spent with the circus had been nightmare
years, notwithstanding the fact that the man who was my
boss is one of the finest human beings in the world. Phil
Statler had saved my life by helping me up off a series of
psychiatrists' couches where I'd been trying to discover just
what the hell I was supposed to do in a world of giants.

Born into a perfectly normal Nebraska family, I was
the product of a pairing of recessive genes. Nature had
compounded her bad joke by endowing me with a fairly
well-muscled intellect, and considerable gymnastic skills
which I'd parlayed into a black belt in karate. By the time
I reached my early twenties, I was in the circus and earning
a living. It was Phil Statler who'd discovered the control I
had over my body, and who'd groomed me into a headliner,
away from the clowns and freaks. The man had given me
dignity.

But simple dignity hadn't been enough. Perhaps because

I was a physical deviate, I was drawn to the problems of other kinds of deviates. I earned a B.S. in sociology, then used my money and time off from the circus to finance my doctorate in criminology. Somewhat to my surprise, I'd been offered a teaching position at the university. There was probably a certain irony in my choice of New York City as a base of operations; my brother, Garth, was a detective on the New York City police force. All disgustingly normal six feet of him.

Garth always maintained that I had a tendency to over-compensate; that was how he explained my private investigator's license. I'd lucked out more than a few times in my life. I wasn't rich, as they say, but I was reasonably happy.

I caught Garth just as he was leaving the station house. He was almost an exact replica of our father: big, rawboned, a wheat-colored thatch of hair atop a head that despite his considerable size seemed too big for the rest of his body. After all his tough years in a city of cold stone, steel, and glass, he still walked with the ambling gait of a farmer. I loved the man; he'd carried me on his broad shoulders through a tortured childhood brimming with jeers and cruel jokes.

Despite his bellowing protests, I managed to maneuver Garth back into the tiny broom closet he called an office. There were dark rings under his blue eyes. Garth always looked tired; maybe it had something to do with being an honest cop who felt a personal responsibility toward eight million people.

"Hello, brother." I flashed my largest grin.

"Don't give me that 'brother' crap, brother," he growled. "You always say that when you want something."

"One reason you're such a good cop is your uncanny perceptiveness."

Garth grunted. "Perceptive? I read you like a book; make that a cheap pulp thriller."

"Tut-tut. Compliments won't get you anywhere. I *would* like to find out a few things."

"This isn't the public library, Mongo. You're a private snoop; you can't just walk in off the street and pump me for information"—he allowed himself a thin smile—"like you always do."

"Now, don't get righteous on me. A retired cop working private could come in here anytime and get information."

"You're not retired, and you're not a cop."

"I'm a colleague, and I'm your *brother*." I tried to put a little whine in my voice; that usually got to him.

He wasn't moved. "I'm hungry, and it's my dinner hour."

"You've grown callous, Garth. I'll buy you whiskey sours and a steak. Consider that an official bribe."

"What the hell do you want, Mongo?" Garth asked wearily.

"Well, now that you mention it, I would like to see the file on—"

Garth shook his head determinedly. "Uh-uh. You know I can't actually let you look at any files."

"Then you look for me. See what you've got on the murder of a Dr. Arthur Morton. It would be early August, about five years ago, so you may get your uniform a little dusty."

"Morton ask you to find his killer?" The question was a typical way of his asking what my concern in the matter was.

I filled him in on Victor Rafferty and Arthur Morton's relationship to him, emphasizing the fact that both had died violent deaths a few days apart.

Garth frowned. "You think there may be some connection between the deaths?"

"Can't say, but I do think it's worth a little digging. Somebody else apparently got hurt in connection with Rafferty, and it upset some important people." I showed him

36

the Xeroxed copy of the photo taken outside Rafferty's home.

Garth studied it. "They do look important."

"And they had the juice to keep everybody away from whatever was happening. That's Rafferty's house. Quite a gathering, huh?"

"Which one is Rafferty?"

"He's not there," I said. "That picture was taken two days before his dive into the furnace. I'd like to find out where he was, and what those men were doing at his house."

"Who's the creep in the winter coat?"

"Beats me. I'm just playing a hunch that there could be a tie-in with Morton's death. Morton was killed in his office—at three-thirty in the morning. What the hell was he doing in his office at that hour? And who would bother to break into a neurosurgeon's office in the first place? No money, and damn little chance of finding any narcotics. Now, isn't that enough to make a cop's nose twitch?"

"I'll pull the file," Garth said seriously.

"When?"

"First thing in the morning," he said, starting to rise. "Right now I'm going to take you up on that bribe offer."

"Rain check, brother," I said. "I'm in a big hurry on this one. I plan to be in Acapulco on Thursday, and I want to earn as much of my client's money as I can before I leave."

"You're going to roil the waters and then swim away? That doesn't sound like you."

"I'm hoping there won't be a week's worth of mud. If there is—well, I need a rest and my colleagues need the work."

"There goes the last of my illusions; I thought you were indestructible."

"What time can I get to you tomorrow, Garth?"

He considered it, then said: "Make it ten. And bring black coffee."

Now I needed a phone directory. I stopped in a bar around the corner from the station house and ordered a corned beef on rye and a beer, which I took into one of the phone booths in the rear.

Harold Q. Barnes was the name of the watchman who'd seen Rafferty fall off the catwalk. But there was only one Harold Q. Barnes listed, and his name was in large, black type in front of the words FILM COMPANY. The address was near Washington Square. I finished my corned beef sandwich in the cab.

Harry Barnes's combination house–movie studio was a converted brownstone in a fashionable district where the remodeling costs alone started at around a hundred thousand dollars. The place was all glitter on the outside and blue funk on the inside; Harry Barnes made dirty movies.

A young, very gay male let me in the door, examined me with an air of jaded disbelief, then motioned me over to where a crowd of actors and actresses were waiting, shuffling their feet. Nobody else paid any particular attention to me. These people had their own problems; the room smelled of sour hope and anxiety.

I recognized a casting "cattle call" when I saw one. The men and women were waiting in line for parts in an X-rated quickie that would probably be shot in forty-eight hours over the weekend. The men were uniformly good-looking and wore tight pants. Most of the women were well past whatever prime they might have had; many were young and just looked old—would-be discoveries on the run from places like Des Moines and Peoria. Or Nebraska. They'd come to New York to chase a star and had washed up, a thousand disappointments later, on the barren shores of the flesh trade.

I waited until the young man's back was turned, then made my way past the crowd, down a fluorescent-lighted corridor that looked as if it led to where the action was. There were now a few giggles from the women; they were speculating as to what role I was going to play in Harry Barnes's next film and what my qualification—singular—might look like.

Barnes was enjoying himself in a large, soundproofed studio deep in the bowels of the brownstone. He was gnawing on a hamburger as he directed a scene involving two big-breasted women writhing on the floor in the tepid embrace of an obviously bored, pimply-faced boy of nineteen or twenty. Again, nobody paid the slightest bit of attention to me: the people on the floor because they didn't care; Barnes because he was totally absorbed in his art.

Barnes was a big man with red hair, moustache, and goatee. He had small eyes that only looked red because of his hair and the bright lighting. Beads of sweat marched like drunken soldiers down his forehead. He turned and spotted me.

"Hey! What the—?" He almost choked on the last bite of his hamburger. He finally got it down, but the sight of a strange, uninvited dwarf standing next to him seemed to have short-circuited his vocal cords. He rose halfway out of his director's chair, his hands flapping nervously at his sides, and sputtered.

"My name's Frederickson," I said quickly. "I'm a private detective. I'd like to ask you some questions about a man named Victor Rafferty. I'll only need a few minutes of your time."

Pay dirt. He stopped sputtering and his hands grew still as he tried on a variety of expressions and settled for surprise. He obviously recognized the name. The three people on the floor continued to writhe around one another as he came over to me.

"All right, dwarf, what did you say your name was?" Barnes's voice was deep, well modulated, pleasing; it clashed with the rest of the package.

"Frederickson." I extended my hand, but he ignored it.

"You said you wanted to talk to me about Rafferty. I'm a busy man."

"I can see that. This won't take long. You worked for Victor Rafferty five years ago. Is that right?"

Barnes turned to watch the fleshy tableau behind him. "Yeah," he mumbled. I seemed to be losing his attention.

"Mr. Barnes, is there someplace we can go to talk?"

He hesitated, then nodded in the direction of a closed door across the corridor from the studio. I followed him through it, leaving the two women and the boy alone in their curious circle of hell.

The cork walls of the spacious office were covered with glossy pornographic photographs. I shut the door of the office behind me as Barnes settled down behind a large oak desk and folded his hands across his ample stomach. He didn't invite me to sit, but I considered myself ahead of the game as long as he was talking to me.

"Yeah, I worked in the Rafferty lab," he said. "But Rafferty himself didn't hire me. I only knew him by sight. There were mostly technical people there; they tested different kinds of metal alloys."

"I understand that. But you claim to have seen Rafferty die."

"I don't claim, I *did* see him die. What's your interest in Rafferty?"

"It's an insurance matter; a few old loose ends that were overlooked at the time and have to be straightened out. Some people don't think Victor Rafferty is dead."

His hands rose, fluttered like wounded birds a few inches above the surface of his desk, slowly came back to a landing. It was the most curious gesture I'd ever seen, and it struck me that it could be learned, practiced, purposely exaggerated. Aside from his voice, Harold Q. Barnes was almost *too* gross, too vulgar, as if he consciously worked at it. The man would bear closer study.

"What the hell does *that* mean?" Barnes snapped. "Somebody calling me a liar?"

"Insurance people are professional skeptics," I said soothingly. "They like to keep going back over the same details."

"That's crazy," he said, a distant look on his face. "Rafferty died five years ago. Who'd be interested now?"

"You were the last person to see him alive. Is that correct?"

"That's what I told the cops, and that's what I told the insurance companies. I don't—"

"Mr. Barnes, would you tell me exactly what happened?"

Barnes shrugged, then spoke as if he were reciting. "He was walking on the catwalk over the smelting furnaces. He stopped and leaned over a railing, like he was looking at something down there. All of a sudden he reached for his head, like he was dizzy. I tried to get to him, but I was too late. He fell over the railing into one of the open vats. His body exploded when it hit that hot metal. There was nothing left of him. I called the cops, but there wasn't anything anyone could do for him."

Barnes seemed immensely pleased with himself, like an actor who has learned his lines well.

"This was on a Sunday, wasn't it?"

"Yeah. I only worked there on weekends."

"Was there anyone else around?"

"No. The lab was closed on Sundays. I kept an eye on the place and checked the furnaces; they have to be kept hot, y'know."

"Why did Rafferty take you along with him, Mr. Barnes?"

"I had to let him on the catwalk. There's a steel door."

"He owned the building. Why didn't he have his own key?"

"Hell, I don't know. He must have forgotten it."

"*Why* did he want to go on the catwalk?"

41

"He never said."

"What was Rafferty doing there on a Sunday?"

"I don't know. I wasn't being paid to ask the boss questions. They tell me he was a weirdo. Maybe he just wanted to make sure everything was running like it should."

I didn't seem to be making much progress in that vein, so I gestured around the office to change the subject. "This is quite a setup you have here."

His eyes clouded with suspicion. "Yeah, I make out. What's it to you and the insurance company?"

"I'm interested in making movies myself."

Barnes's face brightened. "Hey, you ever think of acting? I might be able to build a whole film around you. Something really *kinky*."

"No, thanks. How do you get started in a business like this?"

"Good luck and clean living," he said with a smirk.

"And a little money."

"Some." Barnes was getting nervous again; his hands were beginning to twitch, ready for takeoff.

"About how much, would you say?"

He shook his head. "I don't discuss my personal business. You said you wanted to talk about Rafferty; okay, we talked. You said you don't want to be a movie star; that's all right too."

"It's quite a career jump from watchman to movie producer. I was hoping you might be able to give me a few tips. Who gave you your big break?"

Barnes rose threateningly from his chair. "I'm tired of this conversation. You found your way in here; now find your way out!"

I found my way out and waited a few feet beyond the entrance to the brownstone until one of the women who had been on the studio floor emerged. I almost didn't recognize her with her clothes on. She was big and lumpy, didn't wear a bra and should have. She hadn't bothered to clean off her theatrical makeup, and her face looked like a cake that had been forgotten in the oven. I stepped in front of her.

"Excuse me, ma'am. My name's Frederickson. I'd like to talk to you for a minute."

She stared down at me over the twin peaks of her breasts for what seemed a long time. "I saw you inside the studio, buddy. Whaddya want?"

"Just talk."

"I ain't no hooker, mister. I'm an actress."

"Anybody can see that right away," I assured her. "I said I just want to talk."

"No offense, but you ain't, uh, *normal.* I don't know how you get your kicks."

"I'd get a big kick out of your talking to me."

She sniffed. "The street ain't no Times Square rap parlor, buddy. I'm busy; I got another job to get to."

She started to walk past me. I flashed a twenty and she almost broke a platform heel stopping.

"Twenty bucks, sister, for twenty minutes of your time. A buck a minute."

She took the bill and stuffed it down the front of her dress; I wondered if she'd ever find it again.

"What do you want to talk about?" She could turn her tone on a dime; her voice was now positively saccharine.

We started walking toward Third Avenue. "Tell me about Harry Barnes."

She seemed relieved; I think she'd been expecting me to grab her leg. "*That's* all you want to talk about?"

"That's it. What do you know about him?"

She darted a glance sideways at me. "You ain't going to tell him what I say, are you?"

"Not a word, love. Cross my heart."

She made a face. "He's kinky."

"Oh-oh," I clucked. "What does that mean?"

Her breasts bounced violently as we stepped down off a curb, and then settled back into their normal, quivering

43

rhythm as we crossed the street. "He ain't no professional," she said, demurely supporting her breasts with a forearm as we stepped up on the opposite curb. "I mean, there's lots of guys making skin flicks. Most of them treat *you* like a professional. Harry ain't like that. He likes to touch his girls, sleep with 'em, that kind of thing."

"What's his product like?"

Another face. "I don't know how he makes any money on the shit he turns out. The stuff he makes would have been okay a few years ago, but everything now is synch sound and color. Real Hollywood. It's like Harry makes 'em as a hobby." She shrugged. "Still, he pays pretty good. Standard."

"Where do you suppose he got the money to get started?"

"Gee, I don't know, mister. I ain't interested in the business end. He just *started* is all."

"When?"

"Oh, I don't know. A few years ago."

"Five years?"

"Maybe. Yeah, that sounds about right. I hear he used to be a janitor, or something like that. One day he was just there in the business. Maybe some mob guys set him up, or something like that."

"Or something like that. Thanks, sister." I started to walk away.

"Hey, Mr. Whatever-your-name-is! You still got ten minutes left!"

I blew her a kiss.

It was a little before ten. I took a cab back to the university; I found one of the night guards, and he let me into the building where I had my office. On the way up to the third floor, I took off my jacket and removed the miniaturized tape recorder I kept in a pocket sewn into the lining; the recorder had been running throughout my talk with Harry Barnes.

44

The recorder was a component of a machine called a Stress Evaluator, and it was the latest invasion-of-privacy wrinkle. It was reputed to be far more accurate than the polygraph, and was certain to arouse more controversy. What it did was measure the relative stress in a person's voice, then relay that information to the operator by means of a line graph fed out of the machine on a paper tape. It was assumed that a person was under more stress when he or she was lying. A recording was played at low speed into the machine, and the paper tape came out the other side. All the operator had to do was to compare the spikes on the graph with the corresponding response to any particular question to determine whether the person had, in all probability, been lying. Instant Truth. The machine was a long way from courtroom use, but I was impressed by its potential uses—and abuses. That was what I'd told the American Bar Association in the evaluation report they'd asked me to write.

Using the pause control between each question and answer, I played the Barnes tape into the machine, then scanned the readout. The parts of Barnes's story where he talked about Rafferty's supposed death were consistently skewed toward the high end of the graph.

According to the machine, Harold Q. Barnes had been lying through his teeth.

5

Dirty Harold bothered me all night. There was a recurring dream in which I had somehow become a film director; Barnes was an actor who couldn't remember his lines. He was naked, sitting in a pool of grease and gnawing on a hamburger while I harangued him.

"Are you now, or have you ever been, an architect?"

No answer.

"Are you an actor, Harold? Are you *acting*? What the hell are you all about, Harold?"

No answer.

The alarm rang precisely at eight. I slapped it into submission and went back to sleep. The phone woke me up fifteen minutes later.

"You'd better get your ass down here, brother," Garth said in his cheery morning growl. "I think I've got something that'll interest you."

"You said ten."

"I'm saying *now*. Where's your sense of dedication? Get it down here!"

"All right. Let me get some coffee."

"*Bring* coffee," Garth said. The line went dead.

I fell into my clothes and made my way downtown to the station house. Garth was sitting at his desk, studying the contents of two pea-green manila folders. He held out his hand as I entered and I stuck a container of coffee into it. He didn't look up.

"What have you got, Garth?"

He motioned for me to sit down as he passed one of the folders over for me to see. "Read it, Mongo," he said seriously.

The field report on the investigation into the murder of Dr. Arthur Morton was about as brief a report as I'd ever seen; all it contained was the bare facts of Morton's death.

The neurosurgeon had been killed by a single bullet in the brain. The bullet markings indicated that it had come from a gun equipped with a silencer, which probably made the killer big-league professional. The caliber of the gun was British. There had been no signs of a forced entry into the office, and as far as the investigating officers could tell, nothing had been taken or disturbed. There had been no clues, no suspects. The title page of the file was stamped UNSOLVED.

Garth didn't object when I took out my notebook and wrote down the name of Morton's widow, along with a few other details. "There's not a whole hell of a lot here," I said.

"That's what I thought would interest you. Whoever killed him was no amateur."

"Obviously. Morton decided to stroll into his office at three-thirty in the morning so he could get himself killed by a professional." I pointed to the second folder. "What's that?"

"Oh, *this*?" he said with a gesture of mock surprise. "This is Victor Rafferty's file."

"Victor Rafferty had a police record?" My voice reflected my shock.

"No," Garth said. "But there was a Missing Persons report filed on him."

"What's the date?"

"August 15, 1969."

"The same day that weird picture outside his house was taken." I reached out for the folder. "Can I see?"

"No," Garth said, placing his hand on it. "This is pretty heavy; it's flagged."

"A Missing Persons report flagged? Who flagged it?"

Garth looked grim. "I can't even discuss it. I'm probably risking my job just having this file on my desk." He rose. "I've got to go to the john. Just remember, you haven't seen any police files on Morton or Rafferty. Understood?"

I winked. "Understood."

Garth walked out of the office and I opened the Rafferty file. The first thing that caught my attention was a line that read REPORTED BY ———. It had a code number instead of a name.

I was suddenly conscious of Garth looking over my shoulder. "I thought you'd gone to the head."

"I'm still there."

"What's that?" I asked, pointing to the number.

"I don't know," Garth said evenly.

"What the hell do you mean, you don't know? Don't you work here?"

"It's a code number that has something to do with the Feds. That's why it's flagged. Ordinary detectives like your humble brother aren't even supposed to look at these things. My guess is that it's the D.I.A.—Defense Intelligence Agency."

"Can you find out for sure?" I asked.

"No way."

"Who would put a number like that on?"

"The Commissioner, m'boy, and you're *not* going to question the Commissioner."

"Garth, do you think the Feds could have been after him?"

"It looks that way."

"So, with government agents presumably after him, Rafferty shows up on a Sunday at his metallurgy lab to inspect the furnaces." I tapped the report. "Doesn't make much sense, does it?"

"Not when you put it that way."

"It wasn't even his wife who reported him missing."

"Maybe she didn't miss him," Garth said wryly.

"She might have *known* where he was, or at least why he left."

Garth shrugged. "Why don't you ask her?"

"I can't," I said, suddenly feeling foolish. "That's one of the conditions of my employment. Her present husband's the one who's interested, and he doesn't want me to talk to her. He says he's worried about his wife's mental state, and I believe him."

"She must have a lot of answers."

The phone rang. Garth picked up the receiver and began speaking with the person on the other end. I took the copy of the newspaper photo out of my pocket and studied it. It was as inscrutable as before, but I was convinced Rafferty had been somewhere nearby when the picture was taken. If true, it meant he'd probably had something to do with the two men on the ground.

"Rafferty was picked up," Garth whispered, his hand over the receiver.

"Where?"

"It's in the report."

Garth continued his telephone conversation and I resumed my reading. What followed in the report was even more intriguing. Rafferty had been picked up by ambulance in a restaurant on the morning of Saturday, August 16. He'd been taken to Roosevelt Hospital—where he'd escaped from the custody of an officer named Patrick O'Connell. There was no report from O'Connell, and no indication of how Rafferty had escaped from what was described as a maximum-security ward. There was also no mention of why

49

Rafferty had been taken to the hospital, or why a Missing Persons had been filed in the first place.

There was a name: *Lippitt*. Below the name was a telephone number. I copied it down.

"Interesting, isn't it?" Garth said drily as he hung up.

"Why isn't there a report from this O'Connell?"

"It could have been pulled," Garth said, looking directly at me. "Or he could have been ordered not to write one up."

"Why do you say that?"

"The file is flagged; top priority, very sensitive."

"You recognize the area code on this telephone number?"

"Washington, D.C.," Garth said quietly. "There was a directive to call that number the moment anything turned up on Victor Rafferty." Garth rose and walked to the window. He stared out at the blaring traffic, the pedestrians, the hookers, the pimps, the thugs and murderers, all caught up and swirling in the polluted bloodstream of New York City. "I don't like it, Mongo," he said at last. "The whole thing stinks. Why don't you get your ass to Acapulco?"

"My ass will be toasting in Acapulco soon enough. First it would be interesting to hear what this Lippitt has to say."

Garth turned back from the window. "I don't like your being involved with it, Mongo."

"You know," I said, watching him, "the Morton investigation just doesn't make it. It was closed out three days after Rafferty's supposed death, which makes it just about the shortest unsolved murder investigation on record. You think it got choked off?"

Garth nodded absently. "Could be. Morton was pretty famous in his own right. You'd think they'd have spent a lot more time than they did looking into his murder."

"A police cover-up, Garth?"

"Christ, I hate to think so, but it could be. Ordered at the highest level. If the police were ordered to cut off the investigation, they probably weren't even told why."

"Hey," I said quietly, "maybe we should try to find out."

Garth slowly shook his head. "There's a lot of juice and muscle in that file."

"Power's never bothered you before. A man's been murdered, and his killer was never caught; another man who's supposed to be dead may be alive. Those seem like pretty important considerations to me."

Garth's eyes went cold. "I wouldn't have showed you this stuff if I didn't feel the same way. But I'm official, and you're not. I just don't think it would be a good idea to call that number; you could end up with more trouble than you're bargaining for."

Or Garth might, although he didn't say so. Rafferty, dead or alive, was a broken man who cast a large shadow. "I don't want to start using information that can be traced back to you."

The silence was prolonged. Finally he said: "Shit. Go get 'em, Mongo. Use your discretion as to what information you think you can use."

The tension that had been building inside me suddenly evaporated. My brother had signed on, and it gave me a good feeling. No more games. "What about this O'Connell?" I asked. "Can I talk to him?"

"That's up to O'Connell. He's retired." Garth took a neatly folded paper out of his pocket and handed it to me. "Here," he said. "I got that out of the P.B.A. directory."

The address was a retirement community in southern New Jersey called Sunny Acres. I stuck the paper in my pocket and rose.

"What about that steak, Mongo? It would go good with eggs this time of morning."

"Don't cash that rain check yet, brother," I said, heading for the door. "I'm still on a tight schedule. You wouldn't want me to miss that Aeromexico flight." I hoped it sounded lighter than I felt. I realized now that I'd been a fool to take Foster's money in the first place; I'd hoped to skip a stone across a dark lake and have simple answers come rippling

51

back to me. Instead, I found myself sinking steadily deeper into a quagmire of lies, fear, and murder.

I was already making a list of enemies I could turn the case over to when I left.

Outside, I dug Foster's business card out of my pocket as I crossed the street to a phone booth. His answering service informed me he was home that day. It was becoming obvious that I was going to save a lot of time—and Foster's money—if he'd let me talk to his wife.

I dialed his home number and a woman, presumably Elizabeth Foster, answered. The tone of the single "Hello" was tense and hollow. Unless the Fosters had been fighting all morning, it was the trembling voice of a woman teetering on the edge of emotional breakdown.

"Mrs. Foster?" I said gently; I felt as if I were talking to a patient.

"Yes? Who is this?"

"My name is Robert Frederickson, Mrs. Foster. I've done some business with your husband. May I speak with him, please?"

"Just a moment, Mr. Frederickson."

After a short pause, Foster's tightly controlled voice came on the line. "What do you want, Frederickson?"

"Can you talk?"

"I'd rather not." The tone was hard, clipped. "Why the hell are you calling—?"

"I think it's important, Foster." I was getting a little testy myself.

"Hold on a minute."

It was almost five minutes before he came back on the line. "All right," he said. "Elizabeth's out in the garden. You talk and I'll listen."

"I think it may be time I talked to your wife."

"No." There was a strange note in his voice; the hard

52

edge was blunted. "In fact, I've been thinking the whole thing over and I think I may have been making a mountain out of a molehill."

"This molehill is bigger than you think it is."

I heard him catch his breath. "You've got something?"

"Yes." I didn't want to lay it all out yet, but I didn't want to fold my tents either. "Can you meet me?"

"Where?"

"I'm at Eighth Avenue and Fifty-fourth."

"I'll be there in a few minutes." He hung up.

I called the number in Washington without giving myself time to think about it. The phone was picked up on the first ring.

"Aptown Florists," a woman answered.

That didn't sound quite right. I hung up and dialed the number again, double-checking each digit.

"Aptown Florists." It was the same young, cheery, woman's voice.

"I'd like to speak with Mr. Lippitt."

There was dead silence at the other end. The idea of a phone blind hadn't occurred to me; I had a vision of a lot of flower cutters suddenly stopping work.

"I'm sorry, sir." Her voice had aged; it was now professional, wary. "We have no Mr. Lippitt working for us. Perhaps you'd like to speak to Mr. Raines."

"I doubt it. Mr. Lippitt was the man who took my order."

"What order was that, sir? I don't believe you gave me your order number."

I could *feel* the woman listening very closely. "The flowers were for Victor Rafferty," I said slowly. "I can't remember the order number. It was five years ago. The order may have been premature, and I'd like to discuss the whole matter with Mr. Lippitt."

There was another silence. Then: "Isn't it a little late to be discussing a floral order that went out five years ago?"

53

"No, missy, I don't think so. These flowers were for a funeral, but the man may still be alive." I paused for effect. "That's what I want you to tell Lippitt if he happens to drop by the shop."

This time there wasn't any argument. The woman's voice was fast, sharp. "May I have your name and a number where you may be reached, sir?"

I gave her the information and hung up just as Mike Foster pulled up to the curb in a late-model blue Oldsmobile.

I slid in beside him. He checked the rearview mirror, then pulled out into the traffic and drove uptown toward Harlem. His face was set in a scowl. The muscles under the brown skin of his face and arms worked, and his hands were clenched on the wheel.

His voice shook. "I thought I'd made it clear that this was a matter between you and me."

"It could save a lot of time—"

"I will *not* permit you to talk to my wife!" he said slamming his hand against the steering wheel. "Elizabeth is worse; I'm afraid she's going to have some kind of breakdown. Damn it, you *agreed* that you wouldn't talk to her!" He sucked in his stomach. "Now, if I didn't make it clear before—"

"Stop the car, Foster."

"Huh?"

"Stop the car."

Foster pulled the car back over to the curb. I opened the door and got out. When I looked back he seemed uncertain.

"I don't like being bawled out before the fact," I said quietly. "In fact, I don't like being bawled out at all."

"Uh, look, Frederickson—"

"I took your money and you're entitled to what I found out, along with an opinion or two. First, Richard Patern did

54

design the Nately. Museum, but he admits to getting the idea and inspiration from someone else. He says he doesn't know who, and I believe him. I *don't* believe the man who claims he saw Rafferty go into the furnace. By the way, did you know Rafferty was reported missing two days before he's supposed to have died?"

"No," Foster said sheepishly. "Elizabeth?"

"No. A very heavy government agency that doesn't mess with small fry. Also, the neurosurgeon who saved Rafferty's life was murdered a few days before Rafferty's supposed final accident. I think there's a connection."

"You do?" Foster said weakly.

"And I'll tell you something else: I think there's a good possibility that Victor Rafferty *is* alive, but the smart money says to forget it. That's up to you. Goodbye."

I slammed the car door shut and started hoofing it back down Eighth Avenue. There was a squeal of tires as Foster's car backed past me and screeched to a halt beside a fire hydrant. Foster got out and hurried up to me.

"Frederickson," he said, breathing hard. "Just hang on a minute. Please."

I stopped. A cop appeared from the shadows of a storefront and began writing out a ticket. Foster ignored him.

"I ... I don't know what to say," Foster continued. "You're telling me Rafferty may be *alive*?"

"In my opinion, it's a reasonable possibility."

"Do ... you think Elizabeth knows for sure?" His voice cracked.

"Maybe. We won't know until we talk to her, Mike. It all comes back to that." We were standing in the middle of the sidewalk being jostled by people going in both directions, but Foster didn't seem inclined to move.

"Look, I'm sorry about the way I came on back in the car. I *am* really worried about Elizabeth. It's incredible what you've found out in such a short time."

"There's much more. There has to be. Your wife could have all the answers. You know, Mike, sometimes it's better to face up to a problem."

He looked pained. "I just don't want to take that kind of a chance. If anything should happen to her—"

"Something has already happened to her, Mike. It was five years ago, and it's still eating at her. She's obviously a principal in this case. Sooner or later, I think the police are going to be back in on it."

"Why do you say that?" he asked sharply.

"Because of the murder I mentioned; the man's name was Arthur Morton. If I continue this investigation, I think it's going to open the lid on a can of worms someone tried to close five years ago. The process may already have begun."

"Why?" he said, alarmed. "Have you been to the police?"

"No." It was only a half-lie; I didn't consider talking to Garth going to the police.

"Then how do you know all this?"

"Mike, I don't think you really want a lecture on detective work. You've got a decision to make. If you want me to continue, you're wasting my time and your money by keeping me away from your wife; it's like walking around the world to get across the street."

Foster looked shaken, and I felt sorry for him; I'd been beating him over the head with two razor-sharp horns of a dilemma. But it was Garth who might take it upon himself to reopen the case, and it could cost him his job. In light of that possibility, I didn't mind putting a little pressure on my client.

Foster was staring at his feet. I nudged him and pointed to his car, which was decorated with a buff-colored thirty-five-dollar ticket. "You'd better get your car out of here before the tow truck shows up," I said.

He looked at the car absently, as if it belonged to someone else. "Can you keep on working a little while longer?"

"If that's what you want. It's your money, and I don't leave until Thursday. May I talk to your wife?"

"Would you wait on that just a while longer?" he said, a plea in his voice.

I shrugged. "All right, Mike." It *was* his money, and I'd given him my best advice.

He seemed relieved. "Can I buy you breakfast?"

It was after ten; I hadn't eaten, but I wasn't hungry. "Some other time. If you're still my client, I've got work to do."

"I'm still your client, Mr. Frederickson. Can I drop you someplace?"

"The nearest car-rental agency. You might as well come along, since you're paying for it."

"Where are you going?"

"South Jersey. I want to talk to the cop who had Rafferty."

Foster blinked. "The police had Victor?"

"I don't want to take the time to explain now, Mike. I'd like to get on the road."

Foster nodded toward the big Olds with the buff decoration on the windshield. "Use my car. I'll take a cab home. Tomorrow's Sunday. Leave it in the street in front of your apartment house and I'll pick it up in the morning."

"What about your wife? Won't she wonder where the car is?"

"I'll tell her it broke down. Go ahead and take it."

I removed the ticket, got into the car, and pulled the seat up all the way. In the rearview mirror I saw Foster, hands jammed into his pockets, staring after me. I liked the man; he was groping blindly, sifting through the ashes of the past because he thought it could help his wife. I was convinced those ashes weren't cold, only banked; they could still burn.

I turned at the corner and Foster blinked out of sight.

6

The Olds was big, powerful, smooth-riding. Slipping out of Manhattan through the stone umbilical of the Lincoln Tunnel, I made good time in the light weekend traffic. Within an hour I had passed through the depressing yellow air of northern New Jersey and was immersed in the flat, deadly monotony of the New Jersey Turnpike.

I was off the Turnpike by two thirty. A gas-station attendant gave me some directions and I headed northwest.

Sunny Acres was a pleasant retirement community, spacious and clean, at least on the outside. I parked in a visitor's space and approached an elderly couple who were walking hand in hand. I introduced myself and asked about Patrick O'Connell. After a few giggles, they went into conference and eventually agreed that O'Connell could probably be found shooting pool in the recreation hall. They gave me directions, and we wished each other a nice afternoon.

Inside the recreation hall, I immediately spotted O'Connell as the lion among the lambs. He was silver-haired, with the aura of a good man slightly tarnished by the residue of cynicism and roughness that being a New York City cop leaves on you like a second layer of skin. His ruddy complexion blended with the garish colors of his short-sleeved Hawaiian shirt. Doughy flesh that had once been muscle now swung loosely under his arms, but there was still plenty of strength there. He limped slightly; the sides of his shoes had been slit to make room for his bunions.

O'Connell and a few of the other men in the room turned to stare at me, but they soon turned their attention back to the game in progress. O'Connell was the star; it was obvious that he was used to the role, and enjoyed it. He took ten minutes to beat a wily-looking old man at Rotation, interspersing a variety of trick bank shots with a running stream of banter delivered in an exaggerated Irish brogue. When he got tired of the game, he turned his cue over to another man and made his way to a small self-service bar in a corner of the hall.

He found a beer in a small refrigerator in the back, then came around and sat down on one of the stools with a contented sigh. I sat down beside him. His gray eyes flicked over my face, then returned to gaze at the foaming beer can in front of him. He was too much of a New Yorker to ask what a dwarf was doing in a retirement community, sitting beside him at the bar.

"My name's Frederickson," I said as I took out my P.B.A. courtesy card and laid it next to his elbow. "I'm a private investigator working out of New York. I'd like to talk to you about a case you were involved in."

O'Connell examined my card like a cop looking for evidence of forgery; finally he nodded his approval. "I've heard of you, Frederickson." The Irish brogue had acquired a heavy Brooklyn accent. "Don't you have a brother on the force?"

"Garth," I said. There was nothing the matter with O'Connell's mind. "May I ask you some questions, Mr. O'Connell?"

"You want a beer, Frederickson?"

"Yeah. Thanks."

"Get it yourself, if you don't mind. My goddamned feet are killing me. Bunions."

I helped myself to a beer and returned to the bar. The beer was warm.

"Don't think too much of private cops," O'Connell said, staring at me hard. "Some of them have been known to interfere with the work of duly appointed police officers."

"You check with Bardeen," I said, invoking the name of Garth's precinct commander. "He'll tell you I always cooperate with the police." I cleared my throat, swallowed some warm beer. "I'd like to talk to you about a man named Victor Rafferty."

That struck a chord. He grunted and spun around on his stool to face me. "What's up?"

"Frankly, I was hoping *you* might be able to tell *me*. I've been hired to investigate Rafferty's background. I know you were involved with him, at least for a few hours."

"Craziest few hours I've ever spent in my life!" O'Connell said with feeling, his eyes coming alive.

"Those are the hours I'm interested in. I can see they stick in your mind."

He nodded his gray head slowly. "And that's for sure."

"You were in Roosevelt Hospital with Rafferty. Do you know why he was taken there?"

O'Connell shrugged. "I suppose he was sick."

"With what?"

He seemed slightly embarrassed. "I haven't got the slightest idea. As far as I was concerned, it was a routine bit of business. I just happened to be the closest cop to the restaurant when Rafferty had his accident. Somebody pulled me in off the street."

"Do you remember the name of this restaurant?"

"Uh, Cakewalk. Jack's Cakewalk, I think. I'm pretty sure it was near West Thirty-fourth. Anyway, I walked in and found this guy lying on the floor, out cold."

"Had anybody inside the restaurant seen what happened?"

"A waiter. Must have been ninety if he was a day. It was hard to understand him because he didn't have any teeth, and he'd left his bridge home that day." O'Connell shook his head in admiration. "Tough old son-of-a-bitch. Still working. He'll probably live forever."

I hoped he'd made ninety-five. "Do you remember his name?"

"No, but I do remember that he told a weird story. Didn't make a bit of sense. He kept on babbling about Rafferty throwing food."

"*Throwing* food?"

"Yeah. Throwing food. I told you it didn't make sense. The ambulance boys were just loading Rafferty in when I got a call from the precinct house. The chief told me in no uncertain terms that I was to stay with Rafferty and make sure they locked him up good when we got to Roosevelt."

"He was on a Missing Persons list, right?"

"I guess so."

"The police don't usually go around locking up missing persons, do they?"

"No. I was curious too, but I had my orders. I got in the ambulance and went with Rafferty to the hospital. I made sure they took him up to the security ward on the fourth floor."

"How secure was security?" I asked.

He thought about it for a moment. "Roosevelt isn't really set up for that kind of thing. Security? I'd say maximum inside the room, minimum outside. There weren't any gates in the corridors, no bars on the windows. But the room was bolted from the outside, and the door was absolutely solid, flush to the wall on the inside."

"Was Rafferty admitted by a particular doctor?"

"No. I think they had their orders too. They just wheeled him in and locked us both up."

A feisty old man with a moustache and wearing red

Bermuda shorts three sizes too big for him came over, cue stick in hand, and tried to entice O'Connell back to the table. O'Connell promised him a game later, and he tottered away.

"Too many old guys here," O'Connell said quietly. "Nice guys, but . . ." He let the sentence trail away.

I tried to keep his mind from wandering off. "What were your instructions, besides keeping an eye on him?"

He removed a handkerchief from his pocket, slowly and methodically wiped up a puddle of beer. "That was it," he said when he'd finished. "I was just told to keep him on ice until this guy got there to relieve me."

"Was this man coming from Washington?"

"Yeah. They told me that."

"Was his name Lippitt?"

O'Connell was clearly impressed. "Yeah! Hey, how'd you know that?"

"Oh, I've been talking to some other people. How did Rafferty get away?"

O'Connell flushed angrily. The memory still bothered him. "Somebody let him out."

"Then you must have seen who it was."

"No," O'Connell said defiantly. His eyes glinted. "Those bastards wanted to be so goddamned secretive, well, they paid the price! Nobody told me Rafferty was a hypnotist."

Nobody had told me, either. "What makes you say that?"

"Because he put me to sleep, that's why!" He'd begun to tremble. O'Connell settled himself and addressed his beer can. "I was told to shoot him in the legs if he tried to escape. Whatever he'd done was that serious. Naturally, I pulled my gun on him when he woke up; I wanted to show him right away who was in charge. But when I saw he wasn't going to give me any trouble, I kind of relaxed. That was my one big mistake."

I got us two more beers. "How did Rafferty react when he first woke up, Mr. O'Connell?"

He shook his head. "Cool, he was. No more concerned than if he was waking up from a nap in his own bed. Pretty strange."

"He wasn't hurt?"

"Not that I could tell. He just woke up, looked me over, then started to get out of bed. I stopped him pretty damn quick when I pulled my gun on him, but he didn't give me any arguments. He said it was obviously a mistake that would be cleared up." O'Connell paused, frowned as he looked at the memory. "He didn't even seem surprised to find himself in a locked hospital room with a cop. That's when I started thinking that they'd locked me up with some kind of nut."

We sat in silence for a time while O'Connell ran a finger around the rim of his beer can. "What happened then?" I prompted.

"He just started talking. He was a good talker."

"You mean, he was just making conversation?"

"That's right. Came on like a real nice guy." O'Connell's lip curled contemptuously. "That's what I thought at the time. Now I can see what he was up to. He started talking about how tired I must be, like he was reading my mind. He was right. I was just starting in on a second tour of duty, and probably looked like hell. He suggested I sleep. I didn't intend to do any cooping on *that* job, but all of a sudden I couldn't keep my eyes open. Dropped right off. You see what I mean about his being a hypnotist?"

"Yeah." It was an interesting thought; I remembered Rafferty's black, brooding hawk eyes. But he hadn't hypnotized the door open. "And Rafferty was gone when you woke up?"

"Like a big bird," he said with some bitterness. "He'd locked *me* in."

"You're absolutely sure there was no way he could get out of that room by himself?"

"Absolutely. There wasn't even a hinge on the inside, and no way to jimmy that outside bolt. Somebody *had* to let him out."

"How many people could have known he was in that particular hospital?"

He considered it, finally said: "Just the two guys in the ambulance and a few people in the hospital, besides whoever knew about the orders. Maybe whoever it was found out some other way."

"With all that secrecy?" It didn't seem likely.

"I know it sounds like I'm making excuses, but somebody just had to help him get out of that room. Once out, all he had to do was walk down one of the fire exits to the street."

"Maybe *you* helped him." I let it drop cold and watched O'Connell's growing anger. His face blotched pink and white.

"You're calling me a liar, mister," he said in a choked whisper.

I stared at the clenched fist that had suddenly appeared under my nose. "You must have been asked the same question before."

"No, mister, I wasn't. *Damn*, that makes me angry! I may be a fool, but I don't give up prisoners! I ain't no crook! I'm telling you, they *knew* he was a hypnotist. Christ, I was sound asleep when this Lippitt walked in on me!" O'Connell squeezed the beer can until foam squirted out of the opening and rolled down over his hand. "I think you just asked your last question, Frederickson. I don't like being called a liar."

"C'mon, O'Connell," I said quietly. "I'd have to be an idiot *not* to ask that question."

O'Connell exhaled sharply and looked away. "What else do you want to know?"

"Tell me about this Mr. Lippitt."

"Real weirdo. There was something wrong with him: Here he is wearing a heavy overcoat in August. You could see him shiver every once in a while." He paused, staring hard into the past. "When he found out Rafferty was gone, he chewed my ass good."

Lippitt was beginning to sound like a stand-in for Boris Karloff. But he was real enough; he'd certainly made an impression on O'Connell. "He actually *shivered*?" I asked. "Even with the overcoat?"

"Sure did. And it must have been eighty-five or ninety degrees; he still seemed cold. Didn't make him any less mean, though," he added as an afterthought.

"Did he say what agency he worked for?"

"No, and I didn't ask."

"Don't misunderstand me, Mr. O'Connell," I said, touching his elbow, "but I'm surprised you weren't disciplined in some way."

"The Department was thinking about it, I'm sure of *that*. My guess is that the weird guy talked them out of it."

"Why should Lippitt have done that?" I asked.

"I suppose he was decent enough not to want to see me punished for something that wasn't all my fault. *He* knew Rafferty was a hypnotist."

"Were you asked to file a report?"

He laughed. "Hell, I was told *not* to." He paused, coughed. "I probably shouldn't be talking about it now."

"I appreciate the fact that you did, Mr. O'Connell. I won't keep you any longer."

I shook his hand and started for the door.

"Frederickson!" I stopped and waited while O'Connell shuffled after me on his sore feet. "I just remembered something else," he said. "Whoever helped Rafferty get out of that room may not have been his friend."

"Oh? What makes you say that?"

"I think they hurt him. There were spots of blood all over the floor and scratches on the doorjamb, like a man would make with his fingernails. It looked to me like Rafferty'd put up a struggle. Maybe he didn't *want* to go."

My firm intention was to kill half of Sunday in bed, but I found myself wide awake at eight thirty, thinking about Victor Rafferty. So I got up, brewed a pot of strong coffee, and fried two eggs. One of my neighbors had been kind enough not to steal my paper that morning; I ate over the *Times* sports and editorial sections.

I'd planned to spend the day getting my packing out of the way and recording my notes on the case, so that whoever took over for me would have a solid foundation of information to work with. At the moment I didn't feel like doing anything.

When I went to the window and pulled back the curtain, I could see that Foster had already been around to pick up his car, which made me suspect that he wasn't sleeping too well either. Directly across the street, two men were sitting in a black Chevrolet. It seemed an odd thing to be doing on a Sunday morning, so I got my binoculars out of a drawer and looked the men over. Both were well dressed in light summer business suits and had close-cropped hair; they'd popped out of the same cookie cutter as the men in the newspaper photograph. I was under surveillance.

My telephone rang and I picked it up.

"Garth, Mongo." My brother's voice was tense and low. In the background, I could hear the distinctive sounds of the station house. "I see you've been goosing elephants with your usual casual abandon."

"What's the matter, Garth? I thought you were off today."

"Well, let's say there's a lot of unusual activity around here this morning. I got called in. The Chief's been in and out all morning asking about the Rafferty file. The funny thing is, I get the impression he's not even sure what he's talking about. I had to tell him you were in here asking questions about it. It didn't make him happy. I take it you called that Washington number?"

"Afraid so, Garth."

"I figured as much. They asked me if I'd given you a copy of the file. I said no."

"That's true enough. Has anyone mentioned the Morton case?"

"No. And I can't bring it up without admitting that I at least pulled some files for you. I just wanted you to know what the reaction's been like around here. I'm playing dumb, so I don't think I'll be lining up for unemployment. You just be damn careful where you're digging; you're liable to hit a land mine, if you haven't already."

"Thanks, brother. I appreciate it. I owe you a couple."

"You owe me a gross, but I'll settle for the steak dinner you promised."

"Lawdy, lawdy, I haven't forgotten."

"I'll be mighty glad when you're gone to Acapulco," Garth said, and hung up.

I checked through the phone book, looking for Jack's Cakewalk. There was a listing for a restaurant with that name on West Thirty-sixth. I decided to go for a walk.

Three minutes after I hit the street, the black Chevy passed me; it had lost one passenger, and I'd undoubtedly grown a tail. I did a quick-shuffle around a corner, down into a subway station, and up to the street on the opposite side, where I hailed a cab. There was no black car in sight, but the exercise had been wasted; a crude hand-lettered sign on the window of Jack's Cakewalk proclaimed that the restaurant was closed on Sundays.

The Chevy, with its full contingent, was waiting for me across the street when I got back to my apartment house. Neither man looked at me, but I thought their faces seemed slightly redder than normal.

The rest of the day I spent packing and taping. I went to bed early, lulled to sleep by the thought that big wheels turning just might grind out a few answers.

The possibility that those same wheels might run me over

left me relatively unperturbed. Some years ago a psychiatrist had told me that finding out things other people didn't want known was my way of trying to stay even with a society filled with people bigger than I was. The remark had been meant to startle, to provoke insight, and eventually to alter my behavior.

Instead, I'd simply found that I thoroughly agreed with him, and had gone out after a private investigator's license.

The next morning I ate breakfast out, just to see who was on the surveillance team's day shift. The men had changed, and they were using a pink Pinto, but the haircuts had remained the same. The man who actually got out of the car and followed me into the restaurant wore a black-and-white checked suit and open-necked red shirt.

After breakfast, with the man in the checked suit in tow, I took a short bus ride downtown to the United Nations. Since the man made no effort to disguise the fact that he was following me, I didn't bother losing him; he provided a kind of comforting reassurance that I was doing something right.

At the U.N. I walked under the rainbow of flags, across the plaza, and into the lobby of the Secretariat building. My companion stayed outside. He looked bored as he leaned against one of the concrete barriers, crossed his feet and arms, and heaved a huge sigh.

During my years with the circus, I'd participated in more than my share of benefits for UNICEF. The U.N. official I'd worked with most closely was a Pakistani by the name of Abu Bhutal; if Abu was still with the U.N., he'd be a valuable contact.

I sat down on a polished marble bench in the lobby and took out one of the copies of the conference program Richard Patern had given me. I took a quick count and came up with about two hundred and seventy-five names, from every part of the world. That was just too many names to work with. I knew it was risky, but I winnowed the list down to around fifty Americans, including aides. I put a double line under the name ELLIOTT THOMAS; that certainly looked like two first names to me. Then I went looking for Abu.

An attempted end run around the security guard at the elevator didn't work, so I used a phone to call the UNICEF office. I gave Abu's secretary my name. There was a short pause, I heard a few clicks, and then came a booming "Mongo the Magnificent! How are you?"

"Fi—"

"*Where* are you?" I had to hold the receiver away from my ear. Abu Bhutal's good nature was habitually expressed at a decibel level higher than the human ear could tolerate.

"Downstairs, Abu," I said. "I'd like to talk to you if you've got a few minutes."

"A few *minutes*? I am your *servant*, Mongo! You just wait right there! I'll be right down!"

Less than a minute later, Abu emerged from the elevator, went up on the toes of his patent leather Gucci shoes, and started looking around for me. His jet-black hair flashed blue highlights in the fluorescent light of the lobby. He was wearing a vested sharkskin suit. Abu had a taste for expensive, well-cut Western clothes, and he looked well in them.

He spotted me and took off across the lobby at collision speed. There were tears in his eyes when we shook hands. His effusiveness and warmth embarrassed me; I was the one who'd broken off contact.

Abu ushered me past the security guard, into the elevator, and up to his office, where he sat down behind his desk and sighed expansively. "It's good to see you, Mongo."

"And you, Abu. You look wonderful."

"I thought we were friends, Mongo," he said quietly, tapping his fingers lightly on the top of his desk.

"We *are* friends."

"Then why haven't I heard from you?" he asked reproachfully. "It's been years. I discovered you were no longer with the circus only when I called to try to get you to do another benefit."

The bitterness and tension I'd felt in those years, the bridges I'd burned, were not among my favorite subjects. I mumbled some apologies and promised not to let it happen again.

He seemed appeased and grinned broadly. "So, my friend, I suspect it's more than old times' sake that brings you here."

I cringed. "You never were one to be fooled. Abu, I could use your help."

"There is no way I could refuse. How can I help you?"

"Have you ever heard of Victor Rafferty?"

Abu thought about it, then shook his head. "I can't say that I have."

"He was an architect. I understand he did a lot of volunteer work for the U.N., so he definitely had connections here. I'm trying to find out who those connections were. I'd like to go over a list of names with you."

"May I ask why, Mongo?"

"I'm investigating Rafferty for a client who's in trouble. Some of these people may have information that could be useful to me. Abu, do you know a man by the name of Elliot Thomas? He may work here."

"No, my friend, I can't say that I do. But wait just a minute." He took a U.N. personnel directory from a drawer and thumbed through it. "Aha!" he exclaimed, stabbing the page with a bejeweled, stubby finger. "Elliot Thomas! He's on the American staff of UNESCO. Came here in '71. It says here he has an office on twenty-six."

"Does it mention in there what he does?"

"He's a stress engineer."

"Now, what do you suppose a 'stress engineer' does?"

Abu grinned. "How do you say? 'Beats me'?"

"Don't give me any of that 'ignorant foreigner' crap, Abu. You know more American slang than I do." I wrote down the information on Thomas in my notebook, then handed Abu the conference list. "Do you know any of these men personally? For now, just the names I've circled."

"Yes, I remember this conference well," he said as he thumbed through the program. "It was very successful." He moved a thick finger down the page of names. "Samuel Atkins is with UNESCO now. Ronald Tal is Special Assistant to the Secretary General, and Hillary Peterson, I believe, left a year or so ago."

Abu continued down the list of names he was familiar with while I took notes, crossing off the names of men Abu characterized as under thirty-five, Oriental, black, or Puerto Rican. I ended up with twenty-three names.

"Abu, do you suppose any of these people would agree to talk to me?"

"I can ask. Who would you like to speak with first?"

"Why not start at the top? What about Tal?"

Abu picked up the telephone. "I must warn you that Ronald is an extremely busy man. I'll have to tell him who you are and what you want."

"Of course."

Abu spoke to Tal on the phone, and I listened. I couldn't catch Tal's words, but his voice was low and well modulated, like that of a man who does a lot of public speaking—which Tal did, much to the distress of a good many Americans who didn't like what he had to say. Abu did a good job of building me up, then mentioned Victor Rafferty and why I was there. When the conversation was over, Abu slowly hung up the phone and looked at me. He seemed vaguely surprised. "Your fame and reputation for good works precede you. Ronald recognized your name and is most appreciative of what you've done for this agency. He'll see you in"—he looked at his watch—"forty-five minutes. His offices are part of the Secretary General's suite. You'll be expected. In the meantime, I'll make inquiries as to who may have known Victor Rafferty." He clapped his hands once, loudly. "*Now!* You've got forty-five minutes to kill. What say we have a little drink?"

"For *breakfast?* Thanks, Abu, but give me a rain check. I want to see if I can get a line on this Thomas. I'll be in touch." I made a mental note to call him for dinner after I got back from Acapulco, if I didn't hear from him first.

Now that I was actually inside the working quarters of the U.N., internal security didn't seem to pose a problem. I had no trouble getting to the twenty-sixth floor, but once there, I wasn't sure how to proceed. There was no receptionist, no directory—just a long antiseptic-green corridor with small offices on either side. I ambled down the corridor, hands in my pockets, trying not to look like a lost tourist. I rounded a corner and almost bumped into a man who was wearing a pale blue, three-piece suit. His full auburn beard just reached the top button of his vest.

"Excuse me," the man said as he backed up, gripped my shoulder solicitously, and limped around me.

"Mr. Thomas?"

He turned and smiled quizzically. "Yes?" He had a kind face with kind eyes that were the wrong color—brown. But he could have been wearing contact lenses; the hair and the beard could be dyed, or phony altogether. I knew very well what wondrous things could be done with cosmetics and plastic surgery.

"*Elliot* Thomas?"

"Yes," he said easily. "Can I help you?"

"My name's Frederickson," I said quickly, stepping forward and offering my hand. "I'd like to talk to you if you have a few minutes."

72

"Sure," he said, shaking my hand tentatively. The hair around his mouth parted slightly to reveal a set of even, white teeth. "What is it that you'd like to talk to me about?"

"I, uh . . . uh . . ." Clever detective that I am, this marvelous stroke of luck found me totally unprepared; I hadn't thought up a cover story. I went right at him with, "I'm looking for Victor Rafferty."

It got a response. The teeth disappeared, and I thought I saw something move behind the earth-brown eyes. But then, I was looking pretty hard; I didn't want to be fooled by my own expectations.

"Interesting," he said pleasantly. "Why don't you come into my office?"

He led the way into a small but neatly appointed office with a nice view overlooking Manhattan. My reflexes were quicker than my thinking had been; as he moved around his desk, back to me, I reached out and snatched a cheap plastic protractor from the midst of a pile of papers and drafting tools. I was hoping he wouldn't miss it as I dropped it into my inside jacket pocket.

"Is this a joke?" Thomas asked as he sat down. His smile was wearing thin, but that seemed understandable. "Victor Rafferty has been dead for some years."

"But you *are* familiar with the name?"

"Of course," Thomas said, gesturing to indicate that the answer was obvious. "I'm a stress engineer."

"I'm sorry, but I don't know what a stress engineer does."

"*I'm* sorry," Thomas said evenly, still smiling, "but I don't know what *you* do, either."

A quick search of my mental resources still failed to turn up a plausible cover story. "I'm a private detective," I said. "I've been hired to investigate the death—or, uh, disappearance—of Victor Rafferty. I thought you might be able to help me."

Thomas' chuckle was easy, good-natured. "What ever

gave you the idea that *I* could help you? I never even met the man."

"But you asked about him at the dedication ceremony for the Nately Museum."

He thought a moment, then snapped his fingers. "Patern! The architect! *That's* where you got my name. But I didn't *ask about* Victor Rafferty; I said the building reminded me of his work." He reached inside his beard, tugged at his lower lip, frowned. "I don't remember telling Patern where I work."

"Mr. Thomas," I said quickly, "will you tell me how you happen to know so much about Rafferty's work?"

A shrug. "Why not? You see, a stress engineer evaluates the *structural* requirements of a given design, and the geographical location where the proposed building is to be erected. First, I tell the architect whether it's *possible* to build from his design; if it is, I give him the strength requirements of the materials to be used, depending on the location. For example, any building erected in an earthquake zone is going to have to be stronger than garden apartments in, say, Hoboken. I'm the person who makes those kinds of judgments."

"Then you're not an architect yourself?"

"No. But any stress engineer would be absolutely familiar with Rafferty's work. His 'Rafferty angles' made possible a whole new approach to the construction of very strong but relatively lightweight structures. I could see a relationship to Rafferty's work the minute I saw that museum, and that's why I asked Patern about it. By the way, I found him rather snooty."

We sat and stared at each other for a few moments. Then Thomas shrugged again. "That's it," he said. "Sorry I can't be more helpful."

"You've been very helpful," I said, heading for the door, "and I thank you."

"Just a minute," Thomas said. I turned, waiting. "No offense, Mr. Frederickson, but are you *really* a private detective? I'm still not convinced someone isn't playing a joke on me."

"Oh, I'm a private detective," I said. "And I'm very serious."

7

Although I was on my way to meet Ronald Tal, it was impossible not to think of the Secretary General himself; the two men were as inextricably linked in my mind as they were in the American press.

Having been disappointed by too many famous and powerful men, I wasn't usually moved by reputations or the trappings of office. But Rolfe Thaag, the boss and mentor of the man I was going to see, impressed me, at least by way of accomplishment. A vigorous man in his sixties, Thaag had entered the field of international diplomacy after the Second World War, during which he'd fought in the Resistance in his native Norway. He'd attained his high office almost by accident, as a compromise candidate that all the Big Powers could agree on. Once in power, he'd surprised a lot of people; he was the most activist Secretary General since Dag Hammarskjold.

Thaag owed his power to the fact that he seemed to have an almost uncanny ability to determine who was speaking with forked tongue and who was telling the truth in any given situation; it was a faculty that had earned him a list of enemies almost as long as Ronald Tal's. But even the member nations who screamed the loudest at Thaag's periodic, and often scathing, "assessments of the situation" usually backed off once they'd been caught with their political pants down on the well-lighted stage of world opinion. Above all, Thaag had a reputation for being scrupulously fair. He was called "magician" in a hundred different languages; usually it was a sobriquet, often a curse.

Tal was the Secretary General's Chief Assistant, and he wasn't exactly what you could call eclipsed by his boss's fame. He was far and away the favorite hate object of the American right wing, but he'd been called "traitor," at one time or another, by national figures all along the political spectrum.

According to a *Time* capsule biography I'd read, Tal had been born in Norway of American parents. Orphaned at an early age, he'd been brought up by Rolfe Thaag, a friend of the family. Since joining his mentor at the U.N., Tal—as an American operating, as it were, in his own backyard—had caused almost as much controversy as Rolfe Thaag himself. It was Tal who delivered most of the speeches critical of the West; despite the fact that it was common knowledge that Tal was acting as no more than a mouthpiece for the views of Rolfe Thaag, it was Tal who took his countrymen's heat for these speeches. The man had guts, in my opinion, and I was anxious to meet him.

The elevator I was riding sighed to a stop and opened directly into a suite of offices where Ronald Tal was waiting for me. I knew biographies could be faked, and I immediately started looking for resemblances to Victor Rafferty. Except for eye color, there weren't any. There were no signs of scar tissue on the handsome face. His hair was brown, fuller than Rafferty's had been, and there was no indication he was wearing a toupee. His piercing black eyes reminded me of Rafferty's, but Tal was considerably heavier than Rafferty, with what I judged to be about a hundred and ninety pounds evenly distributed on an athletic six-foot frame. There was a sense of movement about him, even when he was standing still; I suspected he spent a lot of time out of doors and in a gymnasium. There was a quiet dignity about him that hadn't come across in the newspaper photos I'd seen.

"Dr. Frederickson," Tal said, shaking my hand. "It's nice to meet you."

"My pleasure," I said. "I'll try not to take up too much of your time."

"If I understood Abu correctly, you'd like to discuss Victor Rafferty."

"That's right. You've heard of him?"

"Certainly." He motioned me over to a leather settee and sat down in a straight-backed chair across from me. "Rafferty was a seminal force in modern architecture, to say the least. Like you, he did a great deal of volunteer work for U.N. agencies. I believe he died a few years ago. May I ask what your interest in him might be?"

"There's reason to believe Victor Rafferty may still be alive."

He took a green wooden pencil from his breast pocket and began to twirl it slowly back and forth between his thumb and forefinger. Tal was right-handed; Victor Rafferty had been right-handed. Elliot Thomas was right-handed; most of the world's population was right-handed. "I don't understand," he said. "I can't remember the exact details, but I thought he died quite violently in the kind of accident no man could survive. It was reported on quite extensively."

"If the accident ever happened," I said as I showed Tal the photograph of the Nately Museum Foster had left with me.

He looked at the photograph, nodded approvingly. "I don't know much about architecture," he said, "but it *looks* like a beautiful building. Who's the architect?"

"A man by the name of Richard Patern got the credit, but the building is almost certainly Victor Rafferty's idea."

"Are you saying you believe this Richard Patern is actually Victor Rafferty?"

"Not exactly."

"I don't quite understand how you think I can help you."

The conversation was beginning to sound disturbingly similar to the one I'd had with Thomas. "Patern admits he got the idea from a rough drawing he found here a couple of years ago," I said. "He was participating in your Seminar on Inexpensive Construction Techniques for Underdeveloped Countries." I filled Tal in on a few of the details Patern had given me.

Tal shook his head. "Wouldn't it be virtually impossible for a man as famous as Victor Rafferty to simply disappear without leaving a trace? And why would he want to do such a thing?"

"Because some people were after him; they wanted him very badly." I handed Tal the list of names. "If Rafferty was—or is—here, the name he's using should be on this list."

Tal studied the list for a few moments, then said: "I don't believe Rafferty can be any of these people. Obviously, they wouldn't have been invited to participate in the conference if they weren't established professionals in their own countries. I'm sure the careers of all these people predate Rafferty's supposed death."

"You're probably right. Still, I'd like to do some preliminary checking. Do you know any of the people on the list?"

"Of course." He smiled broadly. "I see you have a circle around *my* name."

"You're an American, about the same age as Rafferty would be. You don't look anything alike, but plastic surgeons work miracles these days. I'm just trying to narrow down the possibilities."

Tal chuckled and held out his hands. "Why don't you fingerprint me? That should dispel any doubt in your mind."

I could feel my face grow hot. "I didn't bring my fingerprint kit with me. Thanks anyway."

Just then the phone on a desk at the other side of the office rang. Tal excused himself and rose to answer it. His back was to me as he spoke, and to be sure his offer to fingerprint him wasn't a bluff I picked up the pencil he'd left on the coffee table between us. Holding the pencil by the eraser, I dropped it into my pocket. Then I rose and moved toward the elevator; I didn't want to get caught pilfering pencils from the Secretary General's suite.

Tal finished on the phone and came over to me.

"I've used up enough of your time," I said.

"May I keep this list of names?" Tal asked, smiling.

"Sure. I have another copy."

"I'll look it over more carefully," he said. "If I think of anything I may have forgotten, I'll call you."

I gave him my card and thanked him again.

Abu was in his office when I stopped back in. We had coffee, we reminisced a bit, and then I went out into the late morning. I intended to go to Jack's Cakewalk, and I didn't want company.

The man in the checked suit was studiously pretending to read the *Daily News*. He was chomping on a hot dog, and a strand of sauerkraut was pasted to his chin. He blinked rapidly as he watched me out of the corner of his eye.

The direct approach was called for. "Hi," I said pleasantly as I walked up to him. "Why the hell are you following me?"

He didn't like it; I'd caught him with his mouth full. He chewed furiously, swallowed hard while his face auditioned a variety of expressions, and finally settled for a mixture of surprise and indignation. "Excuse me, sir?"

"I asked you why the hell you're following me. You've got sauerkraut all over your chin."

He swiped at his chin. He was getting mad; he did Mad

80

better than Surprise and Indignation. "What are you talking about, pal?"

"Does it have something to do with Victor Rafferty? If you'd just tell me *why* you're following, I might not have to do so much walking around and we could all go home and relax."

His eyes narrowed. "Nobody's following you. You're crazy."

"Uh-uh. It's a sin to tell a lie. You're following me—and so is he." I pointed across the street to where the man's partner sat in the pink Pinto staring hard at the two of us.

"You're out of your mind, fella."

"Oh, good. Then I know I won't be seeing the two of you around anymore. Have a nice day."

I walked half a block, then stopped and looked back. The two men were having a heated conversation. The one I'd confronted reached inside the car and snatched a mobile telephone. He spoke into it quickly.

I hustled along, ducking into and out of a few storefronts on the way, just in case they had a third man on the job. When I was sure I was clean, I headed for the restaurant.

Jack's Cakewalk was open, crowded with laborers enjoying a late coffee break or an early lunch. There were two rooms, a lunch counter in front and a dingy, dimly lighted dining room in the back. I sat down in an empty seat at the lunch counter and exchanged a little friendly banter with the big boys around me who wanted to know if I was old enough to drink coffee.

The waitress, a pretty young thing with an astounding bust, finally worked her way down to me. She looked at me, smiled warmly. "What'll it be, little man?" she asked, shoving her chest at me amidst a chorus of cheers.

I grinned. "The little man would like a bun."

"A bun?" she singsonged. "Only one?"

"The cinammon variety." I put a five-dollar bill on the counter. "I'm looking for the old man."

"Barney?"

"Is Barney old?"

She pursed her lips. "Barney's *old*."

"That's him. Is he around?"

She waved her hand in the direction of the dining room. "He's probably in the john; Barney's got weak kidneys. He takes care of the back, if you want to talk to him. Go ahead. I'll bring your food and change back to you."

I thanked her and walked into the gloom at the back. There was an empty table near a dirty window, and I sat down at it. A few seconds later there was a flushing sound from the men's room to my right. Ancient plumbing clattered, and a man who looked like a contemporary of the plumbing emerged, drying his hands on an equally ancient, greasy apron. He looked around, squinting in the dim light, saw me, and came over. Through the wet, rheumy windows of his eyes he studied me. Then he rubbed his belly and cackled.

"Circus in town?" he wheezed.

"Funny, I was about to ask the same thing. You've got to be the oldest waiter I've ever seen."

He liked that; he carried his age around with him like a trophy. He gave me a gummy grin and slapped the top of the table with his hand. "Been workin' steady for seventy years, not countin' the Depression when nobody was workin'. Been right here for twenty-five. Can't afford to retire. You ever try livin' on Social Security?" He answered the question himself. "You can't do it. Then you go on Welfare and somebody's always stickin' their nose into your business." He paused, frowned. "You ain't from Social Security, are ya?"

"No, Barney, but I'd still like to talk to you. My name's Mongo."

He looked around. The dining room was beginning to fill. "Bad time, mister. Lunch crowd's comin' in pretty quick."

I laid another five-dollar bill on the table, pushed it toward him. "This won't take long."

He looked at the bill greedily. "Why you want to talk to me, mister?"

The waitress brought me my coffee and bun, with a glimpse of cleavage on the side. Barney ogled her as she walked away.

"I'm a private investigator," I said loudly in an attempt to get his attention back.

He cackled again. "That's the funniest thing I ever heard."

"I've got lots of friends," I said. "Big spenders with a sense of humor. I want to talk to you about a man named Victor Rafferty."

"That's easy," he said, quickly glancing at the bill as if it were about to be taken out of his reach. "I never heard of him."

Barney's hand came closer as I touched the five-dollar bill. "It would have been about five years ago. The man passed out on you."

He snapped his fingers; his eyes were suddenly clear, excited. Memories moved there like tides beneath their wet surface. "The guy that bounced the food!"

"I think that's the one," I said. "Is he the one who passed out on you?"

"Yessir, that's the guy I'm talkin' about! He zonked out after he bounced the food!"

"What do you mean, he 'bounced' the food? He didn't like it? He sent it back?"

The old man looked injured. "No! I'm tellin' you, the food *bounced* off him, like he was standin' behind an invisible wall. Didn't have a spot on him!" He paused, frowned. "You don't believe me, either, do you?"

"Who else didn't believe you?"

"The cop who came."

Whatever Barney meant, it was obvious that the incident had left a lasting impression. "Why don't you tell me about it from the beginning?" I said, putting a ten-dollar bill next to the five. My wallet was emptying fast. "I'd like to hear what happened from the time that man walked in here."

"I didn't see him come in. All I know is that he ended up at that table." He pointed to a table on my left. "He didn't look good. You could tell right away he was sick. You know, he was a little green around the gills, and he looked like he'd slept in his clothes. *Nasty* scar down the side of his face; looked fresh-cut, if you know what I mean. At first I thought he was a bum, but he had a touch of class about him. He ordered a cup of coffee, bacon, eggs, and some orange juice, I think."

"Then it was morning?"

"Yeah. And it was summer. I remember it was summertime because of this far-out joker that came to talk to me. I mean, everybody in the city's sweatin' like a pig, and *this* guy's bundled up in a fur coat. Bald-headed guy. Kind of leaned on me when I started tellin' him what I'm tellin' you."

"About the food?" I asked.

"Yeah, about bouncin' the food. First he tried to make out I was nothin' but a crazy old man, like he wanted *me* to believe that. I told him to go screw. Then he offered me money if I'd promise not to tell anybody else about the food. I told him I didn't want his money. I told him I just wanted to be left alone so I could earn my *own* money." He glanced at me suspiciously. "You sure you ain't from Social Security, mister? I *need* this job and the pension just to keep body and soul together."

"C'mon, Barney. You're looking at the last word in neglected minority groups. Tell me what happened after Rafferty ordered breakfast."

"Well, I was bringin' his food over to him on a tray. I was just a coupla feet away from the table when I tripped over a loose board." He pointed behind him into the gloom. "Damn thing's still there. I didn't see exactly what happened because I was fallin' down myself—"

"Then, you didn't actually *see* any food 'bouncing' off Rafferty?"

He stiffened. "No, but I'll tell you what I *did* see. When I got up, this guy didn't have any food on him. The tray was flyin' right at him, so the food *had* to bounce. You get my meanin'?"

I waited, but it seemed that was all there was to it. "You're saying the food didn't get on him?"

He clapped his hands hard, once, then rubbed them on his apron as if he'd hurt himself. "*Now* you got it!" He seemed upset that I wasn't more impressed. "You see," he continued eagerly, "that's what really stuck in my mind. I was worried he'd been scalded by the coffee, but he wasn't. I could see. The food and the coffee were splattered all around him, but he didn't have a spot on him, not a single stain." He frowned, clucked. "But he was hurt; he was moanin' and hangin' on to his head. Then he just passed out. Almost fell on top of me. I tried to bring him around, but he was out cold."

"And you're absolutely *sure* that the food was going to land on him?"

"Yep."

"How do you think he managed it, Barney?"

"Jesus Christ, I don't know, mister. Nobody ever asked me that before." He thought about it for a moment, then cackled at me again. "He must have had one of those 'invisible shields' they talk about on the deodorant commercials!"

"Is there anything else you remember?"

"Nope. Have I earned my money, mister?"

Barney had earned his money, and I'd earned a headache. I got up and shoved the bills into his shirt pocket. "Thanks, Barney. You're a tiger."

"Hey, you really a private detective?"

"Barney," I said, slapping him on the back, "it's hard for me to understand why everyone keeps asking me that question."

The waitress blew me a kiss on my way out.

8

Wanting to clear Barney's laugh and the gloom of Jack's Cakewalk from my mind, I decided to walk the twenty blocks back to my apartment to check the mail. It was a mistake. The noon streets of New York were hot, filled with the stench of exhaust fumes, the tension of constant hurry. By the time I reached my apartment, my headache had evolved from a dull throb to a sharp pain that flashed back and forth between my temples like arcs of electricity.

The man sitting on my couch was short—five feet six or seven. The eyes that had looked so dark in the newspaper photograph were actually a deep, glacial blue, made to seem even larger and colder by the high dome of his forehead. His eyes were like blank screens hiding his thoughts and emotions. I'd seen eyes like that before; they were either the mirrors in front of a psychopathic mind or the result of years of training, tempered by more than a little pain. He was completely bald.

He was a man who seemed totally at ease with himself, even in someone else's living room. He wore a light blue poplin suit with matching shirt and tie. There was no bulge under the armpit, but I was certain that was due to good tailoring.

He rose and put aside the magazine he'd been reading. "I'm Mr. Lippitt," he said, eyeing me steadily.

"I know."

"How do you know?" he asked quietly.

"You've changed your wardrobe. I almost didn't recognize you without your overcoat."

"The newspaper photo," he said. There was a hint of annoyance in his voice, and something that might have been an emotion passed quickly across the blue surface of his eyes and was gone. "The phone number had to come out of the police file. Your brother must have given it to you; very unprofessional of him, but I'm rather glad he did it. Why do you want to know about Victor Rafferty, Dr. Frederickson?"

"You're pretty goddamn abrupt for a guy who's sitting uninvited in my living room."

"Come, come," Lippitt said. His voice had dropped a half octave, the whisper of silk across a knife blade. "You indicated you wanted to talk to me and I'm here. My circumstances don't allow me to stand around on the street waiting for you."

"I can believe that."

"Who are you working for?" Lippitt asked suddenly. His tone had shifted again. He used his voice like a weapon: reasoning, entreating, bludgeoning.

"Why do you care that I'm investigating Victor Rafferty?"

"It upsets me," Lippitt said evenly. There was just the slightest whisper of menace, and I had no doubt that it was intentional.

"Personally?"

"Personally."

"Why, Lippitt?"

It took him a long time to answer. He saw me watching the dark shadows move behind his eyes and looked quickly away. "I feel a responsibility to make certain that people who have been involved in this matter are not physically harmed." He added pointedly: "That includes you."

"Is that a threat, Mr. Lippitt?"

"You might call it a warning."

We could dance around each other's words all day, so I decided to feed him a little information. "Rafferty may not be dead," I said, watching him.

"What are you talking about? Of course he's dead." The impatience and incredulity in his voice seemed genuine, and it surprised me.

"Other people aren't so sure," I said.

He stared at me. "What other people?"

"Myself, for one."

"Who else?" Lippitt persisted. There was something else in his tone now, and I was sure it was fear. Of what? For whom?

"I can't tell you that," I said quietly.

"What *can* you tell me?"

"My turn. Tell me about Rafferty."

"Rafferty is *dead*," Lippitt said forcefully. It seemed to me that he hadn't blinked for a long time.

"He supposedly fell off a catwalk into a furnace filled with molten metal. Did you actually see him fall, Lippitt?"

"Yes," the bald man said calmly; "as a matter of fact, I did. I watched the whole thing."

"Why is it that I didn't see your name in any of the reports on the accident?"

His thin eyebrows arched slightly. "Would you really expect to?"

"Was Harry Barnes with you?"

"The watchman? Yes." He finally blinked. "You've been very busy, Dr. Frederickson. And resourceful."

"I'm a good reader; I was a Bluebird all through first grade. I'm also good in math. If I were to add two plus two in this case, I think I'd end up with a bribe. Did you set Harry Barnes up in the dirty-movie business in exchange for his forgetting the fact that you were there that Sunday?"

"All right," Lippitt said quietly, his eyes shifting. "I suppose that does become obvious."

"Was Barnes even there?"

A long pause. "No," he said at last. "But I was."

"Who the hell *is* Harry Barnes?"

"An ex-watchman who worked in Victor Rafferty's lab, as advertised. That much is true; and the story of what happened to Rafferty is true. I simply could not afford to become involved. You see, you've reached a wrong conclusion from your otherwise astute deductions."

"Have I? Let's take a look at it. A government agent and a world-famous architect are standing around on a catwalk over open smelting furnaces on a Sunday afternoon. You're having a pleasant chat when—whoops!—the architect falls into one of the furnaces. I'll bet that sounds silly even to you."

Lippitt abruptly sat down in a chair, crossed his legs, and lighted a thin cigar. He didn't appear to be amused, and it occurred to me that the man could be dangerous. "Often, what seems silly is the truth, Dr. Frederickson," he said easily, puffing on the cigar.

"Not in this case."

"Why not? I *am* telling the truth about the most important point: Victor Rafferty died five years ago."

"Lippitt, I don't think *anybody* saw Rafferty fall into that furnace." He'd stopped blinking again. "For some reason, you and your people want the world to think Rafferty is dead. Why?" I decided to take a wild swing at a ball thrown in from the bleachers. "Is Harry Barnes really Victor Rafferty?"

He almost smiled. "Are you serious?"

"Yeah, kind of. I admit it would be quite a transformation from the Victor Rafferty I've heard about, but I suppose playing porno-film maker is as good a cover as any."

"Cover for what?"

"For whatever work he actually performs for you."

Lippitt rose, put his hands in his pockets, and walked to

the window. He didn't turn around when he spoke. "We've prepared a psychological profile on you, Dr. Frederickson. It's sketchy because of the limited time we've had, but it's fascinating nonetheless. Your karate, your Ph. D., your obvious need to achieve. You're aggressive, occasionally hostile, but I suppose that's understandable. You have the mind of a giant trapped in a dwarf's body. A pity."

"My mother thought so too," I said testily. "What's your point?"

He slowly turned and dropped his dead cigar into an ashtray. "My point is that we consider you a dangerous man. I'm not sure how to handle you."

"A suggestion: Try telling me the truth."

"The truth here is irrelevant!" he snapped. Then he sucked in a breath. "It is absolutely essential that you drop this investigation!"

"Essential to whom?"

"To the well-being of innocent people," he answered without hesitation. "Do you know what a 'freak' is?"

"Who would know better?" I said drily.

Lippitt didn't smile. "The term 'freak' has a special meaning in my field. Put simply, a freak is a terrorist, a torturer. Most of the ones I know of are truly psychopathic. They're used on occasion by all countries. Their assignment is simply to spread havoc, but only under special circumstances. Such a man was brought into this situation five years ago but—thankfully—never used. That doesn't mean that he won't be used now if it's discovered that this matter has been brought up again."

"As far as I know, you're the only heavyweight who knows about my interest in Rafferty."

Lippitt laughed shortly, without humor. "Yes, but who knows where your questions will lead? My good man, you have no *idea* how dangerous this business could become. The others have resources." He tapped the tips of his fingers together a few times while he stared at me, then dropped his hands to his sides. I had the feeling he'd made some kind of decision.

"I'll tell you the truth that you seem to think is so important and I say is irrelevant," he continued. "I know Rafferty is dead because I killed him."

I studied the map of Lippitt's face, but there was no key there to indicate whether or not he was lying. My mouth had suddenly gone dry. "How?" I asked in a cracked voice.

"I shot him to death," Lippitt said evenly. "He was trying to kill me. It was after I shot him that he fell off the cat-walk into the furnace."

"Why did you kill him, Lippitt? Why were you after him in the first place?"

"He was about to defect to the Russians. He forced the issue; he backed me into a corner."

"But what would the Russians want with an architect?"

"Rafferty had certain invaluable information. We could not let him share that information with anyone."

"What kind of information?"

Lippitt shook his head. "I can't tell you that, Frederickson."

"Maybe you haven't had the time to cook up that part of your story."

He ignored the barb. "I won't argue with you over something that can't be proved," he said quietly. "Perhaps you should simply give me the benefit of the doubt."

"Why should I do that?"

"To save lives." His even tone lent weight to his words. I suddenly felt brushed back and on the defensive. "Other governments knew that Rafferty had this information," Lippitt continued. "What developed was a race to control Rafferty."

"That would explain the Missing Persons report with your name on it."

"Correct. A number of governments were involved; like

us, they would have spared nothing to find him. What Victor Rafferty knew was that valuable. Now, if you continue to stir things up, certain parties may begin to suspect that Rafferty *is* still alive and they'll begin looking for him. If *that* happens, Dr. Frederickson, people will die. I guarantee it."

"Is that what happened to Dr. Morton?"

Lippitt caught his reaction a split second too late. "Who is this Dr. Morton?"

"He *was* Rafferty's neurosurgeon, and I think you know it. He was murdered a few days before the time you say you shot Rafferty. I believe the two cases are linked."

"I wouldn't know anything about that."

I was sure he was lying, and I wondered why. "Somebody else must have shared Rafferty's knowledge," I said.

"Why do you say that?"

"Somebody helped him get out of that locked hospital room," I replied. "If Rafferty had an ally, it seems reasonable to assume that the ally knew what Rafferty knew."

Lippitt shook his head. "Rafferty worked alone. There's a simple explanation for what happened at the hospital: The officer responsible for guarding Rafferty didn't do his job. The door wasn't bolted properly, and the officer fell asleep."

"That's your version. He says he was hypnotized."

"That's rather creative, but it's nonsense. What excuse would *you* use if you'd been in his place?"

"He also believes that you kept him from being sacked."

"Then he's a senile fool."

"You know, Lippitt, you make it easy to suspect that you and your people have Rafferty and don't want anybody to find out about it."

"And what if we did?" Lippitt snapped, anger flaring in his voice. "There would be nothing you could do about it! The only thing you'd accomplish would be to bring trouble—maybe death—to innocent people. The *first* person they might go after could be his widow."

"Why? Because she knows what Rafferty knew?"

"Because the others might *think* that she does, or think that she knows where he is. *You* could be in great danger as a result of what you're doing, but that doesn't seem to bother you."

"On the contrary," I said; "you're scaring the hell out of me. I don't want anyone to get hurt, and that includes me. But I don't like to be threatened, either. You're not what I'd call a disinterested party."

"Why did you go to the U.N.?"

"If Rafferty is alive, he may have been working there two years ago. He may even be working there now."

"What are you talking about?" In his voice there was disbelief mixed with concern.

Lippitt seemed to grow agitated as I showed him the picture of the Nately Museum and gave him a quick rundown of what I'd learned.

"Impossible," he said when I'd finished.

"Why?"

Lippitt's body suddenly convulsed, and for a moment I feared he was having an epileptic seizure. He was shuddering, as if suffering from a bone-cracking cold blowing in from some subterranean region of his mind. I moved toward him, but he held out his hand to keep me away. I watched with horrified fascination as Lippitt struggled to bring his body under control. Gradually, the shuddering abated, his teeth stopped chattering, and blood came back to his face. He leaned hard against the wall, then straightened up.

"You must excuse me," he said quietly.

"Can I get you something?"

"No, thank you. I'll be all right." He took a deep breath. "Have you discussed this matter with anyone at the U.N.?"

"Maybe," I said after a pause.

"Then you've made a terrible mistake. I understand that you mistrust me and my motives, and that you think I'm lying. But I want you to consider what *your* burden of responsibility will be if I'm telling the truth."

"I'll give it a lot of thought," I replied, meaning it. "One more question: Do *you* know what it was that Rafferty knew?"

"That will have to remain a mystery." He turned and walked to the door. He hesitated a moment and I thought he was going to add something, but he didn't. He stared at me for a few seconds, then left. The air in the apartment suddenly felt oppressive and dank, as if Lippitt had left behind some of his private cold.

9

Lippitt had done his homework well; although he never said so, I was convinced he knew about my last case. He'd repeatedly warned me about the possibility of people getting hurt, and his words had had their intended effect. I sat on my couch for a long time after he left, thinking, staring into space. Finally I got up and went to the phone.

There was no answer at Mike Foster's office, so, reluctantly, I called his home. Elizabeth Foster answered in her hollow-sounding voice. I felt strange talking to her, knowing that she probably held the secret to the riddle of Victor Rafferty. I was beginning to see the dimensions, if not the exact shape, of the nightmare she was living.

Foster was out on a job, but his wife gave me a number where he could be reached. I dialed and finally got through to him.

"Frederickson here, Mike."

"Right." He sounded anxious.

"We should talk," I said. "Can we meet sometime today?"

There was a short pause. His breathing was rapid and shallow, as if he'd been running. "I can't get out of here now. Later?"

"How about dinner?"

"All right," he replied after another pause. "I'll tell Elizabeth I have to entertain a client."

"Can you stop home first?"

"Probably. Why?"

"You mentioned a safe containing some of Rafferty's personal effects. Can you get into it?"

He thought about it. "I don't know, Frederickson. I can't go rummaging around without Elizabeth asking why."

"I need something with Rafferty's fingerprints on it."

"I'll do the best I can," he said. "Have you got a suspect?"

"Just taking a wild shot. Do you know where Danny's is?"

"West Seventy-second."

"Is seven good?"

"Seven it is."

Next, I called Abu's office. His secretary told me he was out to lunch. "I want to leave a message," I said. "Tell him that Mongo called." I spelled it for her. "Right. Tell him I said to *lay off* our project. He'll know what I mean. Ask him to call me when he gets in, or whenever it's convenient." I gave her my number, thanked her, and hung up.

My talk with Lippitt had left me a little shaky. I certainly didn't want to be responsible for anyone's getting hurt, so I thought it better to ease off on any inquiries until I'd had more of a chance to determine whether Lippitt had been telling the truth or was just trying to bluff me.

Not wanting to miss Abu's call, I stayed in the apartment; I made myself some lunch and picked at it. The phone didn't ring. I tried reading a book and fell asleep; it was past five when I woke up. It wasn't likely that I'd slept through a ringing telephone, but I called Abu's office anyway. He hadn't returned from lunch. I sat by the phone for another forty-five minutes, then showered and tried to put the worry out of my mind as I went to meet Foster at Danny's.

Foster was sitting in a back booth, under an autographed picture of Mel Tormé. I sat down next to him under a photo of Jack Dempsey. Foster's light hair was unkempt, as if he'd been running his fingers through it. He pointed silently to a package wrapped in oilcloth on the table in front of him. I carefully unwrapped the cloth. He'd brought me a draftsman's tool kit. I used the tip of my table knife to lift up the cover; inside was an array of drafting tools. Most of the surfaces were thin and round, but there were just enough flat surfaces to make me think there might be latent prints there.

"I imagine a lot of people have handled that box since Victor's death," Foster said, "but there may be some of his prints on the tools inside. Nobody would have had a reason to handle those."

I thanked him and slipped the thin box into my jacket pocket.

"Whose prints are you going to compare those with?" Foster asked.

"I told you it was a wild shot," I said, evading the question. "In any case, I think it's a good idea to have some kind of fingerprint record on Rafferty. The police didn't have him long enough to print him."

Over vodka martinis I brought Foster up to date. He absorbed it all in silence, occasionally stirring his drink. When I finished he grimaced and slowly, emphatically, shook his head.

"This Lippitt character is lying."

"Why do you say that?"

"I knew Victor Rafferty as well as anybody. He wasn't any Russian agent. He *couldn't* have been a spy. Architecture was his whole life. My God, Victor just didn't have *time* to be a spy."

"He did a lot of traveling, didn't he? His career would have given him a perfect cover."

"I'm telling you he wasn't a spy," Foster said determinedly.

"Actually, Lippitt never said Rafferty was a *spy*. He said Rafferty was going to defect to the Russians. There's a difference."

Foster spoke hotly. "It's still a dirty accusation! It would *kill* Elizabeth. He's lying, which means he's covering up something. I want to find out what it is."

"It might be better to leave it alone, Mike," I said quietly.

He glanced at me sharply, surprise and anger in his eyes. "I heard you didn't scare off so easy."

"How easily I scare isn't the point, Mike. There are other considerations. I don't know if Lippitt is telling the truth, but I do believe that Rafferty was somehow involved in some very dangerous business. Just for the sake of argument, let's assume that Rafferty *isn't* dead. Now, what's the point of trying to prove it? Do you think it will help your wife's peace of mind if she finds out her first husband isn't dead after all?"

Foster stared into his drink, then slowly nodded his head. "I see your point. Even if Victor is alive, maybe it's better if Elizabeth never finds out about it."

"Also, Lippitt said that it could be dangerous for other people if I continued the investigation. The fact that *he* came out of the woodwork proves his contention that important people take an interest in this case. I'm not sure that you want to take a chance on anybody's getting hurt. I know *I* don't."

"Are you saying that you're dropping the case?" Foster sounded concerned.

"For the time being, at least. I think it's better to let things cool down and sift awhile. I'm leaving Thursday anyway."

"How long will you be gone?" He avoided my eyes.

"Three weeks, unless I get eaten by a great white shark."

Foster wasn't in the mood for jokes. He leaned against the vinyl backing of the booth and pressed a hand to his forehead. "If I drop it now . . . Elizabeth's in really bad shape."

"She could end up in even worse shape if we continue."

"I'd . . . always wonder," he said distantly.

"Maybe you can handle uncertainty better than your wife

can handle the truth," I said. "Still, I've got a file on this, and I've taped a lot of thoughts. If you want, I'll turn them over to somebody else you can trust before I leave."

"Uh-uh. I like the way you operate." He was staring at a large wall mirror across the room, as if searching for truth there, forgetting that mirrors only reflect the truth of the people looking into them. "You'll be back three weeks from Thursday?" He half-smiled. "Unless you get eaten by a great white shark?"

"Not necessarily to work on this case, Mike. I don't think I want the responsibility."

"But it would be *my* responsibility if I wanted to continue. I'd just like to know if you'll go back to work on it when you come back . . . if I decide I want to know more."

"I'll have to think about it."

"Fair enough. Who knows? Maybe I'll be able to convince Elizabeth that *we* should get away for a couple of weeks. I think a change of scenery might do her some good."

"Do you want my file and tapes?"

"Not now," he said. "Why don't you hang on to them until you get back?"

"Okay. I'd also like to keep the draftsman's kit for a while."

"Of course. How much do I owe you up to this point, Frederickson?"

"Why don't you come around to my office tomorrow afternoon? I'll give you an itemized bill. I should also be finished with the kit by then."

We made an appointment for two o'clock.

The relief I'd expected to feel the next morning wasn't there: only unrelieved anxiety about Abu, distracting as a bad hangover. There'd been no messages left with my answering service. It was too early to start calling, so I tried to put the worry out of my mind, at least temporarily.

After breakfast, I went to see my brother. I found Garth looking hurt and annoyed, stuffed into his cubicle writing reports. The typewriter bounced like a toy under the merciless attack of his thick fingers.

"Hey, brother! Guess who's come to visit you."

"Christ," he said without looking up. "I hope you're not here to take up my time or looking for any more favors; I'm out of both."

"What about a fingerprint kit?"

That got his attention. He eased up on the typewriter, and I thought I could almost hear the machine sigh. "Why the hell do you want a fingerprint kit?"

"Just want to check out a couple of long shots." I took out Tal's pencil and Elliot Thomas' protractor and laid them on the desk in front of Garth.

"What's this? Show and Tell?"

"How long will a fingerprint last?"

Garth shrugged. "Indefinitely, as long as it's on a good surface that's been protected."

I took the draftsman's kit out of my pocket and shoved it across the desk to Garth. "Rafferty's prints may be on some of these tools. I'd like to compare them with whatever you can get off the pencil and the protractor."

"The pencil will be tough."

"Can you get partials?"

"Maybe. I'll have to see. Where'd you get the goodies?"

"The protractor from a man named Elliot Thomas, and the pencil from Ronald Tal."

"Tal? You've been traveling in high circles and keeping bad company."

"Careful, brother. Your Midwest conservatism is showing."

Garth whistled softly. "Christ, you think either of these guys could be Rafferty?"

"Doubtful, but I've got to start thinning the herd somewhere. Both men are about the right height and seem the right age; both men are Americans." Garth looked skeptical. "What can I tell you?" I added. "This is known as being methodical."

101

"How the hell do you get mixed up in these things? How the hell do *I* get mixed up in these things?" He rummaged around in his desk drawers until he finally came up with the kit. He used a pair of tweezers to lift the pencil and protractor from the cellophane sleeves I'd placed them in, then laid the items carefully beside the draftsman's kit. He opened the kit and began dusting the flat metal surfaces of the tools inside.

"Can I use your phone?" I asked.

Garth nodded as he continued dusting the implements. I picked up the receiver and dialed Abu's office. Abu still wasn't in; his secretary hadn't seen him since before lunch the previous day. I checked to make sure she had my message right, then hung up. I stared at the phone for a long time. It took me a few moments to realize that what I felt was fear.

Garth broke into my thoughts. "Take a look at these."

I took the magnifying glass he offered and studied the marks he'd raised on the instruments.

"You lucked out, Mongo," Garth said. "You've got good prints on the protractor, and decent partials on the pencil and the instruments. As far as I can see, there's no match anywhere. If you want, I'll have the lab boys take a look."

It wasn't necessary; I could see that the three sets of prints were entirely different. "Don't bother," I said, snapping the kit closed and putting it back into my pocket. "Two down, a few dozen to go. Case closed."

"Case closed?"

"For me, anyway. Too much risk with too little to gain for everybody involved."

"I don't follow you, Mongo. I thought you were really hot to go on this one. I'd have laid odds the trip to Acapulco was going to be postponed."

"Nope. Some folks I liked got hurt in the last case I was working on. I don't want to see that happen again." I outlined for Garth the reasoning I'd presented to Foster. Garth

102

listened in silence, tapping his fingers thoughtfully on the desk top.

"Heavy," he said when I'd finished. "You're worried about me too, aren't you?"

"Has anybody leaned on you since Sunday?"

Garth pursed his lips and slowly shook his head. "Haven't heard a word."

"Lippitt knows you gave me his number. The man works fast, and he's dangerous."

Garth shrugged. "All must be forgiven."

"Or he's saving that kind of pressure as an ace in the hole. I'm pretty sure you'd be out on the street in a minute if he lifted the wrong eyebrow."

Garth's eyes glinted angrily. "We don't run this department to suit some super-Fed!" He paused, laughed to break the tension. "I guess I'm getting a little skittish myself. You think this Rafferty really is alive?"

"I don't know. It's impossible to read this Lippitt. He's playing some kind of game, but I don't know what it is. If Rafferty is alive, I think there's a good possibility that Lippitt and his merry band have him; they just don't want anybody to know it. But Lippitt *says* he shot Rafferty himself."

"Really?" It wasn't a wisecrack; Garth was listening intently.

"One more free opinion," I said. "I'm convinced Arthur Morton's murder is connected with the Rafferty case. I'm sure Lippitt knew what I was talking about when I mentioned it."

"Lippitt said so?"

"No. He pretended not to know anything about Morton. I think he was lying."

"God, you're a veritable lie detector, aren't you?"

"It was a feeling."

Garth reached into his desk and took out two manila folders. He opened them and absently gazed at the contents.

103

The papers inside were photocopies of the Rafferty and Morton files.

"It's pretty risky having that stuff in your desk, isn't it?" I asked. "A lot of people would be unhappy if they found out you were going to nose around."

Garth replaced the folders in his desk and closed the drawer. "Just wanted you to know that a humble public servant is on the job," Garth said with a smile. "When do you leave for the Sunny South?"

"Thursday."

"Remember to send me a postcard."

I tried to shake off the feeling of exclusion, the suspicion that I'd gone gun-shy. "How about that steak now?"

"You hungry?" Garth sounded distracted.

"Not really, no. But I'd like to buy my brother a steak. You mind?"

Garth pushed the typewriter aside and rose. "I thought you'd never get around to it," he said. "But I don't like it when you sound like you're buying a condemned man his last meal."

After lunch I went to my uptown office to wait for Foster. Another call to Abu's office told me he still wasn't in. The secretary wouldn't give me his unlisted home number. I tried to occupy myself by reading the junk mail that had accumulated. Two o'clock came and went. At two forty-five I left a message taped to the door and caught a subway downtown. I was getting edgy. For all I knew, Abu was holed up somewhere with a mistress, but I wanted to do a little personal checking.

A few blocks from the subway station the upended stone-and-glass slab that was the U.N. Secretariat building rose into a cloudless, azure sky—a gigantic symbol of man's striving for something better than the economic and po-litical squalor the majority of his fellows were accustomed to.

Sunlight glinted off the polished windows on the upper stories as a flock of starlings rode an air current up off the East River and across the face of the building. Suddenly another, larger bird appeared, a little behind the others. This bird was surrounded by a glistening shower of what looked like water. The bird flapped helplessly and plunged toward the earth as its companions flew on without it.

I was running before the body hit the ground.

The screams of police and ambulance sirens were closing in as I reached the U.N. plaza. Theirs was a futile, hopeless sound; the man who had fallen would never need an ambulance or a policeman again.

Stunned pedestrians and U.N. guards stood around staring at something just out of my line of vision. I pushed through the gathering crowd and stopped a few paces away from the bloody, broken thing splashed over the concrete apron. The head was a shapeless jam, but one hand lay in macabre, ironic repose atop the caved-in chest. I'd seen the large opal ring on the finger before.

I stared at what was left of the gentle Pakistani for a few moments, then turned away and dazedly groped my way back through the crowd toward the street. Cops and stretcher bearers raced past me in the opposite direction, but it seemed as if they and everything else were going in slow motion. I heard Abu's voice, speaking to me from the opposite end of a long, dark tunnel, telling me how happy he'd be to help me.

Now he was dead. He'd asked the wrong people the wrong questions.

Now I needed some answers. I needed to know why a friend of mine was dead; to find out what terrible knowledge Victor Rafferty had possessed. There was only one person besides Lippitt who I thought could give me those answers, and that was where I intended to go.

Still numb with shock and something like terror, I managed to hail a cab. I mumbled Foster's address, then sank back into the cab's cracked leather seat. I thought I heard Garth yelling at me as the cab pulled away, but I wasn't sure whether the voice was any more real than Abu's, and didn't really care.

Feeling started to return during the long ride to Queens, but I still saw mental flashes of Abu's body plummeting like a wingless bird to be squashed on a hot sidewalk. Garth was going to be asking me some tough questions when I got back, and I intended to ask them of Mrs. Foster first. The toughest questions were the ones I was going to be asking of myself.

I was wound down by the time I reached the Fosters' home: an expensive trilevel on a street with just enough other houses to provide neighbors, but not enough to make anyone feel crowded. I'd originally intended to come on like Dr. J driving for the basket and start firing questions. Now I realized that that wouldn't help anyone. I wasn't going to feel particularly gallant pumping Mrs. Foster for information if she was alone, so I stood on the sidewalk, hands in my pockets, staring at the house and trying to figure out what I wanted to do.

There was no sign of the Olds: just a black Falcon in the driveway, probably Mrs. Foster's. A phone started to ring inside the house. It rang five or six times, then stopped, unanswered. The muscles in my stomach knotted. I walked up to the front door and tried the bell. There was no answer. I rang the bell again, then pounded on the door; still no answer. It suddenly became very important to me that I get inside the house. It was broad daylight, but I was in a hurry and not thinking too clearly; I used a plastic credit card to jimmy my way past the spring lock and into the house.

Not sure what I expected to find, I went through the house room by room. The fact that the door was locked and hadn't been tampered with seemed to be a good sign. Everything inside the house seemed in order; there were no signs of a struggle. The Fosters had apparently left the house under their own power. The question remained as to where they had gone, and why Foster hadn't kept our appointment.

I used the phone to call my answering service. There were no messages from Foster, or anyone else. Next I called Garth's station house. Garth was out. Finally I called a cab, then the airline to cancel my flight to Acapulco.

10

Garth was waiting for me on the steps of the station house when my cab pulled up to the curb. He came down to the sidewalk to meet me. "You knew him, didn't you?" he said perfunctorily. His eyes were opaque, stirred by conflicting emotions.

"Yes." He didn't have to tell me whom he was talking about. "And I think I'm responsible for his death."

"You have an inclination toward self-pity," Garth snapped. "Some bloody bastard pushed him out a window, and I sure as hell know it wasn't you."

"I'm sorry I ran out on you back there," I said, my voice thick with fatigue. "I couldn't . . . handle it at the time."

Garth nodded. "It has something to do with the Rafferty case, doesn't it?"

"I think so," I said, knowing so.

"Then maybe it's time you told me everything you know, right from the beginning."

We went into Garth's office and spent the next three quarters of an hour going over what I knew and a little of what I suspected. A second shock wave of horror rolled over me, taking away my breath. Garth saw and tried to beat it back with words.

"You say you talked with him yesterday morning," Garth

said, poking me on the arm and forcing me to focus my attention on his words. "Then it all happened incredibly fast."

"Somebody inside that building killed him. And it wasn't a visitor—not up on those floors."

"Rafferty?"

"More likely somebody looking for him. Whoever did it probably thought that Abu knew something. God *damn!*"

"You could be the next target."

"I hope so," I said evenly.

"That sounds suicidal."

"No. Homicidal."

Garth looked at me for a long time. "These boys are rough, Mongo, and they seem to be in a big hurry. There was enough left of your friend to determine that he'd been tortured."

"What's going to be done about it?" I whispered hoarsely.

Garth took a long time to answer. "I don't think anything will be done about it; at least not by the N.Y.P.D."

"Why the hell not?"

"Because your friend fell out of the U.N. building. Even if we wanted to, we can't go in there without an invitation. It's like a sovereign state."

"Why *shouldn't* there be an invitation?"

"Because somebody will object; somebody *always* objects. Besides, it wouldn't do any good." He paused, hit his desk in frustration. "Let's suppose we *did* find out something— which is highly unlikely. Almost everyone in there, with the exception of the Americans, enjoys diplomatic immunity. We couldn't do anything with the killer if we *did* find him."

"What about the publicity? Don't the U.N. people want the public to think they're doing something about it?"

"Oh, the publicity will be bad for a few days, but then it'll die down. It would be even worse if they asked for a police investigation; the police would be followed and questioned by reporters for days, weeks, months, however long it took."

"Then the murderer goes free?"

"I'm afraid that's it. Unless he gets called on the carpet for sloppy workmanship; there are a hell of a lot of tidier ways to kill a man than to push him out the twenty-seventh floor of the U.N. building."

"That's what I was thinking."

"Exactly what would that be?"

"That he wasn't pushed. There's no way the people involved in this thing would want to attract so much attention."

Garth studied me. "You think he *jumped*?"

"Yes. As a warning signal to me. He knew they were going to kill him, and he wanted to warn me that I'd be next. He'd given them my name under torture."

"We'll give you some protection."

Garth started to reach for the telephone and I grabbed his wrist. "I don't want it," I said. "Besides, I don't think it would do any good. If they want me, they'll find a way to get me."

"Are you still going to Acapulco?"

"No."

Garth's eyes narrowed. "What do you plan to do, Mongo?"

"I don't know." The next words forced their way out of me. "I'd like to do a little killing."

"That's not hard to understand, but you're going to have to learn to live with it."

"I may not be able to. They must know about me, and they're going to want to know what *I* know. They're going to be watching, waiting."

"You keep your eyes open, brother."

"What about the Morton case?"

Garth tapped his fingers on the side of his chair. He

seemed angry, frustrated. "I requested permission to reopen it. I was turned down flat. The U.N. isn't the only organization that doesn't want local cops nosing around in its business."

"Then there *has* to be a tie-in with Rafferty!"

Garth nodded. I turned and walked out of the office.

Somebody already knew what I knew: My apartment had been broken into and ransacked. The tapes I'd made were gone. They'd ignored my gun. I cleaned and loaded it, then strapped on my shoulder holster. If they had my tapes, they didn't need me. On the other hand, they might want to make sure that I hadn't left anything out. I hoped someone would come for me. It was the only way I could avenge Abu's death.

Waiting: For most of the afternoon I sat in a chair, sweating, watching the door. I called the Foster home four times and didn't get an answer. Mike's office hadn't heard from him either. In the evening, Ronald Tal called to invite me to a memorial service for Abu the next morning at eleven. I said I'd be there.

After rigging up a crude alarm system, I went to bed with my hand on the gun under my pillow. I slept badly, dreaming of a man with a secret so deadly that men were willing to torture and kill almost at the mere mention of his name.

In the morning I took an ice-cold shower and tried to pull myself together. I dressed, ate, and went out into the brilliant morning sunshine. The hard bulge of the revolver in my armpit felt reassuring.

On the steps of the U.N. plaza a woman with blue hair was standing by the spot where Abu had fallen, gesturing excitedly to the two young children she had in tow. I identified myself to a guard at the entrance, and he escorted me to a small, dimly lighted chapel. At the front was a

111

closed casket surrounded by banks of lilies. The symbol of Islam hung on the wall behind the casket, and there was an honor guard of Pakistanis standing by the bier. Taped organ music played softly in the background.

I stood by the bier for a few minutes staring into the reflections in the oiled mahogany surface of the casket, then turned and walked toward the back of the chapel. The pews were sparsely filled with morning-coated representatives of the various member nations. I found a black-suited Tal in the right-hand corner of the last pew.

He rose and offered me his hand. "Hello, Dr. Frederickson," he said quietly.

"Thanks for the call," I said. "Abu was a good friend of mine."

"He was my friend too," Tal said softly. "Which is why I thought you wouldn't mind my asking some questions."

"I don't feel much like answering questions, and I'm not sure this is the proper time or place."

"It won't make much difference to Abu, will it? I'd like to find out who did this to him, but I need information. Assuming you're being watched, I thought this chapel would be the safest place to talk. We both have a reason for being here."

"All right," I said. "Are you doing this on your own?"

"No. The Secretary General would like to know what happened, and why. This has happened in our 'house,' so to speak. Effective steps can be taken to find out who the murderer is and have him recalled."

"I had something else in mind."

"We'll have to settle for what we can get. But the publicity I'll arrange will be very embarrassing to the country involved. I can almost guarantee that they'll punish whoever is responsible."

"All right, I'm listening."

The pew was hard and I shifted in my seat, half-turning toward Tal. As I moved, I caught sight of something out of the corner of my eye that made me turn all the way around. Elliot Thomas' head jerked back almost imperceptibly. There was no way of knowing how long he'd been standing there, watching, but it was obvious that I'd startled him. He nodded slightly, then walked slowly down the aisle toward the bier.

"Is something the matter?" Tal asked.

"No," I said after a pause. "Just uncomfortable. I'm all right now."

"You asked me about Victor Rafferty. Was Abu making the same kind of inquiries?"

"Yes," I said tersely.

"Can you tell me who hired you?"

"Why?"

"Perhaps it would be a clue," Tal said softly.

"I don't think so." I wasn't ready to trust Tal—or anyone else who didn't already know—with the Fosters' name, at least not until I found out where they were.

Thomas remained at the bier for a few moments, head bowed, then turned and walked back up the aisle. He didn't look at me as he passed.

Tal remained silent for a few minutes, thinking. Then he said, "Victor Rafferty was obviously more than just the greatest architect of our age."

Deciding it might be time to open up a bit, I told Tal about Lippitt, and some of what Lippitt had told me.

Tal took some time to digest what I'd told him, then said: "It seems that everyone was satisfied as long as they believed Victor Rafferty was dead. It's the possibility of his being alive that they find so upsetting."

"That's exactly right." I had the feeling I was being watched. I quickly glanced around me, but Elliot Thomas was nowhere in sight. I was surprised to find that almost all the mourners had changed; they seemed to be coming and going in ten minute shifts. At the moment there was a large number of Asians.

"Tell me," Tal said. "On the basis of your investigation so far, do *you* believe that Rafferty is alive?"

"There are two versions of how he died," I said, turning back to him. "In both versions he ends up in a furnace filled with molten metal. Either way, there wouldn't be any trace."

"You mean, if it ever happened."

"Sure. But Lippitt was pretty forceful on that point. He says he shot Rafferty first."

"He could be lying. As you point out, the furnace story would be a handy excuse not to have to produce a body."

"Still, there was something about Lippitt that bothered me. He seemed to be taking the whole matter personally. He told me something like this could happen. I should have listened harder."

"Then you blame yourself for Abu's death?"

"That's right."

"I think your guilt is misplaced."

"Don't patronize me, Tal."

"All right. Feel guilty if it helps you."

My first reaction was anger. Then something happened which I could not understand and which frightened me; for a split second I thought I was losing my mind. I heard a sound that was not a sound; a single soft, dizzying chime inside my mind that cleared away the din of jumbled, jagged thoughts, leaving in its echoing wake an absolute stillness. Into that silence came a voice that was not a voice, an eerie sensation of speech without sound, a series of vibrations echoing in my subconscious and delivering a message I could understand and accept: Abu's death was not my fault; by the time I'd been in a position to warn Abu, it was already too late.

I could feel the guilt being lifted from me, to be replaced by a kind of warmth and gentle sadness that allowed me to genuinely grieve for my friend. I wiped away tears.

114

"Frederickson?"

"Huh?" I'd forgotten all about Tal.

"Are you all right? You look pale."

"I'm all right."

"Do you want to leave?"

"No. Not just yet," I said distantly. I felt strangely disoriented, but at peace.

"Did you finish your investigation to your satisfaction?" Tal asked quietly.

"I'm finished."

"There would appear to be a slight semantic difference."

"No semantics involved. I'm just off the case." Any investigating I did from that point on would be done strictly in secret. I had to find the Fosters.

"Don't you want to find Abu's killer?"

"Yes, but not if it means more people will die."

Tal quietly cleared his throat. "The Secretary General would like to see you continue the investigation. I think you'll find his terms generous."

I looked up, surprised. "Why me?"

"You're the only logical choice. You're already deeply involved; you know the case."

"Why don't you use your own people?"

"Because the Secretary General would like this investigation to be carried on outside of regular channels, for obvious reasons."

"Lippitt was right," I said, looking away. "People get hurt when you start mentioning Rafferty's name."

"That phase of it may be over; there's been too much publicity over Abu's murder. But more people could die in any case. Consider: You're undoubtedly being watched and followed in an effort to see what you turn up. If you cut off your investigation, the others may continue on their own. They won't ask questions as gently as you do. You've seen the results of their work."

I decided to walk around the suggestion and look at it awhile longer. "It seems like pretty dirty business for a Secretary General to involve himself in."

Tal considered it, then said, "Would you agree that Rolfe Thaag is the most effective Secretary General the U.N. has ever had?"

"He's good."

"Well, he's only as 'good' as the information he receives. In the world of international politics and diplomacy, information is the most valuable commodity. Facts are badly needed here if Abu's murderer is to be brought to justice. And, of course, we want to know if Rafferty *is* here at the United Nations, and if so, what he's doing." He paused, drumming his fingers silently on the back of the pew in front of him. "Will you work for us?"

The crowd had shifted again; the Europeans had taken over. I pretended to mull the offer over, even though I knew what I was going to say. The case couldn't be closed for me until I learned the Fosters were safe. If I was going to look for them, I might as well be paid while I was doing it. "All right," I said. "But I'll drop it again like a hot potato if I think there's good reason to."

"Fair enough," Tal said easily, removing a roll of bills from his pocket. He casually peeled off five hundred dollars and handed me the money. "This will be a retainer."

"You'll get my regular rates," I said, pocketing the cash. "How can I get in touch with you easily?"

He handed me a card. "You can reach me—or someone who knows where I am—at that number, twenty-four hours a day." He looked at me intently. "I appreciate the fact that this is a very dangerous assignment for you."

I knew it was time to steer the conversation into other channels. "Yeah. Tell me, what's an American doing as the Secretary General's top assistant? I wouldn't think that would go down too well with about ninety-five percent of the membership."

Tal smiled wryly. "Now it is the Americans who complain the loudest. In any case, I was appointed, not elected. The Secretary General finds me useful."

"There are a lot of Americans who think you're a traitor to your country."

"That's sad," he said quickly, with a hint of feeling. "Americans are no different from any other people in that they don't like to be criticized—"

"Especially by another American who happens to be working for the Secretary General of the United Nations."

"At the risk of sounding pompous, I'll tell you that I consider my constituency to be the people of the world. And myself a citizen of the world. If you'd grown up in Europe—say, Norway—as I did, you wouldn't find that so hard to understand. Americans are extremely chauvinistic, you know."

"Are you really that divorced from any feeling as an American?"

He smiled. "I'll admit that, at times, I feel little tugs of pride, shame, or anger at being an American, but I generally try to fight such emotions; they're not conducive to good work habits, and I honestly reject patriotism intellectually. There is no logic to patriotism in either a practical or a historical sense." He paused, smiled again. "Does that answer your question?"

"When this is all over, we'll have to sit down and discuss it some more."

"I'd enjoy that, Dr. Frederickson."

"Assistants to the Secretary General are allowed to call me Mongo."

"Okay, Mongo."

We rose together to leave. I was halfway out of the pew when I saw the bald-headed man striding up the center aisle. Lippitt saw me a half-second later and stiffened. He glanced back and forth between Tal and me, then abruptly walked out of the chapel.

"Who was that?" Tal asked. "He seemed to know you."

"That's Mr. Lippitt."

"The one who says he shot Rafferty?"

"One and the same," I said, sliding the rest of the way out of the pew. "I'll be in touch."

11

The quiet, solemn organ music from the chapel faded away
as I followed Lippitt out of the U.N. to where the city was
playing a different sound: the mad, jumbled, cacophonous
roar that was the urban symphony. Lippitt was waiting for
me outside on the plaza. The noon sun was hot and bright,
welcoming me back to the world of the living.

"I want to talk to you," Lippitt said tersely.

"Okay." I walked to the edge of the concourse, leaned
on a concrete parapet, and watched the traffic flow up First
Avenue.

"I'm sorry about what happened to your friend," Lippitt
said as he came up beside me.

The sincerity in his voice surprised me. I looked into his
face and, for a moment, he seemed different: no longer
Super Agent devoid of feeling, but a man in his fifties
holding himself together well—a hard, tough man doing a
hard, mean job. I suddenly realized that I wanted to know
more about him; I didn't even know his first name.

"Thank you," I said.

His eyes and voice suddenly turned cold. "Damn it,
Frederickson, I warned you something like this could happen."

"Go to hell. I tried to take your advice, but you warned

me too late. It was one of your colleagues who killed him."

"Don't be a fool," he said contemptuously. "Bhutal was not killed by the Americans."

"What's the difference? You're *all* fucking idiots!" I immediately felt childish, but it didn't make any difference. Lippitt was obviously beyond any insult I could come up with; he didn't even blink.

"How do you know Tal?" he asked calmly.

"How do *you* know him?"

"I don't know him personally," Lippitt said evenly. "I know *of* him. He's not exactly a friend of the United States."

"He's not exactly an enemy, either."

Lippitt picked up a pebble, examined it, tossed it to the sidewalk below. "That depends on your point of view."

"What you mean is that he doesn't always agree with our policies."

"I mean," Lippitt suddenly shot back, "that I'd like to know what you were talking about in there."

"That's none of your business, Lippitt."

"It's your country's business, and that makes it my business." He was angry now, making no attempt to hide it. "When you took on this case, you opened up a Pandora's box that I thought was closed five years ago. Damn it, you've started a chain reaction, and it has to be stopped! Those stains on the concrete could well have been *you*!"

"Don't worry about me," I said. "Why don't you tell me why Victor Rafferty was so important to you? Why did you kill him . . . if you *did* kill him?"

"I killed him, but I can't tell you what you want to know. You *must* tell me who hired you."

"No."

"Will you tell me *why* you were hired?"

"If I tell you 'why,' you'll know 'who.' "

Lippitt scratched a well-groomed fingernail across the pebbled stone in front of him. Again, I had the feeling he

120

was suppressing considerable anger. "Tell me, Frederickson: Have you run across the name Foster in your investigation?"

"Why?" I asked. The word seemed to stick in my throat as wet cold rippled across my belly.

"Foster is the married name of Rafferty's widow." Lippitt was staring out at the traffic, but his voice hummed with guy-wire tension. "She married a construction contractor who used to do a lot of work for Rafferty. Both of them have been under our protection for the past five years, although they haven't known it. Yesterday they dropped out of sight. We don't know where they are, but I suspect their disappearance has something to do with your investigation." He paused, took a deep breath, straightened up, and stared down at me; I could hear the breath whistling angrily in his lungs. His voice was soft but distinctly threatening, like the deadly hiss of a snake. "If anything happens to the Fosters, I am going to hold you personally responsible."

At that point I might have told Lippitt what he wanted to know, but he wasn't listening. He abruptly walked around me and down off the concourse, pushed through a crowd of pedestrians waiting at the corner, and zigzagged across First Avenue without waiting for the light. I stared after him. I wanted to shout at him, tell him that I was already personally responsible. I was on a deadly roller coaster with no way to get off.

A cloud had slipped across the sun and I was cold.

I took a bus crosstown to the *New York Times* building, made a few inquiries, and was directed into an elevator that led up to the third floor, where I got out and walked down a carpeted corridor until I found a door with the name FRANK ALDEN.

Alden was a man in his late fifties who looked as if he'd spent most of his life auditioning for a part in *The Front Page*. He was actually wearing a wide-brimmed hat shoved

121

on the back of his head. Naturally, a cigarette dangled from the edge of his mouth and there were ashes strewn down the front of his shirt. His collar was loose, and a thick clump of gray hair protruded between the open buttons. He had his feet up on a scarred desk and was scanning a racing sheet; he was straight out of Central Casting. The walls of the office were covered from floor to ceiling with blown-up, glossy black-and-white photographs. *They* were fresh, original.

I rapped on the open door. "Mr. Alden?"

He looked up and stared at me with eyes the same steely gray as his chest hair. Suddenly he put his feet on the floor and began to rapidly snap his fingers. "Mongo the Magnificent," he barked in clipped tones. "Retired circus headliner, used to be with Statler Brothers; now a criminology professor and private detective; real name"—he snapped his fingers some more—"Dick Frederickson."

"Try Bob," I said. "It sounds as if you're preparing my obituary."

"Nah. I did a photo essay on you once."

"You've got a good memory, Mr. Alden."

"Call me Frank. You get mixed up in some pretty strange cases."

I walked into the office, stopped in front of his desk. "I've got a strange case now, Frank. I was hoping you might be able to help me with it."

He pulled his battered hat down low on his forehead and peered at me from under the brim. He actually did: I could almost hear the purr of movie cameras. "You name it, Mongo." He made it sound conspiratorial.

I put the newspaper photograph with the question mark on the desk in front of Alden. "This picture has your photo credit on it. It was taken about five years ago. I want to know if you can remember the circumstances under which it was shot."

Again the popping fingers. Both hands. "Rafferty," he said at last. "Victor Rafferty, the hotshot architect. That's his house." He slapped his hands on the desk and corrected himself. "*Was* his house. He died a few days after that picture was taken."

"Right. What's going on there? Do you remember?"

"I remember, all right. But if I'd been able to find out what was going on, they wouldn't have used that question mark as a caption."

"How did you happen to be there?"

"I've got a police radio in the car. Somebody phoned in a complaint about disturbing the peace. It was early in the morning. Anyway, I was in the neighborhood and I decided to check it out." He tapped the photograph. "I saw what you see here. This one guy was on the ground, dead. Another guy looked pretty bad hurt, and the other guys were all standing around him."

"Could you hear them talking?"

"Couldn't get close enough. The guy in the overcoat was the one giving the orders. The police had set up a cordon across the street, and they wouldn't let anybody past it. I just got up on the hood of the car and watched through a telephoto lens. Oh, you could hear the woman, all right. She was standing in front of the house screaming her head off." He paused and snapped his fingers softly. "The guy in the overcoat was a real strange one. There it was the middle of summer, and this guy's bundled up like he's ready to go skiing. His pals didn't even seem to notice. I suppose they were used to it."

"Anything else you remember, Frank?"

The photographer shook his head. "We got hustled out of there right after I took the picture. A few reporters tried to follow up on it a few days later, but they couldn't get to first base. Mrs. Rafferty was under guard. Finally the orders came down from the boss to kill the investigation."

I pocketed the newspaper photo, thanked Frank Alden, and headed for the door.

"Hey, Mongo! What's up? Where you going now?"

I told him I didn't know what was up, and I hoped I was going to the bottom of things.

12

On my way to the bottom of things I took an elevator to the newspaper morgue in the basement.

There was no listing for a Marianne Morton in any of the borough directories. It was possible she had an unlisted number, but I considered it more likely that she'd remarried. If so, there was reason to assume that the marriage had made the society pages; Arthur Morton had been a big name, and he hadn't exactly left his widow penniless. I was hoping she'd decided to stay around New York City.

I started with a newspaper dated a month after Morton's death and worked my way toward the present. I finally found what I was looking for in an issue dated two years to the day after Morton had been murdered. Marianne Morton, the widow of Dr. Arthur Morton, had married an import-export magnate by the name of Khalil Vahanian. The accompanying photographs showed a respectable middle-aged couple. Vahanian was dark, apparently Middle Eastern; he looked embarrassed, like a man who didn't enjoy having his picture taken. Marianne Vahanian's picture was blurred, but I could see that she was smiling.

A Vahanian Import-Export Company was in the Manhattan directory, but there was no home phone listing for its president. I called the company and was told the president was away. They wouldn't tell me where he lived, or how I could get in touch with him. I got lucky when I took a flier and started combing through the directories of the outlying counties. There was a Khalil Vahanian in the town of Tuxedo Park, a small, exclusive, walled-in community of millionaires in Orange County. It had to be the same one.

From what I'd heard of Tuxedo Park, it was going to be difficult dropping in unannounced, but I was going to have to find a way. I couldn't think of a way of sliding into a phone conversation about the death of Marianne Vahanian's first husband gracefully, and I didn't want to turn her off before I'd had a chance to talk to her in person.

I rented a car and drove up the West Side Highway, across the George Washington Bridge, and up the Palisades Parkway. It felt good to be out of the city. The foliage on the trees along the Palisades was lush and green, and the strip of concrete beneath the wheels seemed like a suspended highway snaking through some primeval jungle. It was a pleasant, otherworldly effect, very relaxing. I almost forgot for a few minutes the ugly, bloody threads unraveling behind me.

A glance into the rearview mirror revealed that I was not alone. A green Cadillac was coming up fast. As I watched, its driver eased off the accelerator and the car settled down, about a hundred yards back, to a speed matching my own.

I took my gun out of its holster and put it on the seat beside me, then pulled off onto the shoulder. The Caddy sped right past. The two men in it seemed totally absorbed in an animated conversation, taking no notice of me. They went by too fast for me to get a good look at them, but the man on the passenger's side had curly red hair and was smoking a cigarette in a long holder. I waited until they were out of sight, then drove back onto the highway.

I reached Tuxedo Park at three forty-five. A short drive along the high stone fence brought me to a locked gate, where I honked my horn. A tall, uniformed private guard emerged from a kiosk and peered aristocratically at me from the other side of the gate. He was tall and held his chin high, shoulders back, like a general personally guarding some military installation. He opened the gate but didn't move out of the way as I inched forward; he was a man who would defend the residents of Tuxedo Park with his life.

I braked and smiled up at him.

"Yes?" He said. The "sir" was pointedly missing. He had a slight lisp.

"I'm here to see Mrs. Vahanian."

"Is Mrs. Vahanian expecting you?"

"Of course. My name is Dr. Frederickson." I was hoping the title would get me through the gate. It didn't; the guard went into his kiosk and picked up a phone.

He emerged a few moments later. He looked confused, and I took that as a good sign. "No one answers," he said uncertainly.

"She's probably out in the garden," I said, deciding to take a chance. I watched him carefully as I said, "You know how much time Mrs. Vahanian spends on her roses."

The guard looked up at the sky as if waiting for divine guidance. Finally he cleared his throat and said, "Mrs. Vahanian usually tells me when she's expecting somebody."

"So? Today she forgot. Look, I'm not going to take it kindly if I have to go all the way back to New York without seeing Mrs. Vahanian, and Mrs. Vahanian isn't going to take it kindly if I don't take it kindly." I paused for effect, then whispered conspiratorially, "You know how these rich folks are."

He knew how rich folks were. He made a half-bow and stepped out of my way. "No offense, sir."

"Don't worry about it."

"I'm paid to worry, sir. Please don't forget to honk at the S-turn."

I drove up a narrow, twisting lane, honked at the turn, then emerged into the community proper. I drove around for a while until I found Wood Lane. There were only three homes on the street, and the largest one belonged to the Vahanians. I parked at the curb and walked across a vast sea of manicured lawn toward a white, colonial-style home with an air of decadent tackiness that had probably cost extra.

There was no answer when I rang the bell, so I walked around to the back, politely calling Mrs. Vahanian's name. I found her at the rear of the house standing under a rose bower next to a metal garden table. The pitcher on the table contained a clear liquid that looked a bit thicker than water. The glass in her hand was half empty, which could account for the fact that she hadn't heard the phone, or me. She was sipping at her drink, staring at her roses.

I came closer. "Mrs. Vahanian?"

She wheeled, almost spilling her drink. She was a handsome woman, with hair a shimmering silver that hadn't come out of a bottle. Her eyes were green, momentarily bright with shock, which gradually faded. She stared at me for a long time, then suddenly laughed. It was a hearty, infectious sound. "Who the *hell* are *you*?" she boomed.

I held out my hand. "My name's Frederickson," I said, grinning and making a half-bow. "I tried the front door, but couldn't get an answer."

"How did you get in here?"

"Dwarf charm. I'm a private investigator. I'd appreciate it very much if you'd answer some questions."

Her eyes filled with the kind of fear wealthy people have for strangers and private detectives, and especially strange private detectives. "About what?" Her voice was breathy and the laughter was gone from it.

"Your first husband."

She shook her head quickly. She looked as if she were getting ready to have me thrown off the property. "I don't understand. What is it that you want?"

"There's no trouble, Mrs. Vahanian." I put my hand on the back of one of the garden chairs and spoke quickly.

"I've been hired to look into the death of a man by the name of Victor Rafferty. He was one of Dr. Morton's patients."

"Victor? Victor's been dead for five years. He died soon after ..." Her voice trailed off, and she quickly poured herself another drink. Her eyes had gone out of focus, as though she were staring at something that had leaped out at her from the past.

"I came across the facts of Dr. Morton's death while I was investigating Rafferty. I was thinking that the one death just might have had something to do with the other."

"I've always thought so," she said distantly. Her eyes suddenly snapped back into focus on me. "I've always felt that the police did not do an adequate job in trying to apprehend Arthur's killer."

"There's at least one policeman who's very anxious to solve the case, but he needs more information. If you want, I'll relay anything you tell me to him."

"Why isn't he here himself?"

"This is out of his jurisdiction. He's a New York City policeman."

She turned her face away for a moment. "Would you like a martini?" she asked quietly. "It's the maid's day off, and that's the only thing I know how to make."

"All right, Mrs. Vahanian. Thank you."

She disappeared into the house and returned a few minutes later with a glass. She walked very slowly, as if carrying an invisible burden I'd brought to her. I filled the glass, then set it down on the table.

"What do you want to know?" she whispered.

"Anything and everything you can remember about the relationship between Victor Rafferty and your first husband. Were they friends before the car accident?"

"Oh, yes. They were both very famous men in their own right. Arthur was a neurosurgeon, so it was only natural that he take Victor as his patient after the accident. Arthur

129

told me that it was one of the worst skull fractures he'd ever seen in which the victim had lived. Part of the skull was literally pulverized, and the brain area beneath was damaged."

She paused and emptied her glass, started to pour a refill, thought better of it. She set the pitcher down and moved away from the table. "Arthur was sure Victor would die. He never said so, but I'm almost positive that he wanted to let Victor die on the operating table. He just . . . couldn't do that. Every second Victor lived after that horrible accident was considered a miracle. Anyway, Arthur did a series of operations. He stopped the hemorrhaging, then replaced the missing skull section with a steel plate." She plucked nervously at her print skirt. "After that, Arthur was afraid that Victor *would* live."

"Why?"

"Brain damage is irreversible, and it's dysfunctional: it destroys the capacities of the brain. Arthur was certain that Victor, if he did survive, would be nothing more than a vegetable, kept alive only by machines. Arthur didn't want that for Victor."

"But it obviously didn't work out that way."

"It certainly didn't. For a while it seemed that half the doctors in the world were asking for permission to come and observe Victor Rafferty. Victor was still very weak, of course, and Arthur put him on an exercise program to build up his body. There didn't seem to be anything at *all* the matter with his brain. That was the amazing thing. Arthur couldn't get over that. For all intents and purposes, Victor seemed to be on the way to complete recovery. Then . . . something happened."

"What was that, Mrs. Vahanian?"

"I don't really know. Arthur became very close-mouthed about it. It started with a telephone call he received one night from Victor."

"Did he tell you what Rafferty said?" I asked.

"No. Arthur did mention something about hallucinations, but he didn't seem to take it too seriously. At first."

"But he did later?"

"Yes," she said tightly. "Victor telephoned one afternoon about a week after the first call. Arthur wasn't here, so I took the call. Victor sounded very upset, but coherent. He said he had to talk to Arthur. When Arthur came home he called Victor back, and I believe they made an appointment to meet that evening. Also—and I'm not sure this is related—Arthur called one of his colleagues, Dr. Mary Llewellyn. She's a clinical psychologist with offices in the same professional building. I remember because Arthur asked me to help him find his professional directory. Dr. Llewellyn had an unlisted phone number, and he had to reach her at home. I believe he called her just before he left the house to meet Victor."

"Did he say *why* he wanted to talk to her?"

"No."

"But you think he wanted this Dr. Llewellyn to meet with him and Rafferty?"

"I really don't know." She walked back to the table, poured another drink, and sipped at it. "As I said, I'm not certain the one thing had anything to do with the other. I just mentioned it because I do remember it happening. Anyway, Arthur was very upset when he got home."

"How upset?"

She smiled wryly. "It was always hard to tell with Arthur. He was a stoic type who didn't like to let his feelings show. I suppose that's why he and Victor got on so well; both could seem like pretty cold fish."

"I've heard that about Rafferty."

She glanced up sharply. "If that's all you've heard about Victor, then you don't have the whole story."

"Victor Rafferty is a hard man to get a fix on, Mrs. Vahanian. I'd appreciate it if you'd tell me more."

She dabbed at her eyes, then laughed wanly. "The man

loved cheap hamburgers. He could afford to eat filet mignon three times a day, but he ate fast-food hamburgers. Isn't that strange?"

"Some people might think so, Mrs. Vahanian. I'm more interested in other things."

It was a long time before she spoke again. "It's true that Victor could be cold and aloof. He was also terribly absent-minded about things that didn't involve his work. He was the kind of man who didn't really need other people in a personal way; because he didn't need them, he didn't really have time for them. But that doesn't mean he didn't *care* about them. What most people don't realize is that Victor had a real social consciousness. He did a great deal of volunteer work for the U.N."

"I've heard that, too."

"All right, I suppose you could say he loved mankind in the abstract more than he loved individuals; but that's no crime, is it?"

"No, it isn't, Mrs. Vahanian. Please go on."

"Where was I?"

"Dr. Morton was very upset after he returned from a meeting with Rafferty."

"Oh, yes. He was distracted. I could tell that. It was very late when he got back, but I always woke up when he came home. But instead of coming to bed, he stayed awake for hours, pacing back and forth in his study. I went down once to see if he wanted to talk, but he shooed me back to bed. I finally went to sleep, but I don't think he went to bed at all that night. At the time I thought he was simply worried about Victor's condition. Now I believe it was much more than that."

She stared at a point in space just over my head, listening to the voices in a movie from the past. "Arthur canceled all his appointments for the next few days," she continued. "And he postponed his operations, except for the most urgent. He spent a great deal of time down in his study, and

132

slept very little. Dr. Llewellyn called once, and I'm sure they argued over the phone. I heard Arthur talking loudly, but I couldn't tell what he was saying." She paused. "He also bought a lot of books."

"What kind of books?"

"Oh, they were mostly medical books with long titles. But there was one book he used a lot. It had a single-word title: Psychology-something, or something-Psychology. Yes. It had a P in front of it."

"Psychology has a P in front of it," I prompted.

"No, this was a longer word with a P in front of it." She strained to remember, then shook her head in resignation. "Anyway, Arthur spent hours on end with those books."

"He never said why?"

"No. But it was almost as if he were . . . *studying.* I think he was trying to understand something."

I watched Mrs. Vahanian. The pain of memory moved back and forth across her green eyes in waves. "Tell me about the night he was murdered, if you will, Mrs. Vahanian."

She trembled slightly, then set her drink down beside mine. "I'm afraid there isn't much to tell," she said distantly. "Arthur was so disturbed by . . . all this. In the middle of the night he simply decided he wanted to go to his office."

"Could a meeting have been arranged for that hour?"

"I can't see how. Arthur hadn't set his alarm; he just woke up. It must have been around two thirty. I woke up and asked him what he was doing. He said he couldn't sleep and wanted to go down to his office. That was the last time I saw him alive."

She looked shaky. I took her elbow and guided her into one of the chairs. "We know he was killed in his office," I said gently. "Someone must have been there when he arrived. He surprised them, and he was killed. The police report said nothing was taken from the office. Is that true?"

"I really have no way of knowing. I was cooperating with the police, but they just seemed to lose interest at some point along the way. One day they simply stopped asking questions. I called them a few times, but all they would say was that they were working on it."

"Did anyone else come to see you besides the police?"

"Yes. A Mr. . . . I can't remember his name. A strange man. It was summer, but he was wearing a heavy overcoat. He was always shivering. He said he was from some government agency, but I don't remember which one."

I set my drink down and straightened up in the chair. "About when was this, Mrs. Vahanian?"

"It was August; the second or third week in August, but I can't be sure. That was 1969."

"What did this man want?"

She pursed her lips. "He said the government had an interest in the case and he wanted to ask me some questions about Arthur's work."

"Did he ask specifically about Victor Rafferty?"

"Only once. He seemed more interested in how much Arthur talked to me about his various patients. I told him what I told you: Arthur didn't discuss his work at home. Then he asked me about Victor."

Lippitt had been touching all the bases, I thought; he'd been retracing steps, determining who knew what about Victor Rafferty.

"The house was broken into a few days after the murder," Mrs. Vahanian added. "Did I mention that?"

"No, I don't think you did." And there'd been no mention of it in the police report.

"The only thing they took was a file Arthur had kept at home on Victor. I reported that to the police, but . . ."

Her voice trailed off. She sat in silence for a few minutes, then abruptly stood up, once again in control of herself. She looked at me hard. "It would give me a great deal of satisfaction to see Arthur's killers finally brought to justice,

Mr. Frederickson. I'm happily married now, and, frankly, I'm closer to Khalil—my husband—than I ever was to Arthur. But Arthur didn't deserve to die like that."

"I agree, Mrs. Vahanian."

"I don't know whether this has anything to do with the matter, but Victor was drinking a great deal after the accident. It wasn't like him. I saw him once or twice after the accident and he always smelled like a brewery. It was strange, though: he never seemed to be *drunk*. Even his eyes didn't show it. The only way you could tell he'd been drinking was by smelling his breath. I believe he took to carrying a flask with him." Her eyes went out of focus again and her voice became distant. "Poor Victor. He must have been in a great deal of pain."

"Did you know Mrs. Rafferty?"

"Yes. We weren't really friends, but we occasionally saw each other socially."

"What was her reaction to the first accident?"

Marianne Vahanian cleared her throat. "I'll be frank with you: Victor and Elizabeth didn't have a particularly happy marriage. Which is not to say that they didn't love each other; but it's difficult being married to a man of genius. I know. Their work is always their first love. Victor was like that. Anyway, it became even worse after the accident. Elizabeth became increasingly upset—and aloof. She gradually stopped seeing her friends. I tried to contact her a few times, but she didn't seem to want to talk to anyone. In fact, she didn't even come to Arthur's funeral. I haven't seen or talked to her since. I don't even know if she's still in the area."

"You've been very helpful, Mrs. Vahanian," I said. "Is there anything else? Anything at all, no matter how small?"

She gazed down into the depths of her glass, finally shook her head. "I don't think so," she said carefully. "It all seems so . . . *long* ago."

"I understand."

"There are some books up in the attic," she said. "They were all packed in boxes when we moved, and we've never gotten around to unpacking them. Many of the books were Arthur's. I have no idea what's there, but you're welcome to rummage around if you don't mind getting sweaty and dirty."

I told her I didn't mind getting sweaty and dirty.

Mrs. Vahanian guided me through the cathedral-like house to the second floor, then up a drop ladder to the attic. She pointed to a section filled with packing crates and cardboard boxes, then returned to the cool, air-conditioned world below while I waded through the sea of heat surrounding the boxes.

I wasn't at all sure exactly what I was looking for, and there was always the risk that I'd miss something important just because it had a fifteen-word title. After opening two boxes I estimated that there were more than two thousand books to examine—everything from gothic romances to barely decipherable tomes on brain surgery. Still, I knew I had to make the effort.

Mrs. Vahanian appeared a half hour later with a tall glass of ice-cold lemonade and a towel. I needed both. She looked at the books a little sadly, then left. I wrapped the towel around my neck to absorb the dripping perspiration and went back to work. After an hour I'd worked myself into such a rhythm that I almost missed what I'd been looking for. A large book, bound in black leather, carried the title *Parapsychology: An Inquiry and Overview.* It filled the bill for a book on psychology with a P in front of it.

I opened the volume and scanned the title page. The first thing that struck me was that this book was qualitatively different from the other medical texts, since it seemed written for the sophisticated layman. It was also massively comprehensive, covering a wide range of topics under the general heading of Extrasensory Perception. There were sections on everything from mental telepathy to occult spirit guides, with additional sections on tarot cards and the use of hallucinogens to alter perception.

It was hard to tell what part of the book Morton had been interested in, as I could see by leafing through the volume that, regrettably, he hadn't been in the habit of underlining.

I toweled off, finished the lemonade, then leaned back against one of the packing crates and began to go through the book more slowly. There was a chapter on psychic healers, from Joshua to Oral Roberts to a man known only as Esteban who could affect the growth of enzymes in glass tubes merely by holding the tubes in his hands. In a long section on Research, the Institute for Parapsychology in Durham, North Carolina, was prominently mentioned. It seemed that the Institute had been carrying on research experiments for many years and enjoyed a good reputation.

There was a chapter on dreams, and another one on telekinesis—the ability to move objects simply by willing it. The book mentioned a Russian woman who could supposedly move small objects simply by passing her hands over them, and another Russian woman reportedly able to tell the color of objects by feeling alone.

And still more: the intelligence of plants, and Kirlian photography—a process for photographing the "aura" of life energy around living things. The book ended with a section on witchcraft.

It all seemed like an odd grab bag of fact, speculation, and pure fantasia: curious reading for a neurosurgeon; perhaps not so curious for a psychologist—which could tie in with Mary Llewellyn.

Halfway through the book on my second run-through, a five-by-seven manila envelope fell out. I'd missed the envelope on the first scan because it had been compressed tightly and wedged into the binding, as though whoever put it there had wanted to make sure it wouldn't fall out. I opened the envelope and carefully spread the contents on the floor. There were a half-dozen newspaper clippings which seemed to indicate that Arthur Morton had been interested in rather specific areas of parapsychology—namely, mental telepathy and its ramifications.

I was mildly surprised to find from the clippings that a sizable number of scientists took things like Kirlian photography and telepathy seriously. It seemed the Russians were considered pioneers in the field. The Pentagon, not to be outdone, had ordered up a series of experiments of its own; most of the testing had been done at the Institute for Parapsychology in Durham.

There was also a piece of paper that was not a newspaper clipping. The paper seemed to have been folded and refolded a number of times, as if by someone who had been very nervous; the creases were worn thin.

I carefully unfolded the sheet and studied it. There were four symbols printed at the top of the paper: a square, a circle, a triangle, and a parallelogram; and beneath each symbol was a column of boxes. There were checks in some of the boxes, distributed among the four columns in what appeared to be random order. The checks in the boxes toward the bottom of the page were darker, shakier, heavier, as though the writer had been growing increasingly nervous and had been pressing harder. None of it made any sense to me.

I refolded the paper and slipped it into my pocket, then repacked the books and went downstairs, taking the book on parapsychology with me. I found Mrs. Vahanian in the kitchen, staring out a window. I thought she'd been crying, but her eyes were dry when she turned to me.

"Was your search fruitful, Mr. Frederickson?"

I showed her the book. "Is this the book you mentioned?"

She nodded. "I remember because Arthur spent so much time reading it at home. He didn't usually do that."

"Does this mean anything to you?" I asked, taking the

paper out of my pocket and pressing it across the counter top.

She looked at the paper and shook her head. "Where did you find it?"

"It was wedged into the binding of this book. Did you ever see Dr. Morton writing on this kind of paper?"

"No, I can't say that I did."

"Do you mind if I keep these things for a few days?"

She shrugged. "Not if you think they'll help. Do you really think the book and paper mean anything?"

"It's hard to say, Mrs. Vahanian."

After the sodden heat of the attic, the chill of the air conditioning was threatening me with a terminal case of pneumonia. I thanked Mrs. Vahanian again and left her staring out the window.

Outside, I wedged the paper back into the binding of the book, which I put in the trunk of my car. Then I made a U-turn and headed toward the gate. I was anxious to get back to New York and begin the task of finding Mary Llewellyn.

Slowing down for the S-curve, I honked, then began to accelerate. I was halfway around the second bend of the S when the green Caddy loomed in front of me.

Somewhere along the line I'd missed a move. Or the men in the car had known where I was going all along. There was no one in the car, which meant that the two men were hiding in the bushes somewhere, probably lining me up in their gunsights at that very moment.

There was no way of getting by the car without wrapping myself around a tree, so I jammed on the brakes and pulled the wheel hard to the left; the car's rear end fishtailed and slammed into the Cadillac, but I was turned around. I slammed my foot down on the accelerator and started back up the road.

A short, dark man in a shiny gabardine suit calmly stepped out into the road a hundred feet in front of me. He had a pipe clenched tightly between his teeth and a Sten gun braced on his hip, pointed at the windshield of the car.

There were three choices: try to run the man over and get killed; try to swerve around him and get killed; or stop and maybe live a while longer. If the man wanted to kill me, he could have done it already. I braked to a halt a few feet from where he was standing. His face was calm, almost smiling; I found his air of total self-assurance annoying as hell. Something about him struck me as being distinctly European.

He motioned with his gun for me to get out of the car. I did so slowly, tensing, waiting for some kind of opening while I looked around for his red-haired partner. But the two of them were fast and professional; I never saw or heard the second man move up behind me. There was just a sharp blow to the base of my skull, and then nothing.

13

When I regained consciousness, I was giggling uncontrollably. I found the idea of being ambushed by two men in a green Cadillac outrageously funny. My head felt twice its normal size, pumped full of helium that was carrying me off to a Land of Oz peopled with smiling, gun-toting Europeans who lived in the glove compartments of green Cadillacs. I giggled some more.

In between my flights of hysteria, the two men—who spoke with British accents—took turns asking me what I thought were the most absurd questions about Victor Rafferty. I'd answer, then howl at the thought that anybody should be asking me questions on a subject about which I knew so little.

A few times I thought I heard my own voice talking back to me. That would be my tapes. I tried to get angry at the Englishmen for breaking into my apartment, but everything was just too funny.

I told them about the book and the piece of paper. One of the men left the room while the other went through my pockets. It tickled, and I laughed. The man with the red hair asked me about the Fosters, and I told him what I knew. I thought it was funny that they should know about the Fosters. I laughed and laughed, and finally fell asleep.

I woke up with a wicked drug hangover. My mouth was dry, raw, puckered. My head still felt twice its normal size, but now it was filled with tacks. I lay still and surveyed the room in front of me through half-closed eyes. I wanted to get some idea of the order of this particular universe before I welcomed company.

It seemed to be a moderate-sized room, rugless, with peeling yellow paper on the walls. I was lying on a convertible sofa that smelled of age and mildew. Overhead was a large chandelier that looked as if it had been imported by someone with a droll sense of humor. To my left was a rickety card table on which had been placed two tape recorders. A few feet in front of me, just above eye level, was a dirty window; I could see the tops of trees through it, which would put me on the second or third story of the building.

There were voices coming from behind me. The two men were discussing European politics in their clipped British accents. I continued to lie motionless.

Someone mentioned tea. There was the sound of a chair scuffing against a hardwood floor, then footsteps. I peered through my lids as the darker man paused beside me, then walked out into the adjoining kitchen to my right. I waited until I heard him rummaging around with the pots and pans, then moaned softly. Again there was the sound of a chair being pushed back, heavy footsteps. The red-haired man loomed over me. He was the man who'd hit me; I opened my eyes and smiled dreamily up at him.

"Hey, Georgie!" the man yelled. "The little bloke's awake!"

The little bloke grunted and kept grinning.

"All right, Peter," the answering reply came from the kitchen, "get him up."

"I don't know. He still looks pretty dopey."

"Well, walk him around. I want to ask him a few more questions."

Peter reached down to shake me. I waited until he had both hands on my shoulders before I gave him another big grin, whispered that he was a son-of-a-bitch, and hit him in the jugular with the side of my hand. His eyes bulged and his hands flew to his throat as his face turned purple. He made a series of staccato choking noises that could barely be heard. My head immediately began to feel better.

I swung my legs over the side of the sofa, stood up, and relieved him of the automatic he had in his belt. I hit him in the gut with it, bringing him down to my level, then rapped him on the back of the head. He hit the floor hard with his face and stayed there.

The commotion brought George, pipe still clenched between his teeth, rushing into the room. He braked, skidded on one foot, and finally came to a halt when he saw me and the gun pointed at him. His swarthy face grew still darker as it mottled with blood. His eyes flashed as he did a double take between me and his fallen partner. He hunched his shoulders and started forward.

"Stay," I said quietly, punctuating the sentence with a loud lead exclamation point just over the top of his head. A chunk of plaster fell from the wall.

George stayed, but he bit through the stem of his meerschaum. The pipe, minus half its mouthpiece, clattered to the floor, and George spat out the rest. "He'll kill you," he stammered, pointing to the gasping redhead. "If he doesn't, I will."

"Oh, shut up, George, and sit down," I said, pointing with the gun toward a chair.

George thought about it for a few seconds. I helped him toward a decision by pointing the gun at his stomach. He sat down. I said something witty about clearing his sinuses permanently if he did anything I didn't like, then went across the room and took the sash cord from the broken venetian blind hanging beside the window. The landscape outside looked like farmland, and I wondered where I was. It was dusk. Assuming it was the same day, I hadn't been out more than a few hours.

I used the sash cord to tie Peter and George. George moved once, but froze when I snatched up the gun from the floor and pressed the barrel against his spine. Now it was my turn to ask questions. I walked over to the tape recorders and turned one on. It was my own tape. I turned that one off and the other one on. The first question surprised me.

"Who is Victor Rafferty?"

I pressed the pause control and looked over at George. "What the hell kind of stupid question is that?" I said. "Don't you know?"

George glared at me and said nothing. I took my finger off the pause control and listened as the two men took turns asking me questions. Occasionally they played sections of the tape I'd made and asked me questions about statements I'd made. My own voice sounded blurred and indistinct, like a drunk's. There were about ten basic questions, repeated over and over in different variations. The Englishmen didn't seem to know any more than I did, a fact which I found depressing. Still, they'd known about me.

I pressed the gun squarely to George's forehead, directly between his eyes. "Is Victor Rafferty alive?"

"You tell me, you little bastard."

"Maybe I'll just shoot you."

"Go ahead."

"Take some time to think about that answer, George; use the time to try to remember all you know about Victor Rafferty. You can start off by telling me why everybody is so interested in him."

He spat at me. I sidestepped the wet missile and tapped lightly on the top of his head with the gun. He cursed. "We've been working blind, you bloody dwarf! We just do what we're told to do! We don't know any more about Rafferty now than we did last time!"

"Last time?"

"Fuck you!"

Peter was beginning to look fairly normal, although he kept swallowing and wincing in pain. Spittle had dried and caked on his lips. His eyes never left me; they were blood-shot, bright with hate.

"How did you know about the Fosters?" I asked George, not really expecting an answer.

"You're going to be killed for this," George hissed. "This thing is a lot bigger than any of us."

"Are you making fun of my size, George?"

"You bloody ———! Untie us!"

"First I want you to tell me all about that 'last time.' I also want to know who did the job on the Pakistani."

George's face became a stony mask. "I'll tell you nothing. You're wasting your time."

He was probably right. I decided to look around the house, and the first thing I found was my gun on a counter in the kitchen. Next to it were the book on parapsychology and the mysterious sheet of paper; I hoped that meant they'd brought my car along with them.

I left everything where it was and searched through the other rooms on the floor. They were barren for the most part, except for a few ratty pieces of furniture that jutted out like bits of flotsam floating in a moldy sea of ratty carpet. Outside, a full moon was rising, bathing the sur-rounding countryside in a soft, cold glow. I assumed the farmhouse was some kind of meeting place, or intelligence drop point. Or perhaps it was no more than what it seemed: an abandoned farmhouse that George and Peter had com-mandeered for the purpose at hand.

The lights obligingly came on when I flipped a switch, and I hit the jackpot when I looked in a closet off the main sitting room: there was a large black medical kit. Inside the kit was a pharmacist's delight, with drugs ranging from what I suspected was L.S.D. to the familiar and effective

145

sodium pentothal. I picked up the bag and went back into the big room. George was obviously unhappy with my discovery; his eyes bulged and sweat broke out on his forehead.

"What the hell are you going to do with that stuff?" he asked warily.

"Time for your vitamins, George."

"That's not going to do you any good!" He swallowed, pumped up the volume of his voice. "I'm trained to resist drugs!"

I groped around inside the bag, took out a handful of bottles and three hypodermics. "Well, I think I'll give you a little of this and a little of that, and see what happens."

"Do you have any idea what you're doing?" he said as I picked three vials at random and filled a hypodermic.

"With drugs? Well, I've found I prefer aspirin for the common headache. What about yourself, George?"

"Jesus, you're going to *kill* me with that stuff! Or turn me into a raving loony! I'm telling you I don't *know* anything!"

I held the tip of the needle poised over his arm. "It would be a shame for you to get turned into a pumpkin for nothing, wouldn't it? Who pays you?"

He took some time to answer as his eyes stayed riveted to the tip of the needle. Finally he heaved a deep sigh. "Christ, dwarf, use your imagination. M.I.-5."

He visibly relaxed as I took a step backward. "How did you get on my trail?"

"Contacts at the U.N.," George said sullenly. "The Pakistani was asking questions about Rafferty and your name was mentioned. The Home Office put us on the job."

"How did you find me in Tuxedo Park?"

"We had a beeper on your car; planted it while you were in the rental agency."

"Did you or your friend here kill the Pakistani?"

"No."

I stepped forward again and raised the hypodermic. "I don't think I believe you."

"It's *true*," George squeaked as a few drops of clear fluid dripped onto his arm. "We didn't kill him. That had to be Kaznakov. The Pakistani was tortured; that's Kaznakov's trademark."

"Who's Kaznakov?" I whispered. I suddenly felt choked, short of breath.

George looked at me a long time. "You don't want anything to do with Kaznakov, believe me."

"Come *on*, George. Who's Kaznakov?" I squirted fluid between his eyes.

"Russian. A bloody freak."

"Where can I find this Kaznakov?"

"Soviet U.N. Mission. He's supposed to be a minor aide, but that's only his cover. He's an agent; a specialist. He's a crazy, bloody freak. One of the worst, from what I hear, although you Americans are supposed to have—"

"Tell me about the 'last time,' George. Did you work on the Rafferty case before?" He turned his face away and didn't say anything. I thought of Abu and had a sudden, almost uncontrollable surge of rage. I grabbed his ear, twisted his head to one side, and held the hypodermic like a dagger over his exposed neck. "I'm not shitting you, George!" I shouted into his ear. "I have to find out these things! If you don't tell me, I'm going to drop this load in your neck and go to work on your friend!"

Something in my voice must have convinced him. When I released his ear, he slumped in his chair. "Five years ago," he said, seemingly resigned. "But we thought Rafferty was dead; killed by an American named Lippitt. Now a lot of people aren't so sure Rafferty's dead after all."

"Why does everyone want Rafferty, George?"

"I don't know. We were just told to find him, kill him if he is alive. Didn't much like it, but orders are orders.

There wasn't much chance Rafferty would work for us, so I'm told, so we had to make sure he didn't end up working for anybody else. It was the same five years ago."

"He wouldn't work for the British, so you were told to *kill* him?"

"That's right. *Everyone* had those orders. We were in a big hurry because we knew the Frenchies had a good line on him."

"The *French* knew about Rafferty?" It had obviously been, obviously was, a crowded track.

"Hell, yes. The French have a good man working for them. Been feeding them top-grade information for years."

"What's this agent's name, and where can I find him?"

George shrugged. "Nobody—except some controller—knows. He—or she, for all I know—has a deep cover; you find out, let *us* know. *There's* someone who can tell you what you want to know about Victor Rafferty. Shit, Peter and I are just cannon fodder compared with the Frenchie. You know, you hurt my fucking ear."

"But you don't know *why* all these people had orders to capture or kill?"

"Top Secret. We were just following our orders. Now, that's all I know. I swear it."

I pressed the point of the needle against the thick blue vein on the inside of his forearm. He squirmed, the color draining from his face as a droplet of blood formed on his arm. "You'll *kill* me if you stick me with that! What the hell are you *doing*?"

"George," I replied, "I feel I'm losing your cooperation."

"Then *ask* me something, for Christ's sake! Or go find the Frenchie!"

I kept the tip of the needle just inside his vein. "Five years ago a doctor by the name of Arthur Morton was murdered. Do you know anything about that? Think carefully, George; my thumb is beginning to twitch."

"We killed him," George croaked, his eyes bulging as he

stared down at the hypodermic and the trail of blood running down his forearm.

"Why?"

"It was an accident! The goddamn bloody fool had no business coming to his office in the middle of the *night*. We weren't expecting him. He surprised us. He had a gun. We just didn't have any choice!"

"Why were you in his office?"

"We were supposed to take pictures of Rafferty's medical records," George said hoarsely. "And I *don't* know why. I swear it!"

I removed the tip of the needle from George's vein but kept it where he could see it. "What do you know about the Fosters?"

"The Russians have them. Everybody in the business knows it. The Russians *want* everybody to know."

My mouth suddenly tasted metallic. "Where have the Russians got them?"

"Russian consulate."

"Why? What do the Russians want with the Fosters?"

"Mrs. Foster used to be married to Rafferty. The Russians figure maybe they can pressure Rafferty into turning himself in, if he's alive." George clucked his tongue. "It's a bloody bad business," he said sincerely. "Got everybody and his brother running around."

"How is Rafferty supposed to find out that the Russians have his ex-wife?"

"*You* thought Rafferty was at the U.N. If he is, he'll find out soon enough."

"What if he *isn't* there?"

George shrugged. "You never know what the Russians will do." Suddenly his face went chalk-white as he glanced up and saw something just behind me. "Kaznakov!" he cried in a strangled voice.

I wheeled and froze. The man filling the doorway was huge—well over six feet and better than two hundred and seventy-five pounds, all resting on ridiculously small feet. There was nothing ridiculous about the machine pistol in his right hand. His eyes were like twin moons, pale and lifeless, suspended in an unbelievably ugly, pockmarked face; a large, mashed nose sat in the middle of that face like a broken rocket drifting off to nowhere. The trackers had been tracked, and I doubted that the Russian was looking for information.

14

There was no change of expression on the Russian's face as he fired a single bullet into Peter's brain; he might have been a robot. George continued to gape while I stood, paralyzed with shock, for what could only have been fractions of a second but seemed like hours. I couldn't believe that anyone, even a "freak," could cold-bloodedly murder three men, two of whom were helpless. Then I remembered Abu.

I dived at the same time as Kaznakov efficiently dispatched George with a second bullet. I hit the floor and rolled sideways as more bullets beat a staccato tattoo on the floor inches from the base of my spine. It was Circus Time. There was no way for me to get to the gun I'd laid aside, no time to use it if I could, and no place to go except out the window. Head first.

I covered my face with my arms as I crashed through the glass. Something razor-sharp and white-hot sliced across the back of my left thigh, but I had other things to worry about. I was at least thirty feet from the ground; if I didn't hit the tree, I was dead.

I kept my face covered until I felt a branch lash my forearm. Instantly I reached out and grabbed a handful of leaves. I let myself fall freely, leaves whipping against my face, until I hit a thin branch. I twisted in the air, grabbed hold of the branch, and let it guide me down and onto another, thicker one that would sustain my weight. I hung on, gasping for breath, but not for long. The Russian was at the window above me, firing blindly down into the tree.

I quickly scrambled down the major branches and dropped the rest of the way to the ground, rolling to ease the pressure on my wounded leg. I got up and pressed against the bole of the tree while Kaznakov pumped bullets into the ground around me; leaves and shattered bits of wood showered down on my head, but I was safe for the time being. I used the time to remove a few shards of glass from my arms, then looked around me. My position was on one side of the house, near the front. I could see two cars—the green Caddy and mine—parked at the top of a long dirt-road driveway that snaked across a large, corn-stubbled field to a highway. My guess was that Kaznakov's car was parked somewhere out on the highway and that he'd walked in. He must have been tailing the two British agents from the beginning.

The firing abruptly stopped. I winced with pain as I stepped on my left leg, but the leg managed to hold me. I hobbled to the car. The door was open, but the keys were gone. I started to slide behind the wheel, then thought better of it: Even under the best daylight conditions, it would take me a few minutes to jump the wires; by the time I started the car, Kaznakov would be over me playing Taps with his machine pistol. There was no time, no place, left to run.

Sucking some night air into my lungs, I limped back to the house and pressed myself flat against the side while I peered over a windowsill into the inside. I could just make out the dim, shadowy bulk of Kaznakov moving carefully down the stairs.

A quick search for something with which to defend myself turned up the ragged edge of a two-by-four sticking out from beneath the raised foundation of the house. I grabbed it and pulled. The wood was about three feet long;

it would make a formidable weapon if I could get enough momentum into a swing, and if I could take Kaznakov by surprise. I picked up the beam, inched my way around the corner and along the front of the farmhouse to the door. I positioned the wooden beam slightly behind me as if I were about to make an Olympic hammer throw, gripped it tightly, and waited. I was soaked with a mixture of sweat and blood.

After what seemed an eternity, the door swung open. The Russian stepped out into the moolight, his gun at the ready as he peered in the direction of the cars. I brought the beam whistling around, and it landed with a sharp crack on his shins. He howled with rage, pain, and surprise, but didn't drop the gun. He instinctively reached down for his shins and almost toppled off the stoop. He straightened up again when I brought the end of the two-by-four up into his face, leaving a large red blob where his nose had been. He staggered down off the stoop and collapsed. Incredibly, he was still conscious—but the gun had slipped from his fingers. I picked it up and pointed it at his chest.

The sudden, giddy elation I felt was probably due to loss of blood and shock. But I had the man who'd tortured and killed Abu, and at the moment that was all I cared about; I'd beat what he knew out of him with the butt of the gun, try to use him to free the Fosters, and then kill him. I was in a hurry to ask questions before I changed my mind. No law was going to touch Kaznakov; Garth had made that clear.

But the Russian had the strength and endurance of a bull, and he seemed to have become indifferent to pain. When I saw him struggle to his feet I was reminded of Antaeus, gaining his strength from the earth, rising from the ground again and again until his opponent's strength was exhausted.

Kaznakov was listing a bit to starboard, but he was standing. He spat blood, then fixed the bloodshot moon eyes in his ruined face on me. He stared at me a long time without saying anything, although I could hear strange, guttural rumblings in his chest, as if he were a volcano about to explode.

"You bastard," I said through clenched teeth. "I'm going to ask you some questions, and you're going to answer them. If you don't, I'm going to start shooting you to death. Slowly. One chunk at a time."

Kaznakov spat more blood, grinned crookedly around broken teeth. "You are tough little fucker," he said in labored English with a heavy accent. "But now I got you. I hurt your friend, the Pakistani, pretty good before he jumped. I'm going to hurt you even more. No one will find you for a long, long time."

"That sock in the nose must have mashed your brains, asshole. *I've* got the gun now. You sneeze wrong and you get a bullet between the legs. Now, let's go see if there's a phone in the house. If there is, you're going to call your people and tell them you want the Fosters dropped here. Tell them you're negotiating with Rafferty; tell them anything you want, but I want the Fosters brought here. You understand?"

"I understand what you say," Kaznakov said as he began to shuffle toward me. "But I think I call and say you are dead. How do you like that?"

"You idiot! Don't you think I'll shoot?" I decided I couldn't take any chances with Kaznakov and I pointed the gun directly at his heart.

"I don't care if you shoot," he said, and he kept coming.

The gun exploded and kicked when I pulled the trigger. The bullet made a thwacking sound against his chest and pushed him back a few inches, but that was all. Kaznakov was a man who hedged all his bets; he was wearing a bullet-proof vest.

I aimed for his head, but I'd run out of time. He swatted the gun away with one huge bear paw of a hand and wrapped the fingers of the other hand around my throat. He lifted me off the ground and started to squeeze. I stabbed with my fingers at his eyes, but it was as if someone had pulled the plug on my will and all my strength was draining out. I couldn't even reach his body.

A red cloak of blood was dropping down over my eyes. I kept trying to suck air, heaving my stomach, but nothing was coming in. Kaznakov was still holding me off the ground, and I expected at any moment to hear the sound of my neck breaking. Finally I got tired of waiting. I expected to see flashes of my life, but I didn't even get that. I finally let go of whatever it was I'd been hanging on to and let myself drop into the deep, warm pool of red in front of my eyes.

There was too much pain for it to be heaven, and I doubted I'd done anything in my life to warrant a place in the same circle of hell as Kaznakov, and that's who was walking around me at the moment.

My wrists were tied together behind my back and anchored by a rope that went around my waist. I'd been hauled off the ground by a suspended iron bar lying between my elbows to a point where just my toes were touching the damp concrete of the farmhouse cellar. It was an ingenious truss: if I allowed myself to hang freely, the joints of my elbows caught fire and, with all the pressure placed on my lungs and rib cage, it quickly became almost impossible to breathe. The alternative was to try supporting my weight on my toes, which was only good for about two minutes before pain started shooting up through my ankles and calves to my hips. I would have to release—and then I couldn't breathe. It was a kind of crucifixion; a slow, very painful way to die. It looked as if I were going to be there, as Kaznakov had promised, a long, long time, and the cavalry was nowhere in sight.

Kaznakov was busy with something behind me that I couldn't see, but that I knew I wasn't going to like. I could hear the sound of metal on metal, and it grated on my nerves. Obviously, Kaznakov hadn't yet exhausted his repertoire. He emerged—limping—from the darkness behind me. He was carrying a telephone from which the casing had been removed. Wires from the telephone snaked back into the darkness.

"You wanted a telephone," Kaznakov said. "I found one for you and have gone to trouble of hooking it up down here. It's on what I think you call 'party line.' It will ring when anyone else gets call." He came close to me until his smashed nose was only inches from my face; it stared at me like a red third eye. "It will hurt you very much," he whispered.

I'd been hanging for a minute or so and it was getting hard to breathe again. Hot lightning was flashing through my elbow joints, across my back, through my lungs. I stood on my toes and gulped for air. Within seconds my toes began to cramp.

"If you want answers from me, you'd better get me down from here," I gasped in a voice that creaked like an old man's. "In a few minutes I'm not going to be able to say anything."

"I don't *want* you to say anything," Kaznakov said evenly. "I only want you to hurt. *Bad.*"

"Do you have proof Rafferty is alive?" The pain in the lower half of my body had become unbearable. I released the pressure from my toes; my lungs and elbows immediately began to burn.

The Russian's answer was to tear my clothes open. He then attached two thin wires to terminals in the phone apparatus, and he securely taped the other ends to my body. He'd made me part of the circuit, but I was past caring. I didn't believe that any pain could be worse than what I was already experiencing, and every fiber of my being was assigned to the monumental task of drawing air through my mouth and nostrils.

"Something else for you to think about while you wait to die, dwarf," Kaznakov whispered.

And then the Russian was gone; the door to the cellar slammed shut and I was left alone with the silence and the pain. I would die there, I thought; not from the pain, but from suffocation or thirst. I went up on my toes and tried to catch a quick breath. I could no longer feel anything below my knees, and my stomach had begun to cramp.

The telephone rang. Instantly my body was engulfed in pain bouncing back and forth between my belly and brain like a ball of molten fire. The ball became a column that flashed between rings, expanded between each flash and the next, filling me up, hurtling me toward madness.

The ringing stopped just as the sour taste of bile crept up into my throat. Someone in the neighborhood had answered the phone. I imagined two people talking: about the weather; making plans; exchanging gossip.

I was crying, precious breath robbed from me as I heaved on the bar, gasping with great sobs, spewing mucus. *Now* my life started to pass before me—and I was astonished to find that it had been so brief. Now the last of it was melting away under a searing blowtorch of agony. I passed out. But there was no escape from the prison of pain, as I woke up again almost immediately. My face was wet with tears and mucus; I cursed my endurance and will, whatever it was inside me that wouldn't let me die.

I heard—or imagined I heard—the cellar door creaking open. The phone rang, and once again I was hurled into a dark hole filled with pain and cracking joints. When it was over, my body was consumed by a flame that wouldn't go out.

But there *was* someone else in the basement with me; I was sure of it; I *felt* it. Someone, or some*thing*. Death? Suddenly, as if a switch had been thrown, the pain was gone.

I assumed it was madness, that the sensory paths to my brain had finally, mercifully, burned out. At the same time there was a soft, steady buzzing in my ears; the sound was soothing, like white noise blocking out the terrible pain. The sound suggested that I sleep. It was a good suggestion, and I took it. I let my head slip down onto my chest; I sighed and closed my eyes, allowing myself to drift away into the warm, welcome embrace of death.

Fooled again. I wasn't dead, but I was still hurting, my body wrapped in a blanket of torment. But the pain was not the same as what I'd experienced before; the difference was that I was lying on the cool concrete of the cellar floor, and I could breathe. I drank in great drafts of the cold night air.

I rolled over on my back and looked up toward the ceiling. One of the ropes that had held the iron bar had parted, and I'd been unceremoniously dumped onto the floor. The only explanation I could come up with was that my thrashing under the deadly tickle of the electricity had done the trick. The wires were still attached to my body, but they'd been torn away from the phone terminals when I'd hit and rolled. I couldn't tell if there were any bones broken—there was too much pain all over my body. But I was alive. I waited for some kind of elation that wouldn't come; I felt as though I'd already died.

There was a dial tone when I knocked the phone receiver off its hook with my jaw. The area code on the plastic disk in the center was for Rockland County. I dialed "0" with my nose. My throat felt swollen shut and I wasn't articulating too well. Still, I managed to make the operator understand that I wanted to get through to the New York City police department. I got Garth's precinct, but Garth wasn't in. I talked to another detective, garbled a truncated version of what had happened to me, told him I was somewhere in

Rockland County, and asked him to trace the call and send someone out to get me. Then I passed out.

Later, I became dimly aware of sunlight falling across my face. A big man was standing over me, calling my name. It was Garth. I wept. Garth cut away the ropes from my wrists and ankles, then picked me up in his arms and carried me out.

15

It was night again, and somewhere a phone was ringing. I tensed, waiting for the terrible pain that didn't come. Finally I hurled myself through the darkness toward the sound of the ringing, hit the phone, and knocked it off the stand. I landed on the floor of the room as the lights came on. Blubbering, I blindly scrambled on my hands and knees to the telephone wall socket and ripped the cord out of the wall.

Strong arms lifted me off the floor and forced me back into bed, then held me down until I was calm enough to look at my surroundings. I was in a hospital, and Garth was standing over me. His hair was rumpled and greasy, and there were dark, purplish rings under his eyes.

Garth grinned crookedly and poked me gently on the arm. "I've heard of people getting pissed off at the phone company, but this is ridiculous."

Nothing came out when I opened my mouth to speak. I felt trapped inside myself, surrounded by mushy walls of soft, fleshlike rubber that would absorb any sound I tried to make. A lump welled in my throat. I could barely move my elbows now, and I had a terrible thirst. I suddenly broke into tears, sobbing like a child. Garth stood quietly next to me, his arm around my shoulder, waiting for the spell to pass. It ended with a short fit of hiccuping. I took the tissue Garth handed me and blew my nose.

"Sorry," I mumbled.

Garth shook his head. "My fault. I told them to put the phone in here. I just wasn't thinking."

"What day is it?"

Garth looked at his watch. "We're a couple of hours into Friday. You've been out awhile."

"I'll bet it's raining in Acapulco."

Garth swallowed. "They hurt you bad, didn't they, Mongo?"

I wanted to cry again; the lump in my throat, the tears in my eyes, and a terrible self-pity all kept creeping up on me. I choked them back; I wondered if there would ever again be a time when I could be sure of speaking a sentence without a sob. "I've never been hurt like that, Garth. Never. I didn't think there could be pain like that."

"Who did it to you, Mongo?" Garth said in a savage whisper.

"I don't know," I said without knowing why.

Garth's eyes narrowed to slits. "Don't bullshit me, Mongo. The doctor says you've been shot, hung up by your elbows, cut, and subjected to electric shock. Somebody did that to you, and you're telling me you don't know who it was?"

"He was wearing a hood."

"I don't believe you. Who's Kaznakov? You kept screaming his name."

Tears came again without warning. I covered my face with my hands and sobbed uncontrollably.

"*Kaznakov*," Garth persisted. "That's the man's name, right? He killed the other two, then went to work on you. You must have had a special place in his heart."

The fit of sobbing passed as quickly as it had come. The speed with which my emotions were darting out from behind corners frightened me. "I don't know where I got the name," I said. "I must have been babbling nonsense."

"Your brains are scrambled, Mongo, and I can understand why. But I want to find out who did this to you."

161

Haltingly, I told Garth what had happened, leaving out Kaznakov's name. I didn't want my brother involved with the Russian. There wasn't anything that could be done legally; Garth just wanted to look Kaznakov up personally, and if he did that he'd be dead. Kaznakov was absolutely invulnerable as long as he was attached to the Soviet U.N. Mission. Also, I wanted to keep my own options open concerning Kaznakov.

Garth shook his head. "Christ, brother, you really put your ass in a sling this time."

He had a point. Something was happening to me that I didn't understand. I was getting flashes again: memories of hanging on the pole, of having my muscles and bones pulled out of shape, not being able to breathe, the telephone ringing, electricity coursing through my body. I began to shake. Garth reached for me, but I pushed him away. In a few minutes the tremors passed. Maybe I was dead after all, the person I had been destroyed.

"I'm afraid, Garth," I said simply.

"You may be able to walk around in a few days, Mongo, but it's going to take a lot longer than that for your mind to heal. You have to expect that and accept it. You're only going to hurt yourself if you try to push things."

"What I need is work. You fall off a horse, you have to get right back on again."

"You didn't fall off any goddamn horse! You got taken apart. You don't need work, you need rest. Take it. You feel you owe somebody for this; forget it. No vendettas."

"It's more than that. They've got the Fosters in the Russian consulate."

"How's that?"

My memory seemed to be on the bum too; I couldn't remember whether or not I'd told Garth about the Fosters. I solved the problem by going through the whole case, from its inception.

162

If Garth had heard the story before, he didn't let on. "What do the Russians want with the Fosters?" he asked.

I told him, and asked if the police could do anything about getting them out.

Garth slowly shook his head. "There's no way, Mongo. I'll see that the State Department is notified, but from what you tell me, they probably already know. The problem is that the consulate is sovereign territory. We have no jurisdiction there, so there's no way we can get in. I'll call some people, though. Maybe we can shake things up."

"Don't," I said.

"Why not?"

"I'm not sure. It just seems that the more people who are in on this, the more people die."

Garth cocked his head to one side and stared at me. "What's the story on Rafferty? Have you found out why he's so valuable?"

"Not yet. But I have a feeling that history is repeating itself."

"Meaning what?"

"I'm convinced almost the same thing happened five years ago. The word on Rafferty—whatever that word is—got out, and people started dying. Lippitt warned me that could happen."

"You say the Englishmen didn't know why Rafferty was important. Do you think Lippitt knows?"

"He knows a lot more than he's telling me. But it still doesn't hold together. If Lippitt knew *everything*, then it's only logical to assume that *he'd* be a target. I think everybody was happy with the thought that Rafferty was dead; it's the possibility of his being alive that they can't tolerate. It's crazy. I've been a kind of Judas goat. Everybody thought that Rafferty was dead, and then I went around raising suspicions. Ever since I started making inquiries about Rafferty, I've been followed to see what I know and what I'm up

163

to. I must have convinced a few people that Rafferty's alive; now they've gone independent. I have to get some answers fast."

"Meaning you have to find out what Rafferty knows?"

"It may not be anything he knows." Like Garth, I found myself slipping easily into the present tense when speaking of Rafferty. "It may be something that he *does*."

"Like what?"

"Maybe he does tricks with his head; maybe he reads other people's minds."

Garth looked at me a long time, probably to see if I was joking. When he was sure I wasn't, he said, "What the hell are you talking about?"

"Arthur Morton became very interested in parapsychology around the same time he was working on Rafferty. I think there may be a connection."

"Hell, I can round up at least a hundred 'psychics' within ten blocks of here," Garth said sarcastically. "This is the Age of Aquarius, remember? Last week I could have paid twenty-five bucks to watch some guy bend forks without touching them; the trouble is that I've got a magician friend who can do the same thing—faster. If the Russians or anybody else wanted a 'mind reader,' all they'd have to do is wait outside some television studio. It's a lot of crap, Mongo."

"Well, maybe Rafferty is the real McCoy. The Defense Department takes telepathy seriously."

"I never thought I'd see the day when you'd cite the Pentagon as a paragon of enlightenment."

There was no point in arguing. "Will you do me a favor?"

"Doubtful," Garth said. "Not unless it involves making arrangements for you to take that vacation in Mexico."

I shook my head. It hurt. What I hadn't told Garth was the most important thing: I had to find out if I could finish it, if I could still function as a human being who also happened to be a dwarf. "I want you to call the U.N. and leave a message for Ronald Tal. Tell him where I am and that

164

I'd like to talk to him." I gave Garth the number Tal had given me. I hesitated, then added, "Please, Garth; do it for me."

Garth stared at me, his eyes moist. "Look at you, Mongo," he whispered in a voice that cracked. "*Why* do you need any more of this shit?"

"I have to keep going, brother. Just take my word for it."

Finally he nodded. Reluctantly. He squeezed my arm tightly, then turned and walked from the room.

The sedatives the doctors gave me didn't help. I thrashed all night, soaking my sheets with sweat, suspended in a dirty twilight between waking and sleeping. Kaznakov chased me through my nightmares, always catching me, breaking my body and my mind. I asked for a shot, and whatever they gave me seemed to work. The quality of my dreams abruptly shifted; in the moments just before waking, I had the sensation that I was a child again and my mother was close, holding back the evil. My dreams turned warm and languid, and I rested.

When I woke up I found Tal standing beside my bed.

"Good morning, Mongo," he said quietly. "I came as soon as your brother called me. I won't ask how you're feeling. I can only say that I'm sorry."

"Thanks, Tal."

"I received permission to visit you early, but your brother made it clear to me that I shouldn't stay long. May I ask what happened?"

"It's not important. I ran into a very nasty person by the name of Kaznakov. You know him?"

The muscles in Tal's jaw tightened. "I know *of* him. Sergei Kaznakov is a Soviet agent attached to their mission here. The rumor is that he's a specialist—what some in the community call a 'freak.' Frankly, I'm surprised you survived the encounter."

"He has a taste for torture. I suppose that was a lucky break for me."

Tal smiled. "If you can look at it that way, you must be feeling better already."

Although I hadn't realized it until Tal said so, I *was* feeling better; I was no longer shaking or sweating.

An attractive nurse entered with a breakfast tray. Tal unbuttoned the jacket of his double-breasted gray suit and helped maneuver the swing-armed table next to my bed. The nurse set the tray down in front of me, waited while I took the appetizer of two pink pills in a cup, then left with a backward, inviting glance at Tal.

"I'm sure Kaznakov doesn't know you're alive," Tal said when the nurse had gone. "If he did, he'd be after you; you're a blemish on his record."

"Best news I've had all day," I said around a mouthful of sodden oatmeal that tasted better than caviar. I was ravenously hungry.

"You should get away. I can arrange it."

"I want to fly down to North Carolina for a day or two when I get out of here. What's my expense account?"

"It will cover whatever you need, but why do you want to go *there*?"

"I'd just as soon wait to discuss it," I said. I was starting to experience hot flashes again, visions of Kaznakov dogging my steps for the rest of my life. The train of my emotions was threatening to derail again, and I didn't feel like getting into a conversation on the merits of a visit to North Carolina. "I'll tell you this: the Russians think Rafferty may be alive, and I've got a hunch they just may be right. I still don't know why everybody wants him; whatever the reason, it's big. There's a small world war going on out there."

"Yes," Tal said quietly. "That's why the Secretary General is anxious for you to find out everything you can. Maybe we can stop that war."

166

"The Russians have Rafferty's widow, and her husband."

"The Fosters," Tal murmured. "I know."

"You *know*?"

Tal nodded. "You were looking at the U.N.; they're fishing in the same waters."

"It doesn't make any sense. Rafferty, if he is alive, gave up his identity—and his wife—five years ago. Why do the Russians assume he'll turn himself in to them just because they've got her now?"

"They're probably hoping to put pressure on him, maybe force some kind of mistake on his part. They may be counting on something as simple as residual affection."

"What happens to the Fosters if Rafferty *is* dead?" I asked, not sure I wanted an answer. "Or if he doesn't surface?"

"That's hard to say," Tal replied. "With the exception of people like Kaznakov, the Russians aren't interested in just killing people. The kidnapping has to be some kind of ploy. They may not harm the Fosters at all."

"Then again, they might."

"It's possible, if only to maintain their credibility for the next such operation. That's why the pressure's on Rafferty, if he's alive."

"Is there any way to get them out?"

Tal shook his head. "Not diplomatically; the Russians will simply deny that they have them."

I thought I'd picked up on something in Tal's voice. "Is there another way?"

"There's always another way. It would take a covert operation and require the services of some highly skilled men."

"Well? You've got a whole building full of agents."

"True," Tal said wryly. "The problem is that none of them work for the Secretary General. The best solution, of course, would be for you to *prove* that Rafferty is dead;

then the Russians would have no reason to keep the Fosters."

"Rafferty may not be dead; even if he is, I may not be able to prove it."

Tal buttoned up his jacket. "I'll give it some thought. When do you plan to go to North Carolina?"

"As soon as I get out of here."

"Fine. You'll remember to keep a low profile?"

"Tal, I was born with a low profile."

He smiled, turned, and left the room. I finished my breakfast and leaned back on the pillow. For a moment, my mind was clear and I could pretend that I was all right.

The next face I saw almost gave me a relapse. It was Lippitt.

16

The bald man's face was impassive, but his eyes seemed larger than before, swollen by a controlled but seething anger. He wore a light blue gabardine suit that shimmered almost hypnotically in the morning light that filtered in through the window.

Lippitt approached the bed, shoved his hands into the pockets of his suit jacket, and stared down at me. "How are you?" he asked after a long pause. The anger was in his voice as well as his eyes, but he seemed oddly distracted, as though his mind—and possibly his anger—were directed elsewhere.

"How'd you know where I was?" He didn't seem inclined to answer my question, so I answered it myself. "You've been following Tal."

"Perhaps I should have been following *you*," he said with a trace of irony. "It looks like you've had an accident."

"It wasn't an accident: It was an on-purpose. You lied to me about killing Rafferty, didn't you?"

Lippitt's eyes went distant and cold. "Is that what you've concluded from your investigation so far?"

"Oh, I've got lots of company. The field's crowded, and it's a fast track."

"I warned you this would happen."

"Somehow I just knew you were going to say that, Lippitt. The same thing happened five years ago, didn't it? You were one of the hunters. Maybe you *found* Rafferty, but you didn't kill him." I watched his face carefully. "What the *hell* is so special about Victor Rafferty?"

Inexplicably, my voice broke at the end and I began to sob uncontrollably. There had been no warning; it was as if my emotions were being controlled by someone else, a mad dwarf who looked like me but loved to cry. Mortified by the behavior of this stranger, I turned my face to the wall and wiped away the tears. Finally I turned back to Lippitt and stared at him defiantly.

Lippitt casually lighted a cigarette and dropped the match onto my breakfast tray. "Whoever got hold of you hurt you very badly, didn't he?" he said evenly. There was neither sympathy nor lack of it in his voice; it was merely a statement of fact.

"A few screws are loose, but I know how to tighten them up. Why won't you tell me now about Rafferty?"

Lippitt blew smoke into the air over my head. "I didn't come here to trade information. I came to present a bill."

"What bill?"

"It's for the suffering you've caused. The Russians have the Fosters inside their consulate. You and I are going to get them out. We're going to see just how good a tumbler and acrobat you are; that's the price I want you to pay for the harm you've brought these people."

"What the hell are you talking about, Lippitt?"

"I thought I was making myself perfectly clear. I consider you responsible for placing the Fosters in jeopardy, so you're going to help me rescue them."

"You're putting together a D.I.A. operation?"

"That's not what I said, Frederickson. It's just you and me. I have a plan."

"I can't wait to hear it. Isn't it pretty risky for you? I'm betting your superiors won't be too happy about it if you get caught inside the Russian consulate."

"That's my concern. Will you agree to come with me? I do need you."

"What do you have in mind? I have an interest in the Fosters too."

"Frankly, I haven't figured out all the details. But I'll need a small man with exceptional athletic ability... and courage. From your press clippings, you seem to fit that description."

The fact of the matter was that I found the prospect of going anywhere Kaznakov might be terrifying. But I said, "I'll need some time to get back into shape; I'm a little stiff right now." I was gratified to find that my voice was reasonably steady.

Lippitt's eyes narrowed. "What happened to you?"

"I fell off a mountain called Kaznakov."

Lippitt stiffened. His right hand came halfway out of his pocket, then went back in again. "A madman." He spat the words out. "It's remarkable that you're here. You're the first person I know of who's suffered that particular fate and lived to tell about it."

"He thinks I'm dead."

"Good. It's best that he continue to think so. How did you get away?"

I managed a smile. "Sheer dwarf cunning."

"What did he do to you, Frederickson?"

"If you don't mind, I'd rather not talk about it. As I said, I'll need some time to get myself together."

"Of course. And I'll need time to formalize a plan. You still have my number?"

"I do. When I'm ready I'll order some flowers."

Lippitt ground out his cigarette in my oatmeal bowl. "You *must* pull yourself together, Frederickson," he said quietly. "I can only guess how badly Kaznakov hurt you, but I suspect the real hurt is now in your mind. You can't forget, but you must learn to *control* your fear."

There was something oddly authoritarian about his voice,

as if he were experienced in such matters and knew what he was talking about.

"It shows, huh?" The words blurred together into a whimper.

"I hope you're feeling better," he said formally, then turned on his heel and started toward the door.

"I'll be all right!" I heard myself shouting. "I'm going with you!"

Lippitt stopped, turned. "We'll see," he said simply, and walked out of the room.

Over the objections of my brother and a battery of doctors, I checked myself out of the hospital on Monday. It had reached the point where the hospital's knockout pills weren't working. I didn't want to sleep, because sleep was infinitely worse than staying awake; Kaznakov always visited me in my sleep. If I was going to stay awake, I reasoned it was better to be getting some things done.

The first thing I did was book a seat on a flight to North Carolina for the next morning. I still couldn't bring myself to pick up a telephone, so I decided I'd simply drop in at the Institute and hope to get lucky. I hung around the apartment the rest of the day and drank myself to sleep that night.

The only effect the booze had was to make it impossible for me to wake up when I wanted to. Kaznakov, his face dripping blood, continued to chase me; the difference was that I was drunk in my dreams, easier to catch.

I struggled awake at dawn and promptly threw up. I stood naked in a dry shower, leaning against the tiled wall and shaking. I wanted to cancel my flight, but the travel agency where I'd made my reservation wasn't open until nine, and my flight was at eight. I could, of course, simply not show up, but something told me that much more than the answers to a few questions could be riding on my ability to make myself get out of the apartment and onto that plane. I finally forced myself to shower, shave, and dress. Too sick to eat, I stumbled out into the street to flag down a cab.

Despite a hangover, or because of it, I wanted another drink on the plane. I decided I wouldn't help my cause by becoming an alcoholic, so I settled for two Alka-Seltzers and a lot of tomato juice.

Late morning found me in Durham, strong enough to walk a reasonably straight line. I celebrated my newfound resolve by forcing myself to use a pay phone. Then I rented a car and drove out to the Duke University campus.

It was a lovely campus, with acres of rolling green, a mixture of old and new buildings, and an overall Gothic atmosphere. The summer session had begun and the landscape was decorated with students, most of them wrapped around each other in various phases of lovemaking. Cicadas droned a steady accompaniment to the strains of guitar music and folk songs that floated on the dry, hot air. The liquor from the night before must have lubricated my joints; I walked without a limp.

The Institute for Parapsychology, not actually a part of Duke, was housed in a converted mansion just off the university campus. I asked for Dr. Fritz James, the man I'd spoken to on the phone, and was ushered into his office.

James was a young man with lean features and long hair tied back with a leather thong. He wore a gossamer Indian chambray shirt, tie-dyed jeans, and worn cowboy boots. He was obviously a man who cared little about his surroundings: there was barely enough room in the office for his desk amidst a litter of magazines, books, and abstract sculpture.

James skipped around from behind his desk and shook my hand enthusiastically. "Dr. Frederickson, it's a real pleasure to meet you."

"I appreciate your agreeing to see me on such short notice."

"I need distractions," he said with a deprecating gesture.

173

"It allows the subconscious to surface and do its work. What's a Yankee like you doing down here in the cotton patches?"

I laughed. "Do I detect a Bronx accent?"

James smiled and nodded. "Fordham Road; born and raised." There was a spontaneous warmth about the man that I liked.

"One of my graduate students wants to do a doctoral dissertation on possible uses of parapsychology in forensic medicine," I lied. "Since I'm his adviser, I thought I'd better find out what he's talking about. I just happened to be in the neighborhood and I thought I'd take a chance that somebody might be willing to talk to me."

"I'm glad you did," James said sincerely. "Are you interested in any particular area of parapsychology?"

I finessed the question by taking out my note pad and drawing a replica of the paper I'd found inside the book on parapsychology. When I finished, I handed it to him and asked, "Have you ever seen a sheet of paper like this?"

"Sure," James said, leaning across his desk and opening a drawer. He withdrew a thick blue pad, which he handed to me. The sheets in the pad were the same: circles, squares, triangles, and parallelograms. "Is this what you mean?"

"It sure is. What are they used for?"

"They're score sheets. We use them to test for telepathy. Would you like to take a stab at it?"

I nodded.

James went back into his desk and came up with a deck of what looked like oversized playing cards. He spread them face up on the desk. Each card had a symbol—a circle, square, triangle, or parallelogram—corresponding to one of the columns on the score sheet.

He put the cards back together, tore a score sheet from the blue pad, and sat down behind his desk. He picked up a couple of large books off the floor and set them on edge between us so that I couldn't see his hands. "We usually use a more sophisticated procedure," he said, shuffling the cards, "but I think this will serve our purpose.

"I'm going to turn over these cards one by one and concentrate on whichever one I'm looking at," he continued. "You try to open your mind to mine, try to get a picture in your mind of which symbol is on the card in front of me. When I rap on the desk, you call out what symbol you think it is. Got it?"

"Got it."

James finished shuffling the cards, then abruptly snapped one face up and rapped on the desk.

The only thing I could think of was Kaznakov.

"Quickly," James said with a note of authority. "Don't try to think about it. Just give me your first impression; let your subconscious do the work."

"Parallelogram."

He checked one of the boxes on the sheet, flipped another card, knocked.

"Triangle."

Knock.

"Triangle."

Knock.

"Square."

It took him twenty minutes to go through the deck. Then he pushed the books aside and spent another minute or so tallying the check marks in the boxes on the sheet. He finished and tapped the paper with the eraser end of his pencil.

"How'd I do?"

"About twenty-five percent. That's average for a random selection. Chance. With four symbols to choose from, the average person would get one out of four right."

"You mean I'm not a telepath?"

He smiled. "I'm afraid not. Welcome to the club."

"Are there people who score better than chance?"

"Oh, God, yes. Since we began testing for it in the past few years, people with latent telepathic skills have been

175

crawling out of the woodwork. It really is amazing. We've got three students here who can consistently score between thirty and forty-five percent. That's pretty damn good."

"On symbols," I said. "What about reading other people's thoughts?"

He shrugged. "There are twins in Minneapolis who are apparently able to communicate with each other through dreams. But picking up thought transference—and *proving* that it's taking place—is pretty esoteric. We use this test because it lends itself to hard statistical analysis."

"What about a hundred percent on the cards? Is there anyone around who can manage that?"

He looked pained as he reached back and tugged at the thong on his hair. "Nobody scores a hundred percent. Maybe men did ten thousand years ago—there's reason to suspect that early man may have been telepathic. Or maybe someone will a few thousand years from now. But not today. A score of thirty percent is considered statistically significant. About a year ago we had a young girl who scored fifty-five—but she never got above thirty after that. Fifty-five percent is the record. We're trying to develop training programs."

"How does it work?" I asked.

"The training programs?"

"Telepathy."

He chuckled amiably. "If we knew that, we'd be home free. Actually, it's all quite a mystery. You see the *effects*, but not the cause. We've found that most people tested do best on their first try, assuming they have the ability to begin with. They don't know how they do it. A thought— a picture of one of those symbols—comes into their minds and they report it. A great deal seems to depend on their mood."

"You mean that on a given day one of these people might be able to read my mind?"

"Well, yes and no. 'Reading your mind' is putting it a

176

bit too melodramatically. They might pick up a mood—or sometimes a word, or a strand of thought—better than other people."

"It all sounds pretty imprecise."

"Oh, it is," James said. "Strictly hit-and-miss when you get beyond the technique we use here."

"But you must have some theory about the mental processes involved."

"You see," James said carefully, staring at the wall behind me, "the 'mind,' as we call it, is much more than just a mere biochemical function of the brain. The brain gives off electrical impulses—much like a radio or television transmitter, to use an overworked analogy. There is *energy* emanated, and we can measure that energy with an electroencephalograph. Now, as far as telepathy is concerned, it seems that some people have a 'talent,' if you will, for picking up and decoding this energy. The astonishing thing is that a few of these people can pick up these 'signals' from great distances, almost instantaneously. So thoughts are not completely analogous to radio waves."

I decided it was time to break into his lengthy explanation and threw a curve. "Dr. James, have you ever heard of Victor Rafferty?"

He tugged at his hair band again. "Rafferty . . . Rafferty . . . Architect?"

"Right."

"Died a few years back in an automobile accident. No, he survived that. He finally died in a laboratory accident, something like that. Why do you ask?"

"Was Rafferty ever tested here?"

"No. Not that I know of—and I'd know. Why?"

"Can you think of any reason why somebody might be killed because he was connected with E.S.P.?"

James's face broke into a broad grin. "Sure. I'm threatened all the time—mostly by clergymen and physicists."

I thought of Abu and couldn't even work up a smile. "I'm

177

talking about power. Could a man *do* something with E.S.P. that could cause others to want to kill him?"

"That's a heavy question. Are you putting me on?"

"No, Dr. James. I'm serious."

"I can see that," he said soberly. "No, I can't think of anything like that. In fact, I almost wish the people in this country *would* take it that seriously. The Russians are far ahead of us in the field."

I leaned forward. "They are?"

"Yes. Of course, their government puts tremendous amounts of money into research. They're reported to have a woman with telekinetic ability."

The second subject that Arthur Morton had apparently been interested in. "What can you tell me about that?"

"Telekinesis is the ability to move objects through the power of thought." I must have looked skeptical. James cleared his throat and rapped his knuckles on the desk. "I've seen films of a Russian woman who seems able to move objects by willing it. Of course, films can be faked, but I don't think these were. First, the Russians don't really have a motive. Second, if they were going to fake something like that, they might as well have her move a suitcase or something big, not pins and matchsticks. She moves the objects by concentrating and passing her hands over them."

"To what purpose?"

He shrugged. "No purpose; except that if it's true, I think it's pretty fantastic. Don't you? Mind over matter. *Imagine* man's potential if it can be shown that he can move objects simply by focusing mental energy."

"I think we have more pressing problems."

"No argument there. Would you like to see our facilities?"

"Yes, I'd like that very much."

James came around from behind his desk and held the door open for me; he was a proud father about to show off his baby. I followed him around the complex and tried to look interested and nod at the right times. But my mind wandered as I tried to connect what I'd seen and heard to my knowledge of Victor Rafferty and the dead men around him.

I was going to need a break; there weren't many more places to visit or people to talk to.

It was a few minutes after five when I landed at LaGuardia, just in time for the evening rush-hour traffic. I sat in the back seat of a cab and stewed. I was tired; ready for a stiff drink or three, dinner, and bed.

It was six fifteen by the time I arrived in Manhattan. My mood had abruptly changed: I was suddenly cold and panicky, pent in by the traffic, the noise, and the realization that there was a maniac in the city who would kill me if he found out I was alive. The apartment now seemed too much like a prison or a trap, and I no longer wanted to go home.

I instructed the cab driver to take me downtown to the medical building where Arthur Morton had had offices. I didn't have hopes of finding anyone still there, but checking the building directory for Mary Llewellyn's name would give me something to do. Hers was the last name I had: the last link in a chain that seemed to be made out of air.

The medical building looked deserted, except for a single guard at the doors who was absorbed in the Final Edition of the *New York Post*. He looked up as I entered, then stuck his nose back into his paper. I walked to the directory at the opposite end of the lobby.

Dr. Mary Llewellyn, Clinical Psychologist, was listed. Fifth floor. I decided to see if she was working late. I took the self-service elevator to the fifth floor, made my way around a cleaning lady, and found Mary Llewellyn's office at the end of the corridor. The light was on inside the office. I knocked, then pushed on the translucent glass door.

A woman in her late thirties looked up from a paper-strewn desk. Mary Llewellyn was attractive in a prissy way. Her blond hair was drawn back in a severe bun. Her eyes were a cold sea-green and seemed to form a barrier between herself and the rest of the world. She looked like a career woman who had lost herself in her work and had no desire to find her way back again.

"Dr. Llewellyn?"

"Yes?" Her tone was frosty.

"Bob Frederickson."

She ignored the hand I offered. "I believe I've heard of you. What can I do for you, Mr. Frederickson?"

"I'm a private investigator. I've been hired by a private party to investigate the murder of one of your colleagues."

A tapered, well-manicured hand shot to her mouth. "Someone I know has been murdered?"

"This murder took place five years ago."

The hand slowly dropped into her lap. "You're talking about Arthur," she whispered.

"That's right, ma'am. I'd like to ask you a few questions."

"I'm glad *someone's* finally getting around to looking into it," she said in a voice that seemed burdened with a weight from the past. "It's disgraceful the way nothing was ever done."

"It's hard to catch a murderer when you can't find the motive," I said, watching her hands as they reached out and seized the edge of the desk. "Maybe he surprised a couple of burglars."

"These were no ordinary burglars," she said with feeling.

"Why do you say that?"

I watched a veil drop over her eyes as she suddenly became very wary. "Whom did you say you were working for?"

"I didn't say, Dr. Llewellyn. My client prefers to remain anonymous. What do you suppose the burglars wanted in Dr. Morton's office?"

"I don't think I can be of any help to you, Mr. Frederickson," she said in a formal tone. She jammed her papers into a slim briefcase and shut it, then rose and glared at me. "I can't remember any of the details. How in the world should *I* know what the burglars were after?"

"They were after the records of a very famous patient. Now, you and Dr. Morton collaborated on at least one occasion concerning Victor Rafferty. I thought you might know what Dr. Morton was doing in his office at that hour of the morning."

"I said I can't remember any of the details," she said curtly. "And whoever told you that we collaborated on the case of Victor Rafferty is either mistaken or a liar."

She came around from behind her desk and held out her free arm as if to sweep me out of the office with her.

"You forgot to turn off the lights," I said.

She quickly turned off the desk lamp. "I really must be going," she said icily.

"You *did* collaborate on Victor Rafferty's case, didn't you?" Even in the dim light from the hallway I could see her jaws clench.

"What do you *really* want, Mr. Frederickson?"

"To learn all I can about Victor Rafferty."

"I don't know anything about Victor Rafferty," she said in a voice barely above a whisper.

"I think you're one of the very few people who do, Dr. Llewellyn. It's a secret that could cost you your life. There are some very nasty people asking questions now about Victor Rafferty. You're lucky they didn't get to you before me. They're not very polite. If you'll tell me what I want to know, it could save lives."

"I can't talk to you," she said in a strangled whisper. *"Please!"*

"Why not?"

"I just can't talk about it!"

"Was Rafferty a telepath?"

That stopped her. Her green eyes caught the light from the hallway and glinted like those of a hunted animal. "Whom have you been talking to? Who told you that?"

181

"*Was* he a telepath?"

"Victor Rafferty is dead! Let him stay dead!"

"Were you and Arthur Morton conducting experiments in parapsychology?" My own voice rose, trembled as if in sympathy with her emotion, her fear.

"Victor Rafferty was a *monster*! A monster and a traitor!"

The vehemence of her statement was totally unexpected, and it brought me down. "*Why* was he a monster, Dr. Llewellyn? What did he do?"

She looked at me a long time in silence. When she spoke again, her voice had regained its icy reserve. "Get out of here or I'll call the police," she said evenly.

Something was happening inside my head. The phone had begun to ring. Mary Llewellyn cursed softly and pushed past me. It took her a moment to find the light button; then she picked up the phone.

There was a fire raging inside my brain and it felt as though every muscle in my body were cramping. Once again I was hanging on the bar, electricity coursing through my body, my brain melting under the onslaught of pain. I heard Mary Llewellyn calling me from what seemed a long distance.

"Mr. Frederickson ... ? Mr. Frederickson, are you all right?"

Reeling, my hands pressed to my ears, I tried to say something, but the words wouldn't leave my throat. I wheeled and stumbled out of her office.

There was no longer any doubt in my mind. I was finished.

17

The guard in the lobby looked over his shoulder at me, then stuck his nose back into his paper when I went to the pay phone in the lobby. It was going to take more than a sweating, shaking dwarf running around his lobby after hours to budge him out of his chair.

I took a deep breath and held it, then dropped a dime into the slot and dialed Tal's number. A woman answered. I gave my name and asked for Tal. There were a few whirs and clicks as the call was channeled through what I assumed were a number of different exchanges.

The attack in the psychologist's office had been the worst, and it wasn't over yet. I was still having flashes, falling to pieces. I was going to take Garth's advice and run to a place where there was a lot of sun and no death. After that I was going to check myself into the best psychiatric clinic I could find. I was scared.

Tal came on the line. "Hello, Mongo. I called the hospital and was told you were gone. When are you going to North Carolina?" His voice sounded odd, uncharacteristically weak.

"I've been."

"Did you find out anything?"

"It's finished, Tal. I can't function. I'm taking myself out of this. I'll reimburse you for the plane trip."

"You want to talk about it, Mongo?"

I bit my lip to keep from sobbing. Sweat was running into my eyes, and the telephone booth seemed to be shrinking. "I don't feel like talking about it!" I shouted into the mouthpiece. "I'm just finished! Okay?" I pressed a fist hard against my forehead and forced myself to speak in what I hoped resembled a normal tone. "Sorry, Tal. It's nothing personal. I've got . . . problems. I can't do anything until I get them worked out."

"Where are you? I'll pick you up."

"That won't do any good. I know what I have to do." And I knew I'd end as a catatonic if I didn't do it.

"Of course," Tal said easily. "I understand. But I would like to know what you did in North Carolina, if you feel up to telling me about that. May I pick you up?"

"All right," I said after a pause. "I'm at the Harlick Building."

"I know where it is. Hang in. I'll be there in fifteen minutes."

Tal arrived twelve minutes later in a year-old Pontiac. He pulled over to the curb and I slid in next to him. He looked pale, tired. As he pulled away, I became conscious of my own odor: I smelled of sweat and fear.

"Sorry I turned out chicken," I mumbled. "I have to get away from things for a while."

"You left the hospital too soon," he said evenly.

"It wouldn't have made any difference if I'd stayed there a year; it's not the kind of hospital I need. My body's fine; it's my head that's screwed up."

"You're impatient. It's going to take time for everything to heal properly."

"You want to hear what I found out in North Carolina? It isn't much; in fact, it probably isn't anything."

"Hold on to it for a few minutes, okay? There's someone else who'd like to hear what you have to say."

"Who?"

"The Secretary General."

184

Rolfe Thaag was sitting in a leather armchair in Tal's suite of offices. Perhaps because legends are always larger than reality, he seemed smaller in person than I'd imagined, although he was close to six feet, and hard-muscled. He had a full head of snowy white hair and a neatly trimmed beard to match. His eyes were a pale, Nordic blue; they were sharp and brooding, bright with intelligence, mellowed slightly by compassion. They matched the cardigan sweater he was wearing. The hand I shook was hard and sinewy.

"It's nice to meet you, Dr. Frederickson," he said in a slightly accented voice that was lower than it sounded on radio and television. "I meant to come out and meet you the other day while you were with Ronald, but I was quite busy. I hope you'll forgive my bad manners."

Not quite sure what to say, I mumbled something about knowing what a busy man he was. I was nervous, and afraid that my mind was going to pick just such an inopportune moment to launch another sneak attack.

Thaag said, "Would you like a drink?"

"No, thank you. If you don't mind, I'd just like to get on with it."

"Of course," the Secretary General said.

I moved across the room to a window and began talking in a monotone, reporting on my conversation with Fritz James, concluding by saying that I thought the mystery surrounding Victor Rafferty could well have something to do with parapsychology. When I turned back from the window, Rolfe Thaag was staring straight ahead, and Tal was absently rubbing his temples with his fingers. "If you don't mind my saying so, neither of you seems particularly interested in all this."

"Forgive us, Dr. Frederickson," Thaag said. "We appreciate what you've done and been through. At the moment we're distracted because we have reason to believe that the Russians have delivered an ultimatum to the Americans. If the Americans don't produce Victor Rafferty, the Fosters will . . . disappear. Soon."

For a moment my own anxiety was eclipsed by a growing excitement. "Then the Americans *do* have Rafferty?"

Rolfe Thaag slowly passed a hand across his eyes. "The Russians think so," he said wearily. "Now, I must *appear* to remain neutral, but it has always been my policy to prevent the deaths of innocent people, whenever possible and by whatever means."

"You'll pardon me if I sound cynical," I said, "but it seems to me that you're risking a great deal for the sake of two people."

Thaag and Tal exchanged glances. It was Tal who spoke.

"All right, Mongo; there are other considerations. First, I feel a measure of responsibility for the Fosters because I was the one who urged you to stay on the case. But it's also important that we find out once and for all what power or knowledge Victor Rafferty possesses, and whether or not he is alive. We certainly don't want the Russians—*or* the Americans—to control Rafferty, if they don't already. Rescuing the Fosters may be the only alternative."

Thaag glanced at me sharply. "Ronald tells me he thinks the Fosters might be rescued . . . if you would be willing to help."

"This is the second time I've heard that proposal," I said, startled.

"Really?" Tal said. "Someone else wants to rescue the Fosters?"

"Lippitt. He came to visit me in the hospital."

"What's his plan?"

"He didn't go into details, but it was a two-man operation: himself and me."

"He must have been thinking of the same point of entry," Thaag said as he turned to Tal. "That would explain his need of Dr. Frederickson."

186

"Then Lippitt must have schematics too," Tal said as he went to a desk and opened a locked drawer. He brought out a roll of papers that had been tightly bound with a rubber band, unrolled the sheets, and anchored them flat on the desk top.

What I saw was detailed schematic drawings of the inside of the Russian consulate. I wondered what they'd cost.

"It's no good," I said. "Whatever you've got in mind, I can't do it."

"Your fear?" Tal queried softly.

"It hits me with no warning, and when it does I'm no good for anything. I'm not going into any Russian consulate like this; I could get us all killed."

"I'm willing to take that chance," Tal said.

"*I'm* not."

Tal stared at me. "I think you want to go."

The pressure was building on me, from within and without. It was true that I wanted to go after the Fosters, but it was also true that Kaznakov would probably be inside the building. Try as hard as I might to ignore that fact, my subconscious would remember—and react.

"I have to think about it," I said weakly.

"There isn't time," Tal said. His voice was soft but insistent. "If we're going to go, we have to do it tonight."

I heard someone say, "I'll try," and was shocked to discover that the voice was mine.

Tal looked at his watch. "Good," he said curtly. "Afterward, arrangements will be made for you to go into hiding, if that's what you still want to do." He rose, stretched, winced as if in pain. He immediately caught himself, thrust his hands into his pockets, and smiled. I thought he was favoring his left side. "There are some things I have to get," he continued. "Are you hungry, Mongo?"

Not trusting my voice, I shook my head.

"You may be later. It's eight thirty now. I'll be gone a

couple of hours. I suggest that you try to get some sleep."

"I don't want to sleep," I said. "I want to get this show on the road and over with."

"I'll get you something to help you relax," Rolfe Thaag said, rising from his chair.

He went into a small kitchenette off the office and I heard the sound of water running, a teakettle being filled. Tal nodded to me, then went to the elevator. A few seconds later the elevator doors sighed open; they closed after him and he was gone.

Everything seemed surreal, moving too fast. I sat and tried to think of nothing.

The teakettle began to whistle. The sound died, and moments later Rolfe Thaag appeared carrying a steaming cup of something that looked like tea and smelled sharp and bitter. I made an effort to control hands that had suddenly begun to tremble as I reached for the cup.

"What's this?"

"Tea," the Secretary General said, "with a touch of ginseng. A special preparation made by a Chinese friend of mine. Drink it; it will soothe you and help you to sleep."

The hot tea scalded the roof of my mouth and my tongue, but I welcomed the pain with a kind of masochistic relief: it made me temporarily forget the other, sharper pain in my mind. I set down the cup on the coffee table in front of me.

"You should drink it while it's hot," Thaag said, picking up the cup and handing it back to me. The tone of his voice was almost hypnotic.

I didn't argue but drank some more of the bitter tea. It burned in my stomach, but it was not an unpleasant sensation. I laughed suddenly, without humor. "I can't believe I'm sitting here with the Secretary General of the United Nations, who has just assisted in the planning of a break-in at the Russian consulate, a plan to be personally carried out by his top assistant."

Thaag shrugged. "It's true that it's a risky venture."

"Then why involve yourself? I told you that Lippitt has a plan of his own."

Thaag looked at me a long time, as if I'd said something stupid and he were searching for a way to be polite. "I do not make a practice of depending on American agents," he said at last. "We must all, on occasion, take risks, and responsibility."

"Tal could be killed. If we're discovered in there, it will be the end of your tenure."

"Being Secretary General means nothing to me in itself, Dr. Frederickson; not unless I can be *effective*. I have a lovely home and a profitable business in my native country; I can always return to those. As far as Ronald is concerned, I believe he can guarantee your safety while you're inside the consulate."

"I don't follow you."

"If Ronald is killed inside the consulate, I will take steps to make certain he's regarded as a martyr. I will get up in the General Assembly and tell all I know. And I will be believed. I will admit my role in trying to rescue the Fosters, and then I will resign. Every investigative reporter in the United States will be digging for information about Victor Rafferty. *That* would not please any of the parties involved. I think the Russians, if they *should* catch you, will let both of you go."

"If they stop long enough to ask questions," I said.

"That's a risk we'll have to take."

"You could speak up now."

"I am not prepared to resign unless it is necessary," Thaag said forcefully. "And I cannot make charges without proof unless I *am* prepared to leave. What I say must have impact. If you and Ronald are able to rescue the Fosters without publicity, so much the better. I am hoping the Russians will dump you in the street, if you are caught."

Not Kaznakov, I thought, but I didn't say anything. I was surprised to find that I *was* getting sleepy. I shook my head and it felt as though my brain was sloshing around inside my skull. I mumbled something, closed my eyes, and breathed deeply, launching myself into sleep. Kaznakov came calling, riding in on a black dream. Suddenly I was reliving the torture session.

I knew I was dreaming, tried to wake up, and couldn't. The giant with the smashed nose was hanging me up by the elbows, wiring me to the telephone. I was strangling, writhing on the bar; waves of excruciating pain coursed through every nerve in my body. As before, I thought I heard a door open; someone was with me in the farmhouse cellar.

Then it started all over again: Kaznakov killing the British agents, chasing after me, stringing me up. However, this time there was a difference, however slight: The pain was not quite as bad. It was almost as though I were no longer a direct participant; I was floating outside myself, watching a man who looked like me suffering on an iron bar. I could heartily sympathize with him, but his pain was no longer my own.

The second show ended, then promptly began again. And again. It went on and on until finally I was quite bored with it all.

When I woke up, sweat was pouring down my face and my clothes were pasted to my body. I sat bolt upright in the chair. It was dark and I was sopping wet. But something was different, and it took me a long time to figure out exactly what it was.

Suddenly it came to me that I was no longer afraid.

The burning ball of fear that had taken up residence in my belly had cooled, leaving me weak and warm but unafraid. I could think of Kaznakov and the telephone and the electricity and it had no more emotional impact than the last run-through of the dream. The fever in my mind had broken, and I was whole again.

A telephone rang out in the darkness. I had no emotional reaction; now it was no more than just a phone ringing. A door opened somewhere in the outer suite of offices and I heard the muffled sound of footsteps in a carpeted hallway. The door to the office I'd been sleeping in suddenly opened and the room flooded with light.

Tal moved quickly across the room and picked up the phone on the desk. He was dressed all in black, from his shoes to the seaman's cap he wore on his head. He spoke a few curt words into the telephone, then hung up and turned toward me. "Wrong number," he said. "Wouldn't you know? I'm sorry it woke you." He paused, came closer. "You look terrible. You must have been dreaming."

"I feel better," I said. My voice was weak but steady. I stood up and experienced a sudden wave of dizziness, but it passed. "Where's the bathroom, and when do we go?"

Tal smiled. I thought he still looked pale. "The bathroom's out the door to your left, and we leave soon. I was going to wake you up in half an hour. I've prepared some food."

"Good. I can use something to eat." In fact I was ravenously hungry, and I knew the hunger was the result of the long journey I'd taken during the night, from sickness to health, from nowhere to now.

I went into the bathroom and sponged myself off. There was a surprise waiting for me when I went back into the office; the surprise had pale eyes and a bald head.

"Jesus," I said.

"Hello, Frederickson," Lippitt replied softly.

I looked at Tal as I jerked a thumb in Lippitt's direction. "What's he doing here?"

"An extra hand," Tal said wryly.

"Do you object, Mongo?" Tal asked.

"Who, me? I'm just along for the ride."

"You're the key to the plan," Lippitt said tightly.

"It seems Mr. Lippitt has been industriously following me," Tal said, an easy smile playing around the corners of his mouth. "Since he seems to have come up with a similar plan, it seemed a good idea to pool our resources."

191

Lippitt laughed; it was a sharp, harsh sound. "What resources?"

"If you don't think this is going to work, why did you approach me in the first place?" I asked.

"Masochism, and the fact that I wanted you to start paying some dues."

"I don't think so. The Fosters—or Mrs. Foster—is very important to you, Lippitt: so much so that you'd risk your own life, not to mention mine, to save her. Why?"

"It's none of your business," Lippitt said simply.

"Do you have Rafferty?" I persisted.

Lippitt heaved a deep sigh. "Rafferty's dead. I killed him. At least, I thought I did."

I repeated his words. "Thought you did?"

"You look like hell, Frederickson," Lippitt said, his eyes suddenly cold. "I'm beginning to wonder if this is such a good idea. You're going to get yourself killed, and I'm not as mad now as I was in the hospital."

I stood up straight. "Lippitt, I've never felt better in my life." I looked at Tal. "Where's the Secretary General?"

"In his own apartment, sleeping."

"You mentioned something about food."

Tal nodded. "Steak, eggs, and coffee. We'll go over the plan in detail while we eat."

18

The luminous dial on my watch read four fifteen as Tal pulled his car up to the curb a half block away from the consulate. The street was deserted except for an occasional taxi that sped past, ferrying the night people.

Tal and Lippitt immediately went to the locked glass door of the office building next to the consulate. I followed and waited in the shadows. Lippitt reached into his pocket and withdrew a length of stiff wire; within seconds he'd picked the lock. In a few minutes we were on top of the building and looking down on the roof of the consulate. Across the way, I could see the upside-down Ls of the ventilator shafts glinting in the moonlight. It was a good twenty-five feet across, with a downward angle of about thirty degrees. I would have to clear a two-foot parapet; if I missed, it was eighteen stories to the ground.

"Check your equipment," Lippitt said curtly.

For the third time that evening I opened the canvas flight bag Tal had given me and checked its contents: a small acetylene torch with self-contained gas supply, a bottle of olive oil, flashlight, gun, magnet, and grenade-type incendiary bomb.

"Everything's here," I said, zipping up the bag and rising.

"Once again," Tal said. "You'll keep track of the floors by counting the intersections of horizontal and vertical ducts. When you get to the third floor, you'll go to your *left*. Count ten sections—you'll feel the seams—and cut through in the middle of the tenth section. You should find yourself on a stairwell landing. Go through the door and down to the end of the corridor. That's where you plant the incendiary bomb; it has only an eight-second fuse, so don't waste time after you pull the pin; get down the stairs as fast as you can. At the bottom, you'll find an exit door with a steel bolt. It leads to a service alley. That's where Lippitt and I will be."

"Give me about forty minutes," I said, flinging the canvas bag out into the darkness. It landed with a dull thud on the consulate roof. Before I could give myself time to think about it, I backed up a few paces, ran forward, and threw myself into the yawning, empty night between the buildings. Wind whistled in my ears as the parapet rushed up at me. I cleared it by no more than an inch, tucked and rolled when I hit the tarmac. Using my shoulders and upper back to absorb the force of my landing, I rolled a second time and came up on my feet.

Across the way, Tal and Lippitt gave me a thumbs-up sign, then melted back into the shadows. I picked up the canvas bag and walked to the ventilator shafts.

Both shafts were covered with steel grates. I took out the torch and went to work on the one on the right. The torch sputtered a few times, but finally cut through the bolts holding the grille in place. The shaft looked awfully narrow, and I was going to have to squirm down fifteen stories in it.

I smeared my body and clothes with olive oil, then clambered into the duct feet first, scraping the skin on my elbow. I rolled over on my stomach and, dragging the bag after me, worked my way over the angle of the L. Darkness closed over my head.

The duct sloped slightly, but it was still steep. At one point I began to slide too quickly; I flexed my shoulders and thighs and braked to a stop. The friction had burned through my shirt and pants, and my flesh throbbed. I manipulated the bottle over my head and poured more oil down over my body. I wondered how long the oil would last; if I got stuck, it would take a team of plumbers a week to get me out.

I reached the first horizontal section. Fourteen more floors to go; I lay in the wider section of the duct and panted. There was a slight draft coming down from the top; I waited until the sweat dried, then started down again.

It cost me a lot of pain, not a little anxiety, and a lot of skin when I ran out of oil on the eighth floor. But I made it to the intersection of ducts on the third floor. In the middle of the tenth section, I took out the torch and magnet. I was already considerably behind schedule, and it took ten minutes to get the torch working properly. The fact that I could barely breathe didn't help.

I adjusted the tiny blue-white flame of the torch and went to work on the metal. It quickly became a question of what would burn out first, the metal or me. Within moments the metal under my knees became red hot; I could smell my clothing burning, and I was breathing in quick, nervous gasps.

With about an inch to go, I removed the magnet from the bag, draped the attached leather thong around my neck, and placed the magnet in the center of the circle I'd circumscribed with the cutting flame. Then I cut the rest of the way through the metal and pulled the hot circle up and out.

I waited a few minutes for the metal to cool, then poked my head down through the hole in the duct. Tal and Lippitt had been right on target: my nose was a few inches away from a glowing EXIT sign. A well-lighted stairway led down and up from the landing. I dropped to the stairwell, dragging the canvas bag after me. I immediately took out the automatic, checked the full magazine, then crouched by the door to listen. When I heard nothing, I pushed through.

According to plan, I found myself at one end of a long, carpeted corridor. I had to plant the bomb at the opposite end of the corridor where it would do the most damage, then get down the stairs to let in Lippitt and Tal. I hurried down the corridor, knelt in a corner at the end, and unzipped the bag.

At the sound of a door opening directly behind me, I rose and spun. There was no place to run or hide, so I whipped the gun out of my waistband and aimed it at a point in space where the man's chest would appear in another split second. The door opened and my finger froze on the trigger. Big as death, dressed in the uniform of a Russian major, stood Kaznakov. He looked to me like an ogre from some half-remembered childhood dream.

I looked to him like a dwarf he'd seen before.

He thought and moved faster than I did. While I was still waving my pistol around in space, he reached out and swatted it from my hand as easily as a grizzly smashing fish out of a stream.

That woke me up; I crouched down and started to back up in the few feet I had between Kaznakov and the wall. He didn't even bother to draw his revolver from its holster; he just grinned crookedly and lumbered forward, arms outstretched to cut off any possible avenue of escape.

I wasn't about to let the scabby-faced Russian carry me off gently into the good night of one of the darkened rooms off the corridor. A few hours earlier, I'd have been paralyzed by the mere sight of the man in front of me. Now, thanks to Rolfe Thaag's Miracle Tea and Sleep Cure, I was ready to do a little battle.

When I was backed to the wall, Kaznakov crouched and leaped at me. I ducked under his outstretched arms, spun around, and landed the point of my shoe on his elbow. I'd been aiming for the base of his spine, but the kick on the elbow did some good; there was a crunching sound. Kaznakov grunted with surprise and pain as the arm I'd kicked convulsed, then flopped to the side of his body. I pivoted again and dived for my gun, gripped it, rolled over on my back, and pointed it at a thoroughly surprised Kaznakov. I giggled in hysterical relief and pulled the trigger. Nothing happened; the force of Kaznakov's knocking the gun against the wall had jammed the firing mechanism. I threw the gun at his huge globe head—and missed.

Kaznakov, satisfied that I couldn't get through a door before he shot me, was taking a breather. He cursed in Russian and spat, cradling his broken elbow and leaning against the wall. He looked at me through eyes glazed with pain and hatred. "I am going to tear your arms and legs from sockets."

Slowly, I got to my feet. We stood a few feet apart, panting and staring at each other.

The huge moon eyes slowly blinked. "How did you get out of the farmhouse?"

"Magic, pig!" I shouted, adrenaline bubbling through my bloodstream. "Didn't your pig mother ever tell you any fairy tales about dwarfs?"

Maybe he didn't like my insulting his mother; more likely, he was just tired. He reached across his body for his gun, and I showed him another move.

In the circus I'd leaped over barriers a lot higher than Kaznakov, but I'd had considerably more room to get up a head of steam. As it was, I made it to about the level of his neck, twisted in the air, and kicked at the area of his bandaged nose. The Russian reached out and plucked me out of the air like a fielder snaring an easy pop-up. He immediately began to squeeze.

I came down hard on both his ears with my palms. He screamed and dropped me as he reached for his head. I fell to the floor; as luck would have it, Kaznakov tripped and fell on top of me. I groped in front of me for the canvas bag that was only inches away from my fingertips, but it was no good. Kaznakov had me. Instantly on his feet, he

197

picked me up and hurled me against the wall. I instinctively relaxed to try to prevent broken bones, but it felt as though I'd been hit by a freight train. I bounced off the wall and hit the floor. Everything went dark, as if someone had tripped a wire inside my brain. Huge black waves pounded over my head as I clung frantically to the cliff edge of consciousness, knowing that if I went over that drop I was a dead man.

Some of my vision was coming back, but it was blurred. I heard the Russian's breathing, heavy with hate. Iron fingers wrapped around my ankles and twisted, pulling my legs in opposite directions. Kaznakov intended to literally split me up the middle with his bare hands.

Still blind, I groped for something to use as a weapon, and my fingers found the canvas bag. Pain shot up through my groin to my belly; in a few seconds, ligaments would start to tear. But I was getting more of my vision back. Kaznakov's leering face was very close to mine; he was watching me with a kind of detached interest, waiting for me to start screaming.

Trying to forget the pain for just a moment, I tensed, focusing all my energy into the palms of my hands for one more blow. When I could stand the pain no longer, I screamed at the top of my lungs and again brought my hands around on Kaznakov's ears.

He yelled and released my ankles. I swung at his head with the sack, then somehow managed to get my feet under me; the only problem was that my legs weren't working right. I tried to run, tripped and stumbled, got up, then stumbled again. I needed a time-out; I had my eyes back, but I needed a decent set of legs to go with them. Kaznakov, of course, wasn't inclined to be obliging. He either had forgotten about his gun, or had lost interest in doing anything short of tearing me apart with his hands. He was coming at me full tilt.

I got up and tried to run again, with only slightly more

success. Kaznakov was gaining on me fast. There was only one thing left to try, and it was going to take some exquisite timing—not to mention luck. I tried to judge from the sound of his footsteps just where he was. When I felt his arms reach out for me, I dropped like a stone. Kaznakov went sailing through the air over my head.

I leaped onto the backs of his knees and drove my thumbs as hard as I could into his kidneys. He gargled with rage and pain and started to get up on his hands and knees. I wrapped my legs around his middle and hung on as he started to buck. At the same time, I unzipped the bag and searched inside for the incendiary grenade; I found it and wrapped my fingers around the hard metal.

Kaznakov was on his feet now, writhing, banging me against the wall, struggling to get me off his back. I grabbed his shirt collar and yanked; the shirt and jacket tore open. Still gripping his midsection with my legs, I pulled the pin on the grenade and dropped it down the back of his shirt. Then I jumped off and started hobbling toward the door where I'd come in. When I didn't hear footsteps behind me, I stopped and looked back.

Kaznakov was standing where I'd left him, a dazed expression on his face as it slowly dawned on him that there was a live grenade inside his shirt. He began to dance and claw at his shirt and jacket, trying to get at the small, deadly sphere that was ticking against his flesh. But he knew he was finished; at the last moment he stopped his wild dancing and stared at me. I thought I saw tears in his eyes.

A fountain of flame suddenly shot up from his back. There was a loud whooshing noise, and Kaznakov, without a sound, disappeared into that red fountain. He stayed on his feet a few more seconds, the shadowy outline of a giant petal in a huge crimson flower that was spreading through the corridor; then he sank down. The air was filled with the stench of gasoline and roasting human flesh.

I ran for the exit, pushed through the door, and froze.

Someone was racing up the stairs. I had no gun and no place to hide. I backed up against the wall of the stairwell and crouched, ready to spring if I ever got the chance. The man rounded the bend in the stairs just below me.

"Tal!"

Tal stopped and looked up at me. There was blood streaming from both his nostrils, bright crimson stains on flesh the color of chalk. He swiped at the blood with the back of his hand, then yelled at me. I couldn't hear him above the din of the alarm bell, but I could read his lips: "Follow me! Hurry!"

I scrambled off the landing and down the stairs after Tal. Despite the beating I'd taken, I felt vital and alive, powered by a terrible excitement: I'd killed Kaznakov.

We met Lippitt, his gun drawn, between the first and second landings. His eyes were wide, face flushed. "What the hell?" he shouted at Tal. "I was only gone a minute! How the hell did you get in?"

"The door must have opened automatically when the fire alarm went off!" Tal shouted back. "I just pushed on it and it opened!"

"Why didn't you wait for me?" Lippitt demanded.

"No time! There's no time now! Every second counts!"

Lippitt nodded curtly, turned, and led the way down toward the basement. He paused in front of the basement door.

Tal stepped forward. "Wait here," he said.

"No," Lippitt said. He was looking at Tal suspiciously. "I go where you go."

Tal glanced at me. "Will *you* wait here, Mongo?" There was a note of impatience in his voice. "Fire or no fire, there'll probably still be a guard standing in front of the Fosters' room. I may be able to bluff him, but certainly not if you're along."

I nodded. What Tal said made sense. Still, Lippitt was right on Tal's heels as they went through the basement door. I waited ten seconds, then pushed the door open a few inches and peered down the corridor. The hallway looked the same as the one on the third floor—except that there was a guard standing in front of a door fifty feet down the hall in these, the "living quarters" indicated on the schematics.

Tal walked quickly, with an air of absolute assurance, even when the guard raised his rifle and challenged him. Lippitt was walking a few feet behind Tal, using the taller man's body to shield the automatic in his hand.

Tal spoke rapidly to the guard, in fluent Russian. I felt a little chill up my spine. I could understand Lippitt's sudden nervousness. The discussion quickly degenerated into an argument, with Tal maintaining, from what I could gather from his hand gestures, that the Fosters would have to be taken out of the room because of the fire. The guard was apparently insisting that Tal and Lippitt produce some kind of credentials. Tal made a show of going through his pockets while Lippitt ended the discussion by hitting the guard over the head with the butt of his gun.

Lippitt immediately went to his knees in front of the door and began to pick the lock. I pushed through the door and ran down the hall, arriving just as Lippitt finished his work and opened the door.

The Fosters were standing in the middle of the room. Mike Foster had his arms wrapped tightly around his wife. Both were still in their nightclothes. "Mongo!" Foster shouted when he saw me. "Jesus Christ! *Jesus Christ!*"

Something in Foster's voice caused his wife to push his arms away from her shoulders. She turned slowly to look at us. Elizabeth Foster was a beautiful woman, even without makeup and numbed by sleep. But now her thin lips were compressed by terror, her violet eyes muddy with shock. She gasped when she saw Lippitt.

"*You!*"

"Hello, Mrs. Foster," Lippitt said softly.

Foster's mouth opened and closed without making a sound. He kept staring at me, as if he couldn't believe I was there. I knew how he felt.

"Let's go," Lippitt said.

It was Tal who led the way out. "This way," he said, turning to his right and motioning for us to follow.

Lippitt abruptly stopped in the doorway, blocking our way. I watched the gun in his hand swing up and point at Tal. "Hold it," Lippitt said. "That's not the way out. We go out the way we came in. That's the plan!"

Tal's eyes flashed angrily. "We can't make it that way, Lippitt. They'll be waiting for us! You tripped an alarm when you opened the door."

"How the hell do you know that?"

"Look at the doorjamb!"

Lippitt and I looked in the direction where Tal pointed; there was a thin, almost invisible wire running the length of the jamb.

Lippitt hesitated. "The way you want to go leads right up to the lobby; there'll be a lot of firepower there."

"There'll be more at the other exits," Tal replied. "It's our only chance; the *last* place they'll expect us to show up is the main entrance! *Think*, man!"

Lippitt's gun was still firmly pointed at Tal's chest. "You know too goddamned much about this place to suit me," Lippitt said tensely.

Foster turned to me. "Who do we follow, Mongo?"

"Tal," I said quickly, without really knowing why.

Ignoring Lippitt's gun, Foster brushed past me and pushed the agent to one side. Gripping his wife's hand firmly, he started after Tal, who was already walking toward the open stairway at the far end of the corridor. Lippitt and I exchanged glances.

"You'd better have guessed right, Frederickson," Lippitt said ominously. His gun started to swing around, stopped just short of my forehead.

There didn't seem to be much sense in stopping to argue the point, so I ducked under the gun and started after Tal and the Fosters. Lippitt's footsteps came up quickly from behind me as a contingent of guards suddenly appeared on the stairs just above us. Tal grabbed the Fosters and pulled them to the floor while Lippitt squeezed three quick shots over our heads. The three men fell dead, each with a bullet hole placed precisely in the middle of his forehead.

As Elizabeth Foster started to scream and tremble, her husband scooped her up in his arms and ran up the stairs after Tal. Lippitt followed, and after grabbing a pistol from one of the dead guards, I brought up the rear. I almost bumped into Lippitt as I rounded a curve in the stairs. Tal, Lippitt, and the Fosters were crouched down, backs against the wall, while someone poured shots down the stairwell.

"Two of them," Lippitt barked. "Machine pistols. They've spotted us!"

I was still filled with the giddy, drunken feeling I'd been carrying with me since I'd left Kaznakov's charred, crackling corpse up on the third floor. I lunged up the stairs, leaped, twisted in the air, and pulled the trigger on my own gun. I fired blindly, both hands on the weapon. It must have been a red-letter day on my astrological chart, because I knew even before I landed hard on my back that I'd hit both of them. Tal suddenly appeared beside me. He finished the job with a gun he took from one of the guards, then motioned for the others to follow him. I saw that he was holding his left side.

"You all right?" I asked. Tal nodded. "Go!" I shouted as Foster paused beside me. "Get your wife out of here!"

It was Lippitt who stopped and yanked me to my feet. "Are you hit?"

"No," I gasped, sobbing for breath. "Just knocked the wind out of myself." With Lippitt dragging me by the sleeve, I struggled up the steps and through the pneumatic door above into a mass of milling, shouting bodies.

The wail of police and fire sirens was very loud now, almost drowning out everything else. The main entrance was perhaps sixty feet away, separated from us by a throng of Russians and firemen. The air was thick with smoke that was billowing down the elevator shafts and stairways.

Someone shouted in Russian, and two burly men who had been standing around as if awaiting orders craned their necks, saw us and drew their guns, started in our direction.

Tal and Lippitt stepped forward, and I joined them as Foster pushed through and a semicircle was formed around his wife. Foster had no gun, but he had his fists; he jabbed and feinted in the air as we inched forward.

I was staring up the barrel of a Russian gun as a red-faced fireman with an American flag sewn on his sleeve and a fire ax in his hands suddenly squeezed into the semicircle between Lippitt and me.

"Man, I don't know what you people are up to," the fireman said in a thick Brooklyn accent, "but anybody who's trying to get away from the Russkys has my help."

More firemen joined the circle, and our group began to move forward. The Russians, unwilling to shoot down New York firemen, backed away. In a few seconds we were at the main entrance. A human corridor of firemen's bodies was formed, and Elizabeth Foster went through it, followed by her husband, Tal, Lippitt, and me.

We were out of the consulate.

19

The street was filled with smoke, sparks, and heat. Flames had eaten through the outer walls of the second and third floors; their light cast a small circle of artificial dawn that vied with the real thing. We'd made a journey of thousands of miles merely by stepping through a doorway; it was a journey of the mind and spirit. The New York street was our homeland.

Lippitt cleared a path through the police lines with his credentials, and we walked quickly to the car. Tal slipped behind the wheel and Lippitt got in on the passenger's side next to him. I sat in the back with the Fosters. A fire chief cleared the way, and Tal pulled away from the curb, navigated the obstacle course of vehicles, then turned uptown. The mad energy that had been fueling me had evaporated. I felt weak and nauseated, and I was trembling slightly. I hurt all over; my entire body felt like a bruise, which it was.

At the U.N., Tal drove through a series of linked underground garages and security gates, then parked. Finally he led us into a locked private elevator, which took us to the top floors of the building.

Lippitt was looking more unhappy and distracted by the minute. I didn't trust him. More important, Elizabeth Foster didn't trust him, and I knew why: if Lippitt had his way, the Fosters probably would have been squirreled away someplace else, as incommunicado as if they'd stayed with the Russians. As far as Mike Foster's wife was concerned, Lippitt was but one of several enemies.

Elizabeth Foster was walking around under her own power now, but she never moved an inch from her husband. She was pressed against him, one arm wrapped tightly around his waist.

The elevator door sighed open and we stepped into an apartment that I assumed was Rolfe Thaag's. Sunlight was streaming in through a bank of windows that reached from floor to ceiling and offered a giddy, panoramic view of Manhattan. It was going to be a hot, cloudless day. Somewhere out in that day, the vast resources of many armies were being marshaled: We were into the end game.

A telephone rang. Tal disappeared for a few moments into an adjoining room. When he returned, his face was ashen. "Rolfe Thaag has had a heart attack," he said in a low voice as he came close to me.

"Jesus."

Tal shook his head. "He's being taken care of in a private clinic. He's expected to recover, but he can't be disturbed. I think it's best if we don't mention it to the others."

Across the room, Mike Foster blinked back tears. "I just want you to know . . . I just want to thank all of you."

"He's alive," Elizabeth Foster said distantly in a voice that could barely be heard.

The room was suddenly very still. I wasn't sure I'd heard her correctly. She turned to her husband and repeated it. "He's alive. Victor is alive, darling."

Lippitt wasn't facing the window, but his eyes were half-closed, as if to shut out some bright light only he could see. He suddenly shifted his gaze to me, and our eyes held.

"How do you know, Mrs. Foster?" Tal said gently.

"He *called*." She slowly looked around the room at all of us. Her eyes were wild, drugged with horror. "They told us he called."

"It's true," Foster said, stepping into the center of the room. "I don't think they were lying; they were too damn happy about the whole thing. They said Rafferty was going to turn himself in this morning." He paused, touched his forehead. "Christ, I hope he knows we're out of there."

"I'm betting he knows," I said directly to Lippitt.

Tal slowly shook his head. "It could be a phony. Something the Americans cooked up to buy a little time."

"No," Lippitt said. He looked pale and shaken. A single drop of perspiration had appeared in the center of his forehead. He made no move to wipe it away as it ran down into his eyebrow. "The Russians must have voiceprints."

"How?" Foster asked.

"From the last time. Radio, television. Rafferty was a celebrity, remember?"

"You insisted you'd killed him," I said to Lippitt.

The American agent looked through me as if I weren't there, then abruptly wiped away the streak of moisture on his forehead and walked to the window.

I turned to the woman. "Mrs. Foster, what did your husband know?"

"Know?" Her voice was faint, like a frightened child's. Her violet eyes, paler now in the daylight, slowly came into focus on my face. "What do you mean?"

Tal put his hand gently on Elizabeth Foster's elbow. "You and your husband should sleep now. Try to rest. You can talk to us when you wake up, if you want to."

Elizabeth Foster swallowed hard; her words came in a forced whisper. "It's starting all over again."

I pressed. "What, Mrs. Foster? What's starting all over again?"

Lippitt suddenly turned from the window. "Mrs. Foster, I am going to ask you not to say anything. This is a matter of national security. Does your husband know anything?"

"I don't know beans, pal," Foster said, clenching his fists. "And I don't like your tone of voice. I've got a funny feeling you're the son-of-a-bitch who started this whole thing."

"No, Mr. Foster," Lippitt said evenly. "Whoever hired Frederickson to investigate Rafferty is the person responsible for what's happened. Was that you?"

Foster blanched and looked away from his wife's startled gaze. "It was the museum," he said weakly. "I had . . . to find out what it was. I *had* to find out. . . . I love you so much, Beth."

The woman spat her next words at the bald man standing by the window. "Why couldn't you just leave Victor alone? That's all he ever wanted!"

"We *couldn't* do that, Mrs. Foster." There was real anguish in Lippitt's voice, and it surprised me. "*Others* knew about him. If I hadn't gone after him, he would have been found by someone else. Apparently, that's what happened. God knows where he's been and what he's been doing for the past five years."

Lippitt seemed sincere. If he was telling the truth, it meant the Americans didn't have Rafferty after all.

Elizabeth Foster wheeled around and spoke to me. "Victor could read minds!" she said in a clear, defiant voice. It was clear that she was punishing Lippitt. Her eyes were smoky now, bursting with memories that had been bottled up and festering for five years. "He could read minds just as easily as the people in this room can read books and newspapers. It destroyed him."

Lippitt shrugged in resignation, clasped his hands behind his back, and stared at the floor.

"My God," Mike Foster whispered. "But I still don't under . . ." His voice trailed off.

"You don't have to talk about it, Mrs. Foster," Tal said soothingly.

She shook her head defiantly. "I *want* to talk about it," she said. "I thought it was all over. I thought Victor was dead and it would all be forgotten . . . by everyone except me. When I . . . saw that picture of the museum, I *knew* he was alive. I just knew." She looked at Lippitt with hatred in her eyes. "He was supposed to be dead! *You said he was dead!*"

"I honestly thought he was, Mrs. Foster," Lippitt said. "I'm *still* not convinced he's alive; I don't understand how he can be."

"It was the accident," Elizabeth Foster said, her voice steadily gaining strength, a small tic in her left eye the only evidence of the tremendous emotional strain she was under. "A part of Victor's brain was severely damaged. In most people that would mean death, or life as a vegetable. But with Victor . . . something else happened. Arthur couldn't explain it. The accident didn't debilitate Victor mentally; it just left him with this terrible, growing power, this terrible . . . energy."

She started to cry, stifled it. She waved Mike Foster away when he started to move toward her. "God knows he didn't *want* the gift," she continued. "Victor was not an easy man to understand. His work was his whole life, but I loved him and *tried* to understand." Now she paused, reached out, and squeezed her husband's hand. He moved closer and put his arm around her shoulders. "I suppose I was never *really* happy until I married Mike," she said, looking into her husband's eyes. "But I was terribly *proud* of Victor, and if our marriage took second place to his buildings, I didn't complain. The point is that all Victor ever wanted to do was design his buildings. After the accident"—she gave Lippitt another hate-filled glance—"that became impossible."

She heaved a deep, trembling sigh. She couldn't hold back her feeling; it escaped from her in sighs and shudders like air hissing from a balloon. "I could see the pain in his face," she continued quietly. "Apparently there was a great *deal* of pain associated with the things he could do. He thought he was going mad. He couldn't stand to be physically close to people; that was when it hurt the most. I didn't understand. I thought he was repelled by me. It wasn't that at

209

all; he just couldn't stand to be . . . *close*. When he finally did tell me, it was . . . too late.

"The pain kept getting worse as his powers increased. He didn't know what to do about it, didn't know whom he could go to." She smiled wryly; it was an ugly, pained grimace. "He knew instinctively that he shouldn't tell anyone, but he finally went to Arthur when he couldn't stand it any longer. Suddenly, *everyone* seemed to know. I don't understand how Arthur could have betrayed Victor like that."

"I'm not sure he did," I said. "My guess is that he called in a colleague without telling your husband. That person's name is Mary Llewellyn, and *she* was the source of the first leak." I watched Lippitt stiffen slightly and I knew I was right. "I think Dr. Llewellyn felt it was her patriotic duty to inform someone that there was a man who would make a formidable agent—really an incredible intelligence-gathering machine. Dr. Llewellyn saw the implications from the beginning: Give Rafferty a change of appearance, send him into the diplomatic corps; he goes to a Washington cocktail party, chats with some visiting Russian general, and walks out with more strategic military information than a team of C.I.A. agents could gather in a year. The Ultimate Weapon. The only problem was that there was only one of him, and he couldn't be duplicated."

Elizabeth Foster nodded her head in agreement. "Victor once gave me a demonstration," she said thickly. "He asked me to think of a series of numbers. I did and he . . . rattled them off as soon as they popped into my head. Then he started on my other thoughts. He wouldn't stop; he kept on and on, telling me *everything* that I was *thinking*! You can't imagine how that feels! I had to scream to make him stop. I . . . oh, God, I called him a monster."

Mary Llewellyn, I recalled, had called him the same thing. She had thought it perfectly reasonable that this monster, Victor Rafferty, give himself up to service in the government for the rest of his life. I was beginning to understand the dimensions and horror of Victor Rafferty's situation: A builder, an architect, Victor Rafferty had suddenly, through a quirk of nature, found himself alone, trapped in a lonely city of the mind, with no one to understand, much less keep him company. He was alone, listening to the baying in the darkness beyond the city's outermost limits.

"I . . . I hurt him so much," Mrs. Foster continued. "It crushed him when I said that; I'll never forget the look on his face. *That* was precisely what he'd been so afraid of: He didn't want people to think of him as a . . . freak."

Or a weapon, I thought.

"Victor never understood," she said, slowly turning to look at all of us. "He never could understand why other people couldn't appreciate what things he might be able to do in medicine, psychiatry . . . even criminal law." She started to laugh and it came out a wracking sob. "You wouldn't have to ask a person where it hurt; Victor would *know*. He'd have been able to diagnose symptoms that patients might not have been able to fully articulate. In trials, he would know who was guilty, and—more important— who wasn't. He believed scientists could study him in a laboratory and learn more about mankind; maybe, through him, others could have learned how to do the things he did. But of course, *they* wouldn't let him do that kind of work."

Lippitt winced, as if he could feel the woman's pointing finger jabbing into him. "It couldn't be helped, Mrs. Foster," Lippitt said softly. "When Dr. Llewellyn contacted us, she used lines of communication that are routinely monitored by foreign agents. They found out about Victor Rafferty virtually the same time as we did. It became a race against time. We wanted your husband to work for us, yes; in fact, it was imperative that he do so. A less free society, if they'd caught him, would have been able to force him to work for them. We couldn't allow that."

I glanced at Tal, who appeared to be deep in thought.

He was sitting in a straight-backed chair, staring at the floor and rolling a pencil between his palms.

"One morning, Mr. Lippitt came to our door," the woman continued in an icy voice. "He wanted to talk to Victor. Victor made me leave, but I know what they talked about. Mr. Lippitt gave Victor an ultimatum: Victor would have to work for the United States Government, and we would have to be relocated. Both Victor and I would have to undergo plastic surgery. No one—not family or friends—would ever see us again. We would be required to live like virtual prisoners for the rest of our lives while Victor did . . . whatever was expected of him."

"There are prisons, and there are prisons," Lippitt said. "Some are a good deal worse than others."

Elizabeth Foster wasn't really listening to anything Lippitt had to say. "Victor knew what was in Mr. Lippitt's mind," she continued, taking a deep breath and drawing her shoulders back. "He knew others would be coming for him, so he decided to run. He told me he'd find a safe place and then send for me. After all, we had plenty of money in the bank. Victor planned to use the money to buy new identities, new lives somewhere where *they* couldn't find us.

"He left the house. There were two men waiting for him. I saw what happened, but I still don't understand it." She wrapped her arms around her body as she shuddered. "I was standing on the stoop when one of the men jumped out at him. Victor swung his suitcase at the man, but Victor was still very weak from the operations; he didn't really have much strength to begin with, and the other man was so *big*. The man ducked around behind Victor and grabbed Victor's arm. Victor was struggling to get away, and then . . . the man just seemed to go down. His knees buckled and he fell to the sidewalk. He was holding his head and moaning, as if he were in pain, and then . . . he just lay still. Then another man came running at Victor. I thought Victor was going to be killed, so I ran inside and called the police.

When I came back out, both men were lying on the sidewalk and Victor was gone. I started to scream again. . . . I couldn't stop screaming."

Elizabeth Foster's voice trailed off, and there was silence in the room. I didn't think she would speak again, but she did.

"I knew I'd never see him again," she whispered. "And I didn't." She blinked back tears. "Two days later Mr. Lippitt called and told me Victor had been killed. The day after that, I saw a report in the newspaper that Victor had died in an accident in his laboratory. Now the Russians say they've talked to him on the phone. I just don't understand how that can be."

She looked at Lippitt, who stared back at her for a few moments, then glanced quickly away.

Tal spoke quietly to Mrs. Foster. "Do you have any idea how your first husband managed to escape from the two men?"

The woman shook her head.

It was Lippitt who answered. "He killed one and he knocked the other unconscious," Lippitt said into the stillness. He paused, then added: "And he did it with his mind. Victor Rafferty could kill with his mind."

Tal gestured impatiently. "That's insane."

"Nevertheless, it's true," Lippitt replied calmly. "You see, Victor Rafferty could do much more than just 'read minds.' He discovered through a series of accidents that his mental powers were growing. First, he found out he could kill by willing it when he was attacked by my men. I don't believe Rafferty meant to kill, but he panicked; he saw himself being captured. He literally reached out with his mind into the other man's brain. I don't know *what* he did there, or how he did it—an autopsy showed that my man died of a massive cerebral hemorrhage. But Rafferty knew, because he was able to control it within the space of a few seconds; remember that the second man was only knocked unconscious. Can you see the implications of this power, Dr. Frederickson?"

"Assassination," I said quickly. "The same general or diplomat Rafferty leached his information from could suddenly die of a cerebral hemorrhage."

"Without anyone having laid a hand on him," Lippitt said tightly. "It wouldn't have to be a general; it could be a president, a vice president, a cabinet member. Victor Rafferty would be able to kill anyone he could get close to, and never be caught."

20

"He *wouldn't* have!" Elizabeth Foster cried, violently shaking her head from side to side. "You know what he did to the first man was an accident! He didn't know what he was doing!"

"But he had the *capability*," Lippitt said. "That's the whole point. It was conceivable that he could have been *forced* to use his powers against us. If they had *you*, Mrs. Foster, they would control him. That's what the exercise of the last few hours was all about. For as long as he lived, Victor Rafferty could conceivably be forced to spy and kill for whoever controlled him, and no nation but the one he was working for would have a military secret left. Can you understand our position now, Mrs. Foster?"

Elizabeth Foster continued to shake her head, but her eyes betrayed her: She did understand, perhaps for the first time.

"Every nation that knew of his existence had only two choices," I said. "Force Rafferty into its camp—or kill him."

Lippitt gave a curt affirmative nod, and Elizabeth Foster's head snapped back against the cushions of the sofa as though Lippitt had struck her a physical blow. Mike Foster swore softly under his breath.

"There were orders," Lippitt continued quietly. "They

215

were the same type of orders that I'm sure went out to the intelligence divisions of the other countries."

"Victor didn't die in an accident," Elizabeth Foster whispered. "When he refused to cooperate with you, you killed him. Or you *tried* to kill him."

Lippitt made an end run around the implied question. "We almost had him again," he said. "We were . . . so close."

"The restaurant and the hospital?" I asked.

"Yes." Lippitt fixed his eyes on me. "I believe Rafferty discovered one more facet to his powers in that diner."

My mind flashed back to the old waiter, Barney, and his insistence that Rafferty had made food 'bounce.' "Telekinesis," I said, the breath catching in my throat. "He learned he could actually move objects by willing it."

"Correct," Lippitt responded evenly. "Again, an accident that enhanced Rafferty's knowledge of his own powers. He was tired and on the run. He'd lost his suitcase in the struggle with my men, and his bankbook was in that suitcase. He had no place to hide and no funds, except what he had with him. He had only the clothes on his back. When the waiter tripped and Rafferty saw that food flying at him, he instinctively reached out and pushed it away with his mind. It was a reflex action, and it must have hurt him terribly; he passed out from the pain. The waiter got a cop, who called an ambulance. Finally the cop recognized Rafferty from the description we'd sent out. I was eventually contacted in Washington . . . but you know the rest. By the time I got there, it was too late."

"Why hadn't the police been briefed?" Tal asked.

"Because all pertinent information concerning Victor Rafferty was—and is—Top Secret."

"That's almost funny," Tal said sardonically. "Apparently everyone knew about Rafferty except the people who could have helped you."

Lippitt ignored him. "No one was aware at the time that

216

Rafferty could actually move objects. Also, it must be said that he learned very quickly how to control his powers. He put the guard to sleep, then used telekinesis to open the bolt. That's how he escaped from the hospital."

Lippitt, with his flat narrative, made it sound too easy. I remembered O'Connell's description of the fingernail scratches on the doorjamb, the blood on the floor: Rafferty had been in agony.

"Poor Victor," Elizabeth Foster murmured. "Poor, poor Victor."

"How did you know Rafferty was at the metallurgy lab?" I asked. "Or is that all a story too?"

Lippitt looked at me oddly for a moment. "Rafferty called on the phone and told me he'd be there," he said simply. He took a deep breath, as if preparing to swim a long distance underwater. "It was a Sunday morning. He said that he wanted to meet me in his metallurgical lab. I had a plane bring me from Washington, and I went to the building at the appointed time."

"Alone?" I asked.

"Yes, alone. He insisted on that, and I didn't want to risk losing him again."

"Didn't you think that was rather dangerous?"

"Despite what had happened, I did not consider Rafferty a dangerous man," Lippitt said quietly. "I believed that the killing of the guard was an accident; there was nothing in Rafferty's past to indicate that he could suddenly become a killer. Now I can see that I was right: He never intended to kill me."

"He was backed into a corner," Tal said softly.

"True, but I still don't think he ever intended to kill me. He had a plan, but killing me wasn't a part of it."

"But you were prepared to kill *him*," I said.

"Yes," he said. "If I had to. Those were my orders, and I agreed with them. There would have been no need to kill

217

him if he could have been persuaded to come with us. We'd have given him an entirely new identity. He would have undergone plastic surgery, voice training; even his mannerisms could have been altered. When we were finished, no one"—he nodded in Mrs. Foster's direction—"including his wife, would have recognized him. Then we would have made arrangements for his wife to join him."

"After undergoing the same . . . 'adjustments'?"

"Yes. Naturally."

"Christ, Lippitt," I said, feeling a chill, "you live in an ugly world."

The agent's eyes glinted for a brief moment. "Don't you dare patronize me, Frederickson. I know of too many brave men who have lost their lives; our 'ugly' world exists so that you may continue to live in your rather comfortable, relatively free world." He paused, raised his eyebrows inquiringly. When I didn't say anything, the fire in his eyes cooled and he went on. "In any case, I went to the building and found the door open. Rafferty was waiting for me with a gun, and he got the drop on me as I was going in. He told me he'd finally made up his mind what he was going to do: He was defecting to the Russians."

Elizabeth Foster made a strangled noise. Her husband started to rise, but Lippitt ignored him. Foster clenched and unclenched his fists, then abruptly sat down again. Foster knew—we both knew—that what Lippitt was saying had a ring of truth to it, and fists were no defense against it. He'd found out what he wanted to know, and now he and his wife were going to have to live with the knowledge.

"Actually," Lippitt continued, "Rafferty's reasoning was quite sound, and I respected him for it; it was a practical, rather than an ideological, decision. No state could better guarantee his safety and his wife's than one which was authoritarian. Since he could not be free anyway, he would ally himself with the system that could afford him the best protection."

218

"Victor never said anything about defecting!" Mrs. Foster cried. "He just wanted to be *left alone!*"

Lippitt smiled thinly and continued. "He indicated to me that his decision was irreversible. He then forced me to go with him up on a catwalk above the foundry floor. He said that he intended to shoot me, then drop my body into one of the furnaces."

"*No!*" Elizabeth Foster cried, springing to her feet. "Victor would never say anything like that! You're lying!"

Mike Foster gently but firmly gripped his wife's arm and pulled her back down onto the sofa beside him. She broke, burying her face in her husband's shoulder and sobbing. "Let him tell his story," Foster said to his wife. "That doesn't mean we have to believe him."

"I knew that I'd have to kill him," Lippitt resumed in a low monotone. "I tried to reason with him right up to the last moment. Then, I simply . . . beat him. We both fired at the same time; I was lucky. He was hit and . . . he fell over the railing into the furnace."

The agent suddenly paused and licked his lips. Lippitt now seemed unusually agitated, and I didn't think it was for the obvious reason that he was admitting to Mrs. Foster that he'd killed her first husband. Something else was bothering him.

"I thought that was the end of the . . . problem," Lippitt continued with a catch in his voice. "I then took certain steps; I reported Rafferty's death through the same channels Dr. Llewellyn had used. I knew the report would be monitored, and I assumed the pressure would ease off. Mrs. Foster, at least, would be safe. It worked." He quickly glanced in my direction. "Then you began asking questions, Dr. Frederickson, and it started all over again." He walked back to the window, as if trying to cleanse the dark business of the past in the wash of bright sunlight. "I *shot* him," he continued in a clipped voice. "I *saw* him clutch at his stomach and fall over the railing into the furnace. . . . But

219

now I understand that it didn't happen. It was an *illusion*. One more trick. My God, he made me see what he *wanted* me to see."

"C'mon, Lippitt," Mike Foster said, scorn and incredulity in his voice. "You're trying to tell us that you saw Victor fall into the furnace, but he didn't actually fall?"

"That's *exactly* what I'm saying. It's the only explanation. And it means that his powers are far greater than even I knew." He paused, turned, and looked at each of us. He must have seen more than a little skepticism; he grew very pale. "You still don't believe me. He *did* have the power to enter men's minds. You know that, because Mrs. Foster has confirmed it. But there were *other* things he could do, things I haven't told you about. Perhaps if you knew—"

"He did something else to you, didn't he?" I said, certain I was right. "Why don't you tell us about that?"

Lippitt abruptly folded his arms across his chest and turned his back to us once again. His voice became stronger, matter-of-fact. "I was captured during the Korean war and tortured with ice baths."

Lippitt shuddered, as I had seen him do once before. He quickly clenched the muscles in his body, and that brought the shaking under control; it had been a spasm, no more, but it had chilled everyone in the room. I remembered the pictures of Lippitt in his overcoat in summer, and I felt cold myself.

"I'm sorry to say they extracted the information they wanted in a very short time," he continued. "I managed to survive, but the ice baths had affected my mind. It seemed to me that I could never be warm. I constantly wore a coat, because I was cold all the time. There was nothing I could do, nothing any doctor could do. I didn't want to retire, and I was of sufficient value to get my way on that . . . but I suffered." He looked over his shoulder at Elizabeth Foster. She glanced up at him, and their eyes held. "We talked for some time," he said, slowly turning, his gaze still locked with the woman's. "Actually, Rafferty did most of the talking. He spoke of the way *he* thought his powers should be used, in the manner Mrs. Foster has already mentioned. Then he gave *me* a demonstration."

"He cured you, didn't he?" I said slowly.

Lippitt nodded, swallowed hard. "He knew *everything*. He talked about it so casually; every thought in my mind. He knew all of it, despite the nail."

"What nail?" I said, looking up.

Lippitt held up the palm of his left hand to reveal a jagged scar running from the mount of Venus to the base of the little finger. "I'd been gripping a sharpened nail treated with acid. I didn't want Rafferty to know what I was thinking—or that *I* had a gun. I thought I could mask my thoughts with pain. I assumed it had worked; for five years I've been congratulating myself on how clever I'd been. Now, of course, I see that it didn't work at all. Rafferty had known about the gun all the time, right up to the moment when I made the decision to draw and shoot." He passed a hand across his eyes; then he continued in a softer, yet still anguished voice. "But while we talked he was working on me; he told me how my suffering was psychosomatic. Then he went into my mind, and there was nothing I could do to stop him. I could *feel* his mind in mine, probing, comforting, making me understand . . . making me well again. He convinced me in less than a minute that there was nothing wrong with my body. Suddenly . . . I wasn't cold anymore."

"And then you killed him," Elizabeth Foster whispered. "That was your way of thanking him."

"He made me *think* that I'd killed him, Mrs. Foster. He created and forced the situation, and now I understand why. I heard him pull the hammer back while I was standing at the edge of the catwalk. I did the only thing I could do, and that was what Rafferty *wanted* me to do. I spun around, drew, and fired at him."

It was clear to me now why Lippitt had been willing to risk his life, along with a good number of government secrets, to get Elizabeth Foster and her husband out of the Russian consulate. He'd felt he owed Victor Rafferty at least that; he'd been motivated by guilt. I suddenly felt a great deal of compassion for Lippitt. He was a patriot, and in the cause of patriotism he'd traded one form of mental torture for another.

But it was Rafferty who'd made the supreme sacrifice, I thought. Ironically, in the cause of freedom; his wife's, and his own. He'd given up everything: his wife, his work, his life as he'd known it. Now that sacrifice had been wiped out. Rafferty had betrayed himself with a doodle on a scrap of paper.

"So Rafferty set you up," I said to Lippitt. My voice seemed unnaturally loud in the sudden quiet. "He made you think you'd killed him. That was an alternative you hadn't considered."

"Then Rafferty is not working for the Americans," Tal said, placing the pencil he had been rolling back in his pocket. "Or the Russians. Assuming that Mr. Lippitt is at last telling the truth . . . where *is* Rafferty, and what has he been doing for the past five years?"

"We know he was at the U.N., at least at the time of the housing seminar," I said. "The drawing proves that."

"It begins again," Lippitt said bitterly.

"The hunt?" Something in my voice—probably disgust—caused Lippitt to look at me sharply. There was a brief glint of pain in his eyes, and then it was gone.

"I have no choice, Frederickson," Lippitt said quietly. "It *is* a hunt. The others will be after him, and you should hope that I find him before they do."

As far as I was concerned, he had a point. I knew where *Lippitt* was, because I was with him. But there were still the Russians, the British, the French with their mysterious agent, and God only knew how many others, all beating the bushes for Rafferty. I had no way of knowing how close *they* were.

"Let him alone!" Mike Foster said, emotion twisting his voice and features. "For God's sake, haven't you done enough to the man? He's shown that he means no harm to anyone!"

"Has he?" Lippitt said. "He's proved nothing of the kind, and I'm not waiting for a nuclear attack to find out whether our defense network has been penetrated; neither will any other country that knows about him."

"What about Mr. and Mrs. Foster?" I asked. "You plan to lock them away someplace?"

Lippitt looked at Mrs. Foster. "They should come with me for their own protection."

Elizabeth Foster shook her head and moved even closer to her husband. "Go to hell, Lippitt," Mike Foster said evenly.

"The Fosters will be taken care of," Tal said. "And you too, Mongo. There are a lot of people, I'm sure, who will want to ask you questions."

"Thanks, Tal. I'll look after myself."

Mike Foster gently pulled his wife to her feet and supported her as they moved into an adjoining bedroom; he closed the door quietly behind them.

There was a sharp, prolonged buzzing sound from Lippitt's direction. The agent took a small beeper out of his pocket and shut it off. He looked vaguely surprised. "I have to go," he said.

"If it's a telephone you need, you're welcome to use the one here," Tal said.

Lippitt ignored the offer, jerked his head in the direction of the Fosters' bedroom. "You've taken on a big responsibility, Tal."

Tal met the other man's cold gaze. "Then perhaps you should keep silent. If you do, there's no reason why anyone outside this room should know where the Fosters are."

"I have other responsibilities."

"Then you'll just have to weigh them against the safety of the Fosters, won't you? Mrs. Foster has told you all she knows; the Americans have no more need of her. Unless *you* risk a leak, no one else will have access to her. Think about that when you report to your superiors."

Lippitt walked to the elevator. He paused at the door as if he wanted to add something, but said nothing. In a few moments he was gone. I wondered what his message could be, where he was going.

Tal put his hand on my shoulder. "You should accept my offer, Mongo. I don't think Lippitt will kill you, but he might not be able to stop one of his colleagues from doing so if the order came down. They will want to make sure you don't share the information you have."

"Sorry. I don't feel like being a prisoner any more than Rafferty did. I'll take my chances on the street."

"I understand."

"It's over, I suppose." There was a flat, metallic taste in my mouth. "You found out what you wanted to know."

Tal looked surprised. "You want to quit now?"

"Rafferty's alive, and everybody and his brother is looking for him. Even if he has been working your turf, he's finished there now. He's blown and he knows it; he's going to be on the run. What's the point of our continuing to look for him?"

"Because we have something the others don't," Tal said firmly. "We have the list of people who participated in that seminar, and that gives us an edge."

"That doesn't answer my question. *Why* should we look for him now?"

He smiled. "Aren't you curious?"

"Rafferty's got enough people looking for him."

"Yes," Tal said seriously. "But you and I are the only ones who might want to help him."

21

Dawn was an hour old, growing into a mean, humid, overcast day. Somewhere out in that gathering light was a man many considered the most powerful and dangerous man who had ever lived, a man from whom no one could keep a secret, a man who could move objects with his mind. A man who could kill with a thought. It was the same man who had rescued me from the farmhouse; I was sure of that now.

I pointed to the papers on Tal's desk. "You want to check out every one of those people who attended the conference?"

"If necessary," Tal said, leaning forward and drumming his fingers on the desk top. "Imagine what a man with Rafferty's capabilities could do for us."

"By 'us,' I assume you mean the Secretary General and yourself?"

"Yes. He'd be able to provide us with vital information. He'd know that we'd use his skills properly."

"It looks as if he already has a job. Maybe he doesn't want to change, or can't."

Suddenly there was a knock on the door behind us. I jumped; I'd thought the door led to a closet. Tal spun around in his chair, a look of astonishment on his face.

"Are you expecting someone?"

Tal shook his head. "Even if I were, he wouldn't be coming through there. That's a second private elevator with a combination warning system–lock on the door leading to it. The only person besides me who knows the entry code is the Secretary General, and he's in the hospital."

There was another knock. I felt the hair prickle on the back of my neck. "Well, aren't you going to see who it is?"

Tal rose from his chair, walked quickly across the room, and yanked the door open. I immediately recognized the man who stood in the elevator portal: It was Yuri Malakov, the Soviet Ambassador to the United Nations. He was trying to look dignified and not succeeding; his rotund face was flushed with excitement, and even beneath his beard I could see the muscles in his jaw working.

"What the hell—?" Tal said.

Malakov drew himself up. "I am here at the request of Victor Rafferty," he announced formally, in good English. "I received a telephone call a half hour ago asking me to come here, by this route. Rafferty said it would prove to you that he is who he says he is."

Tal dazedly stepped back, and the Ambassador entered the suite.

"It means he's been close to me all this time," Tal said distantly. "*Who?*"

Tal's desk intercom buzzed. He pressed the flashing button with some annoyance and spoke sharply into the speaker. "Marge, I thought I told you I wasn't to be disturbed!"

A woman's voice with a Midwestern accent came over the line. "I know, sir; I'm sorry. It's a Mr. Elliot Thomas. He insists on talking to you. He says it's very important. He's . . . calling on the green line."

My chest constricted, making it hard for me to breathe. My heart was pounding as I leaned forward and gripped the edge of Tal's desk.

Tal's brow furrowed. "Elliot Thomas? Who's he, and how did he get the green-line number?"

"I don't know, sir," the woman answered. "He will only say that it's very urgent and concerns a man by the name of Victor Rafferty."

"All right, Marge," Tal said tightly. "Put him through." There was a click. Tal picked up the telephone. "Yes, Mr. Thomas?" he said, excitement making his voice sound thin. "What do you know about Victor Rafferty?"

I couldn't distinguish what the voice at the other end of the line was saying, but Tal listened for a few moments, then gasped in astonishment. He grabbed a pencil and held it poised over a pad.

"*How*, Mr. Thomas? Give me some kind of proof!"

There was more unintelligible mumbling on the other end. Tal scribbled something on the pad, then shoved it across the desk to me. I looked at the paper and felt my mouth go dry despite the fact that I was certain what Tal had written.

There was one word: *Rafferty!*

There was a pause. Then Tal said: "All right, Thomas. The Ambassador's here, but the Secretary General is ill and in the hospital. Will you deal with me? ... Okay. Hang on where you are. Just don't turn yourself in to Lippitt; if you do, no one will ever see you again.... We'll be there as soon as possible."

Tal gently replaced the receiver in its cradle, then clenched and unclenched his fists. He was staring straight ahead.

"That was Rafferty?" My voice cracked. I attempted to swallow, but there was no moisture left in my mouth.

"He's been right here at the U.N. all along," Tal said in a tone of disbelief.

"I know."

Tal raised his eyebrows. "*You* know? *How* do you know?"

I looked back at Malakov, who was standing a few feet

227

away. He looked overcome by it all; his eyes were wide, and he was holding one pudgy hand to his mouth as if he had a toothache. "Thomas' name is on the list of delegates to the seminar. I talked to him before I came to see you. He's an engineer working for UNESCO."

"It's perfect," Tal said distantly. "Or it was. An engineer; with his knowledge of buildings and how they function, he had no difficulty getting the job. First he fooled Lippitt into thinking he was dead; that got him and his wife off the hook. Then he went someplace for plastic surgery, probably Rio de Janeiro. Finally, there would be the problem of a new identity, but money would take care of that."

"But where'd he *get* the money? Lippitt said he had no funds."

Tal thought for a few moments. "I think I can guess. Gambling: horse races, card games, the stock market—you name it. He'd have every advantage, because he was constantly picking the brains of the experts and his opponents. He got together the money he needed for the traveling, surgery, and a whole new set of identity papers. Then he came back here and got a job at the U.N. It was a good, hardheaded decision. He didn't want to always be looking over his shoulder. If a question ever arose about his supposed death, this would be the best place to pick up on it."

"It worked," I said, "until he left a drawing where he shouldn't have."

The Ambassador stepped up behind us. "Wh . . . where is Rafferty now?" he asked breathlessly.

"In an abandoned boathouse in the Rockaways," Tal said softly.

"What's *happening*?" Malakov demanded. "Tell me what is happening!"

"He's found a way to end it," Tal said thoughtfully. "I suppose you could call it the Goldfish Bowl Solution."

"What are you talking about?" Malakov snarled. "And where is the Secretary General?"

228

"The Secretary General is indisposed, Mr. Ambassador. The important thing is that Rafferty is tired of hiding; he knows it can't work anymore, and he wants to come in. He's made arrangements for all of us, Mr. Ambassador—you for the Russians, Lippitt for the Americans, and me—to be together when he turns himself in to me, representing the Secretary General. He's also notified the media, so there'll be plenty of coverage. No more secrets, Mr. Ambassador; it's all going to come out. He intends to place himself under the protection of this office; he'll remain at the U.N. for all to see. The whole world will know about him, so there'll no longer be any reason to kill him. He's willing to use his talents in any country's behalf, provided it's for a peaceful purpose. The Secretary General will screen all requests."

"God," I said. "He'll be like an animal in the zoo."

Tal grunted. "But no longer an endangered species."

Malakov looked grieved. I imagined Lippitt had looked the same way when he'd received the news. "Lippitt must already know," I said. "That was his message. He has a head start on us."

"You're right," Tal said curtly. "We'll have to hurry."

"Just one second," I said, grabbing the telephone. "Can you get me an open line?"

Tal punched a button and I heard a dial tone. I dialed Garth's precinct. Garth was out. I did a lot of screaming about a death in the family and they patched me through to his car.

"Mongo!" he shouted over the line. "What the hell—? *Where* the hell are you? I've been looking all over the goddamn city! Man, have I got some questions for *you!*"

"I'll meet you at"—I looked at the address Tal had written on the pad—"1386 Rockaway Boulevard."

"What's on Rockaway Boulevard?"

"Answers."

"Don't be cryptic! I can't just drive out to the Rockaways!"

"You will if you want to be in on the wrap-up of the Rafferty thing. Make a lot of noise on the way, and bring along as much blue as you can!"

"We go now," Tal said, heading for the elevator as I hung up.

22

The tires of Tal's car squealed as we gathered speed in the underground garage. He was doing close to thirty by the time we hit the street. As we sped down Second Avenue, I hung on and listened to the sirens in the distance ahead of us. Garth was on his way, with company.

"I think this could be a trick," Malakov said. The Ambassador's face was ashen, and he was hanging on to a leather passenger loop with both hands. "The American agent will get there before we do."

The Ambassador had a point. Lippitt had a good half-hour start, and there was no way Tal could drive fast enough to make up the difference. It bothered me. "Lippitt's not going to like our showing up," I said to Tal. "We could both end up in the slammer for the next two hundred years."

"Well, we'll just have to worry about that when the time comes," Tal said. He came up on a lumbering soda truck and veered effortlessly around it while I fought off the impulse to grab the wheel. Malakov gasped. "The important thing is that Rafferty's proposal is reasonable," Tal continued easily. "He'll be highly visible at all times. Whatever he wants to do, he'll be *seen* doing it, and that's the all-important thing. If anyone wishes to talk with him, fine; people with secrets will know enough to stay away."

"There'll be emotional problems for the Fosters," I said.

"They'll be all right. Certainly, Rafferty will make no demands on her." After a pause he added, "He may have loved her much more than Mrs. Foster realizes."

"Uh-huh. And he was legally dead as far as the law is concerned when the Fosters were married."

In twenty minutes we reached Rockaway Boulevard. Tal turned left and we sped down the broad highway. I thought I could hear the deadly rattle of automatic-weapons fire ahead. Tal heard it too, jammed the accelerator to the floor, cursed softly and systematically. The Ambassador leaned forward anxiously. We were speeding along a section of the highway bounded by rocky cliffs on one side and, on the other, dirty, rock-strewn stretches of muddied sand sloping down to the sea. The air smelled of rotting fish.

Tal went into a power slide, straightened out, and fish-tailed fifty yards down the rutted remains of a road leading toward a collection of police cars and men. He stopped behind a patrol car with a siren that was just dying. We quickly got out and made our way around a television camera crew that was just setting up. A police cordon had been erected a few yards farther down the road. Garth was standing off to one side, staring intently down a hundred-yard stretch of sand to where three rotting boathouses jutted out over the water. I ran up to him and grabbed his arm.

"Garth!"

Garth turned and grinned when he saw me. He poked and prodded for a few seconds, presumably to see if I was all in one piece. When he was satisfied that I was, his grin faded.

"What the hell's going on here, Mongo? I've got my neck stuck out a mile."

"It's for a good cause. Garth, this is Ronald Tal and Ambassador Malakov. Gentlemen, my brother."

Garth nodded to the Ambassador and gave Tal a long,

cold stare. "I talked to you on the phone," he said, perfunctorily shaking Tal's hand before turning back to me. "You didn't tell me the Feds would be here."

"Which boathouse is Rafferty in?"

"That's *Rafferty* in there with the machine gun?"

"It is. Where is he?"

"The one on the left," he said, jerking his thumb in that direction.

"Garth," I said, "Tal and I have to get down there."

"I will go too," the Ambassador said anxiously. "I go where you go."

"You'll get your heads blown off," Garth said. "It's quiet now. You should have been here five minutes ago."

"He won't shoot when he sees who it is," Tal said.

Garth snorted. "That's what *you* say."

It was suddenly very still. Somewhere in the distance the raucous whine of a powerboat carried clearly over the water; there was something disquieting, ominous about the sound.

"Garth," I said, "at least get us to Lippitt."

Garth took me by the elbow, led me around the barricade, and pointed twenty yards farther down the beach to where Lippitt and two other men were squatting down behind another barricade made up of the old, rotting husks of rowboats. All three had automatic pistols.

Lippitt!" I yelled. "Let us come down!"

Lippitt's bald head snapped around; the pale eyes found and focused on me. He hesitated a moment, then signaled to Garth, who was still holding me. His hand left my arm. Tal, Malakov, and I hurried across the sand. The two agents with Lippitt gave us a cursory glance as we dropped down behind the rowboats, then turned their attention—and their guns—back to the boathouse.

"What the hell are you trying to do?" I said, grabbing Lippitt's arm. "Didn't Rafferty explain his plan?"

"He didn't explain anything. *He* was the one who started

shooting." He paused. "What's Malakov doing here?"

"Rafferty wants to negotiate," I said. "Malakov got a call too."

"Negotiate *what*, for Christ's sake? He's five years too late! Besides, we've tried to talk to him. He won't answer, and he won't let any of us come down. He may have gone crazy."

"He's *not* crazy! He's been buying time until we could get here. He called Tal, and I've spoken to him before. Maybe he'll talk to one of us now."

Lippitt rested one knee on the sand and looked at me. "When did you talk to him?"

"A few days ago, but I didn't know he was Victor Rafferty. He's been using the name Elliot Thomas. He's been working as an engineer at the U.N. The sketch of the Nately Museum was his. The paper must have dropped out of his pocket, or he just forgot and left it on the table. He's ready to give himself up . . . under the auspices of the U.N."

Speaking in a low monotone, Tal outlined Rafferty's plan to Lippitt. Lippitt's face was totally impassive as he listened. The sound of the powerboat was much louder now, coming closer. Far out in the water I could see sunlight glinting off its metal hull.

Tal finished as Lippitt absently began drawing figures in the sand with his finger.

"What do you think?" I said to the agent.

"I don't know," Lippitt said without looking up. "You're suggesting that the United States give up—"

"You can't have him, Lippitt," Tal broke in impatiently. "Your only alternative is to kill him, and I don't think you want to do that. He won't let anyone use him; he gave up everything to make that point, and he's not going to change his mind now. What he suggests is the only way."

"I can't authorize something like that on my own, Tal," Lippitt said quietly.

"I know. But what do you *think* of the idea?"

Lippitt erased the drawings in the sand, glanced up, and said in the same soft tone: "It could work. What's your reaction, Malakov?"

The portly Russian slowly nodded his head. "I too must have authorization, but what Rafferty suggests does . . . seem to be a viable alternative."

I hadn't realized I'd been holding my breath until it came out of me in a long sigh. My stomach hurt.

Tal stood up. "I'm going down there. I'll tell him what the two of you just said, and I'll see what he has to say. In the meantime, you can contact your superiors."

Lippitt shook his head. "It's going to take a lot longer than a few minutes to make this kind of decision."

"How *much* longer?"

"At least a couple of days. I'll go to Washington myself."

"Let him come with me in the meantime," Tal said quickly. "The important thing is to get him out of that boathouse, right?"

"What if our government says it's no deal?" I asked Lippitt.

"I don't know," Lippitt said evenly. "No promises."

"Do not take us for fools," Malakov said tightly. "One of my men must accompany Rafferty at all times until a decision is made."

"Whatever you say, Mr. Ambassador," Lippitt said coldly. "One of my men will be along too."

"Let's see what Rafferty has to say," Tal said as he stepped out from behind the rowboats, in full view of the boathouse. He cupped his hands to his mouth and yelled: "Rafferty! It's Tal! Don't shoot! I'm coming down!"

There was no answer, no sound at all from the direction of the water except the steadily increasing roar of the speedboat. The craft was close now, no more than three or four hundred yards offshore, and it was making me nervous.

Malakov grabbed Lippitt's elbow. "How do you know he's still in there? He may have slipped away from you again!"

"He's surrounded," Lippitt said, jerking his arm free. "I've got men with rifles on the roofs of the other boathouses; there's no way Rafferty can get out of there without being shot. Rafferty may be a lot of things, but he's not invisible."

"Okay," Tal said softly, "I'm going down."

"Hold it!" I yelled as I stood and pointed toward the water. "What's that boat out there doing?!"

Lippitt tore the binoculars from the neck of the agent squatting next to him and raised them to his eyes. I watched the muscles in his jaw and neck begin to quiver. He threw the binoculars to one side, then turned to the crowd of police and agents behind him. "Shoot that boat out of the water!" he yelled. "Goddamn it, *blow it away!*"

Immediately the air was filled with the din of automatic-weapons fire. Two agents sprinted out onto the sand and began firing down at the water, their guns braced against their hips.

"There's no one in the boat!" Lippitt shouted. I could barely hear him above the clatter of the weapons. "It's a drone, radio-controlled! Somebody wants to blow Rafferty up!"

The pilotless boat zigzagged as the rain of bullets fell into the water around it; there were dozens of hits, but the boat kept coming. It wasn't going to stop until it hit the boat-house.

"He's got to see it coming," Tal said through clenched teeth. "Why doesn't he get out of there?" He again cupped his hands to his mouth and yelled. "Thomas! Rafferty! Get out of there! *Run!*"

A bearded figure immediately recognizable as Elliot Thomas suddenly appeared in the doorway of the crumbling boathouse. He was carrying an automatic assault rifle. He seemed to be groggy as he staggered out onto the sand, fell

236

back against the side of the house, and began firing up the beach in our direction. Bullets whined in the air, chewed up the sand, thwacked into the wooden barricades.

Lippitt yelled, "Hold your fire!"

I caught a flash of movement out of the corner of my eye. It was Garth sprinting toward the boathouse, his arms pumping. Tal's reflexes were faster than mine. He tackled Garth at the knees and both men went down. Garth took a swing at Tal's head, missed, then tried to struggle to his feet again as Tal hung on to his legs. I tried not to think of the bullets singing around my head as I ran forward, jumped on Garth's back, wrapped my arms around his neck.

"You can't just let that man die down there without making an effort to get him out!" Garth shouted, clawing at my arms.

"It's too late," Tal said quietly.

The boat hit the rotting wood structure and exploded. It was something a lot more powerful than dynamite, probably *plastique*. The force of the blast shook the ground around us. The entire boathouse quivered for a moment, lifted off the ground, then disintegrated into bits and pieces of wood and metal. Instantly flames shot up into the temporary vacuum, burning with the white-hot glow of phosphorus or napalm.

Someone had wanted to make certain the job was done right.

23

There was numb, shocked silence in the aftermath of the explosion. The silence, broken only by the fierce crackle of the flames, lasted almost thirty seconds and seemed an eternity. Then Lippitt suddenly sprang forward and punched Malakov in the mouth. The stunned ambassador sat down hard on the sand and put a trembling hand to his bleeding mouth.

"You fucker!" Lippitt growled. "You killed him! I should blow *you* away!"

Malakov struggled to his feet and spat blood. His face was purple. "*We* didn't kill him!" he shouted, ignoring the gun aimed at his heart. His voice trembled with outrage. "It was *your* people who must have done this thing! *You're* a fucker!"

They glared at each other across a distance of less than a yard. Then the tension was suddenly broken when two men with rifles came running up the beach from the direction of the remaining boathouses. One man's arm hung limp, and the other appeared to have singed hair. Otherwise they seemed to be all right.

"Excuse me," Tal said weakly. "I think I'm going to be sick." He walked shakily down the beach toward the undamaged boathouse on the right. He was holding his left arm tightly against his side; his shirt on that side was stained with blood, and the dark patch was spreading. No one else seemed to notice.

Garth nudged me. "All right, brother, let's hear it from the top."

"Huh?" I wasn't really listening. The apparent chaos suddenly did not seem so confused, not in light of some of the things that had begun to bother me. Had Lippitt ordered the killing? It seemed highly unlikely, considering Lippitt's ambiguous feelings toward Rafferty, and Malakov just hadn't had time, even if he'd had the inclination. Then who *had* arranged the explosion?

Rafferty.

He'd staged an apparently fatal end for himself, just as he'd done five years before. But this time he'd arranged for the entire world to look on.

"I want to hear the whole story, Mongo," Garth was saying. "I want to know what happened here."

"Over steaks and drinks, Garth. Just give me a few minutes."

Tal had disappeared from sight into the boathouse on the right. I went after him.

The boathouse was dark and smelled of still, dead air. Tal was standing at the opposite end, silhouetted by the late-morning light streaming in a window. He was smoking a cigarette—the first time I'd ever seen him do so. The smoke curled up around his head like a halo, or a mist from hell.

"I'll be damned," I said, the dank air muffling my voice. "Here I've been following you around all this time and I haven't found a single hamburger wrapper. You certainly did go through some changes, didn't you?"

I instinctively held up my hand and shied away as I felt an almost imperceptible tingling in my head. It was a sensation I'd experienced before and hadn't been able to put my finger on. This time I'd been looking for it.

"I assume you can control what you do," I said. "I'd appreciate it if you'd respect my privacy."

The tingling stopped. Tal was still silhouetted against the window, and I couldn't see his face. I wondered what he was thinking.

"How did you manage the fingerprints on the pencil? That was good. It threw me off the track right at the beginning."

Tal said nothing. He continued to smoke.

"You know that I know."

"*What* do you know, Mongo?"

"I know that you're Victor Rafferty. That was the French agent who died in the boathouse. Elliot Thomas was the 'Frenchie'—an American working deep undercover for France." I pointed to his side. "You're bleeding, but there aren't any bullet holes in your shirt. You've been favoring that side since yesterday; you ripped open an already existing wound when you tackled Garth. My guess is that Thomas—or whatever his name really was—finally caught up with you. After all, he'd been at it a long time, and he'd *really* been digging ever since the Nately Museum went up. He knew, just as your ex-wife knew, that Victor Rafferty had designed that building. Somehow, you got on Thomas' list of candidates; when he got around to checking your background, your cover didn't hold."

Tal remained silent.

"God only knows how Thomas did it," I continued, "but he must have gotten the drop on you. Unlucky for him: Thomas didn't make out any better than Lippitt did five years ago. You've been keeping Thomas on ice for the past few days; Rolfe Thaag's been baby-sitting him while you put this plan into operation. You knew what was in my mind, so you had every reason to think I'd buy it. I can't point to any one thing that convinced me; it's the sum of a lot of *little* things. Considering the fact that you've been winging it for the past few days, you've done damn well. But then, you read minds, don't you?"

"I don't know what you're talking about, Mongo," Tal said quietly.

"Now you're just playing out the string, hoping I'll back off. I won't. Putting Thomas in that boathouse down there was pretty murderous for Victor Rafferty, but you certainly had cause. He's been trying to kill or capture you for years. That would try my patience too."

Tal still hadn't moved, and I stayed where I was, firing long-range verbal artillery. I hated to admit it, but I was afraid to go closer. I liked Ronald Tal, but I didn't know this stranger at the other end of the boathouse.

"When did you arrive at these conclusions, Mongo?"

"Don't you know? Why don't you look in my head and find out?" I waited, but Tal said nothing and there was no tingling sensation. "It suddenly occurred to me on the beach that I was being had. Call it *déjà vu* once removed. Why the hell should Victor Rafferty have come out of that boathouse like it was *High Noon*? It didn't make sense. Thomas was dazed; the man didn't even know where he was. He was like a man who'd just recovered consciousness—or who'd had a few mental circuits burned out. He died trying to carry out his duty, which was to kill *you*. *That's* why he fired up the beach."

"I understand that you think I'm Victor Rafferty," Tal said calmly, "but you're wrong."

"No, I'm not. 'In the world of diplomacy, information is the most valuable commodity.' Remember when you told me that?"

"I remember. What does it prove?"

"Nothing. I just want you to know that *I* know the truth. You see, that's precisely what you've been doing all this time: providing Rolfe Thaag with that valuable commodity. All his diplomatic success springs from you."

"What about the fingerprints on the pencil?"

"All right, that is troublesome. Let's speculate. You had

241

advance warning of who I was and what I wanted when Abu called. You immediately probed my mind when I walked into your office and found out everything there was to know; up to that point, anyway. You started setting me up from that very moment. You put a contingency plan into motion. My guess is that the pencil was Rolfe Thaag's. You'd probably covered the tips of your fingers with cellophane tape. Even dried glue would do the trick. Then you set the pencil down right in front of me; you knew I'd take it, just as I'd taken the protractor from Elliot Thomas' office. You knew I was suspicious of you, and you decided to knock me out of the box right at the beginning."

I tried to see Tal's face, but he was still framed against the circle of muddy light. He didn't move. "You have fantastic control over your emotions," I continued. "I suppose that's just one more thing you had to learn in order to survive. I'm sure you knew that Richard Patern had used your design for the Nately Museum, but you probably didn't suspect that you were in danger of being discovered until I walked into your office. And you never blinked an eye. But you knew what could happen, and you started keeping a close watch on things. You were too late to save Abu, but you were probably trying to find a way when he was killed."

Tal dropped his cigarette to the floor and ground it out under his heel. Then he walked forward and stopped in front of me. His face was impassive, but his black eyes shone brightly in the dim light. He was still holding his side, but the bleeding had stopped. "Rafferty and I don't look anything alike," he said. "Wasn't he quite thin? I must be at least thirty pounds heavier, and I don't think you'll find that much fat on me."

"Anabolic steroids could do that; the drugs, combined with a heavy conditioning program, would build you up. You not only managed to change your physical appearance, you radically altered your whole behavior pattern; you must be some natural actor. Then there would be plastic surgery, hair transplants, and voice training. The works, and all within the space of a year or so. That's cutting it close, but it could be done. It *was* done. I'm betting you looked different—pretty shaky—when you first showed up at the U.N. That—finally—may have been what tipped Thomas off once he thought about it and started making inquiries. I'm going to do some heavy checking on that myself."

Tal lighted another cigarette. His face hadn't changed, but his hand shook slightly. He saw that I noticed, quickly ground the cigarette out, and put his hands in his pockets. The masquerade was over, and Ronald Tal–Victor Rafferty knew it. I wondered why I didn't feel better about the whole thing.

"You could stay on top of what was happening simply by being around the right people—like me—at the right time. You were hoping against hope that I and the others would conclude that you *had* died, but you needed me in order to keep in touch with people you wouldn't ordinarily come into contact with."

I paused and was once again aware of the tingling in my mind. It was slight, but it was there. Tal's eyes had narrowed.

"You got worried when you found out I wanted to bail out of the case," I continued. "You already knew at that time that the Russians had Foster and your ex-wife, and you had to stay plugged into the situation until you could figure out what to do. I was your plug.

"But first you had to change my mind; you had to make me *feel* better; you had to make me see things the way you wanted me to see them. You eased my guilt with that incredible mind of yours. There's a distinct sensation when you touch someone's mind; I first felt it when we were together in the chapel. Of course, I didn't know what was happening at the time, but then I felt it again in the hospital, and still again at the farmhouse. I went into that chapel ready to slit my wrists, and walked out feeling pretty good.

When I stopped to think about it, I knew it wasn't natural. In fact, it was getting to the point—then and later—where I perked up every time you were around. You juiced up my psyche once too often, and I started to put it together after I heard Lippitt describe what you'd done for him.

"You *were* the one who saved me at the farmhouse. I *knew* I heard a door open; it was you. I think I know what you did, but I can't understand how you found out I was there."

Tal shrugged. "Let me speculate along your lines. Rafferty *was* keeping a very close watch on things . . . and who would be better qualified than a total telepath? He knew about the two British agents on your tail, and he knew the Russians had brought in Kaznakov. He became very much concerned and made it a point to make excuses to see—or at least be physically close to—informed British and Russian officials every day. Of course, there had to be a bit of good fortune involved; he may have talked with an Englishman who was nervous because a check-in call from the two agents he controlled was long overdue. Then, naturally, Rafferty would have probed to find out where the British agents were supposed to be." He smiled thinly. "Pure speculation, of course."

Tal seemed calmer now, and I was certain I knew why. He'd made a decision: Tal, in his own way, was telling me I was right. He really had no choice; whether he admitted it or not, what I'd already said was probably enough to get us both killed if I repeated it anywhere else.

"Go ahead," Tal said. "Let's hear the rest of it."

"Again: why don't you just read my mind?"

Tal took some time to think about his answer. "Perhaps it's physically painful, Mongo. Maybe it's a very personal thing that involves simply not wanting to invade someone else's privacy. Or, maybe I'm simply not Victor Rafferty."

"You are Victor Rafferty."

"Why *insist* on being so sure, Mongo? Right or wrong,

you'll pay a terrible price; that kind of certainty could make you responsible for the lives of Victor Rafferty and others for as long as you live. Don't pick up that burden. Rafferty died in that explosion down on the beach. Leave it at that."

"Why not just kill me?"

"You mean if I was who you say I am? Because Victor Rafferty is not a killer." He paused, added: "Except, I assume, when he has no other choice."

I cleared my throat, tried to swallow. My mouth was still dry. "I was in bad shape after Kaznakov played his tune on me. I was finished. I might never have come back. But you took care of that, too... in the apartment, while I slept. I know enough about psychiatry to realize that a mental condition like the one I had couldn't possibly cure itself overnight. Thaag probably put something in the tea to make me sleep. Then you came back and went to work on my head, just the same as you did when you entered Lippitt's mind to cure him of that permanent chill. You fixed me up because you needed me for the break-in at the consulate.

"Incidentally, you probably stole that plan from Lippitt. You were going in anyway because you knew about the ultimatum. That's why you called the Russians, using a voice you hadn't used in five years. Lippitt *had* a good plan, and that's why you co-opted it. You had to make sure that *you* went along, because that was the only way you could help ensure success. After all, your ex-wife was in there, and you still love her."

Tal made an angry, impatient gesture. "Victor Rafferty is dead, remember?"

I went on as if he hadn't spoken. "The most incredible thing was that trick you pulled off at the consulate. If you did what I *think* you did, it's no wonder everyone's turning the world inside out looking for you." I paused for breath; the excitement and anxiety I felt were making me short-winded. "You knew something was wrong when I didn't show up on time to open the door. You waited until

Lippitt got nervous and started to look around—or maybe you planted the suggestion in his mind. He walked away for a few seconds and you threw back that steel bolt with your mind. Telekinesis. *God*, how that must have cost you! You hemorrhaged, just as you did five years ago when you broke out of that hospital room. There was blood running out of your nose. You'd come up to help me. Finally, there was the way you guided us safely out of that building. You seemed to know where everything was, and what was happening; you even knew that a silent alarm had been triggered. You picked *that* up from the guard."

"Who blew up the boathouse?" Tal asked. "Do you believe Elliot Thomas was kind enough to do that for... Victor Rafferty?"

"Rolfe Thaag took care of that bit of business. He's not young, but he's in good shape, and he'd know about firearms and explosives from his World War Two days with the Resistance."

"The Secretary General is in the hospital."

"Is he? We'll see. I think you had something like this as a contingency plan from the beginning, although having Thomas make his move when he did was an added blessing; you had a real body to put in the boathouse. I'm betting a title search will show that this particular piece of real estate belongs to you personally, to Rolfe Thaag, or even to some U.N. agency. You've both had time to plan this thing and make preparations. My guess is that there's an underground passage leading out of that boathouse into this one or the one next door. Rolfe Thaag sat in there for a while with an unconscious Thomas, trading shots with Lippitt and his men long enough for all the invited guests to show up. Then he left through that underground passage—which I think we'll find with a little digging—to wherever he is now. That's where he operated the boat by remote control. Thomas must have regained consciousness before he was supposed to. Hell, for all I know you may have been able to control the poor bastard from here."

Tal suddenly looked over my shoulder and tensed. "Why don't you join us, Mr. Lippitt?"

There was the sound of footsteps behind me, and I turned in time to see Lippitt step out from the shadows by the entranceway where he'd been listening. He walked slowly into the boathouse and stopped a few yards away from where Tal and I were standing. The agent was carrying a large, ugly pistol which was leveled at Tal.

I felt stricken at the thought that I'd been the one to expose Tal.

no, mongo, you didn't lead him here

It was Tal, reading my thoughts as easily as if they'd been spoken aloud.

lippitt has had his own suspicions for some time

I felt a sudden chill as I realized that Tal hadn't spoken at all; the words—the *thoughts*—had simply appeared in my mind, clear, unmistakable. I looked at Tal in astonishment. He returned my gaze and slowly, deliberately ... winked.

so now you know for certain, my friend i need your help with lippitt, we have a real problem

"That door at the consulate *was* locked," Lippitt said. "It was bolted tight. I tried it. There's only one man who could have opened that door ... *Jesus*, Rafferty! What the *hell* have you been up to for the past five years?"

"You know as well as anyone," Tal said easily. "I've never

247

been out of the public eye, and I think my record speaks for itself. The Secretary General has made continued good use of the information I've supplied him with."

"That's a matter of opinion, Rafferty. Thaag's periodic revelations to the world press haven't always been in the best interests of your country. I believe I've mentioned that."

> don't, *mongo* he'll kill you

I'd been thinking of trying to jump Lippitt.

> good ... *relax as you may have noticed, mr. lippitt does tend to get slightly hysterical where i'm concerned argue my case, if you will, but don't try to move on him he's very, very fast he's on his guard now and his will is very strong if you talk to him, distract him, we may get out of this yet trust me*

"I have no country, Lippitt," Tal said. "You took that away from me. But that's immaterial. The point is that our work at the U.N. has been evenhanded and fair. *People* benefit from what I do."

Lippitt seemed to bow his head slightly. When he spoke, his voice was so low it could hardly be heard. "I ... I've never had a chance to thank you for healing me."

"You showed your appreciation to Victor Rafferty by protecting his wife these past five years," Tal said. "You knew you would get no thanks from her, yet you risked your life to rescue her from the consulate. You're a man of loyalty and honor." He paused, smiled. "*That's* a source of torment even Victor Rafferty can't do anything about."

"What will you do now, Lippitt?" I said.

My voice was too loud, too anxious, but Lippitt didn't

seem to notice. He nodded in Tal's direction. "He knows what has to be done."

Tal wearily shook his head. "No, that's not possible. I won't work for you. Besides, there are complications."

"What complications? Everyone thinks Victor Rafferty is dead."

"Except for Rolfe Thaag and Mongo."

Rolfe Thaag's voice rose out of the darkness at the far end of the boathouse, behind Lippitt. "Yes, Mr. Lippitt. That *is* a problem, isn't it? Will you now have to kill us both?"

Lippitt wheeled and crouched, gun in hand, as the Secretary General stepped out of the shadows. Thaag, like Tal, was dressed all in black. The submachine gun he carried was trained on Lippitt's stomach.

Lippitt was still in a crouch, his gun on Thaag, his eyes darting back and forth between Thaag, Tal, and me. Thaag kept coming, stopped a few yards from Lippitt.

do nothing, *mongo   watch*

"Well, Mr. Lippitt?" There was scorn, mockery in Thaag's voice. He casually tossed the heavy gun off to one side; it landed with a crash and skittered off into the darkness. Lippitt, looking thoroughly puzzled, slowly straightened up.

"Why did you do that?" Lippitt asked in a thick voice. "You could have killed me."

"There's been too much death already. You're so unimaginative, Lippitt, such a fool. *God*, if you only knew how tired I get of dealing with fools." The Secretary General's voice suddenly rose harshly. "Answer me! Do you intend to kill us? And after you kill us, how will you force Ronald to do your bidding? Will *you* kidnap his wife? Will *you* threaten to torture her?"

"*Shut up!*" Lippitt shouted. His voice abruptly dropped

to a rasping whisper. "Damn it, Thaag, what choice do I have?" Lippitt suddenly made a gargling sound and stiffened. "Damn you!" The words were choked, squeezed through jaws that suddenly seemed to be locked tightly together. "*Stop it*! You . . . *can't*! I won't . . . *let* you!"

I looked at Tal. His eyes were closed in concentration; his head was thrust slightly forward, and the veins stood out in his neck and forehead. He began to tremble and grabbed at his head as blood spurted from both nostrils, staining the front of his clothing, spotting the boards at his feet. Still he maintained his concentration. Lippitt seemed caught in the grip of some terrible force. He was obviously struggling with all his strength and will, yet the hand holding the gun slowly, inexorably, came down. The fingers, bent into claws, stiffened, and the gun clattered to the floor.

Hearing about telekinesis and *seeing* it performed were two quite different things. This was the last and most terrifying demonstration I'd seen of Victor Rafferty's powers. Suddenly I understood Lippitt perfectly; I shared his fear. The remote-control assassination of a president could be nothing more than a minor exercise for Victor Rafferty. He could actually *move* men and objects with his mind: I suspected he would have less difficulty exploding a brain, as he'd already done on a hot August morning five years before.

"You miss the obvious alternative," Rolfe Thaag said quietly as he stepped forward and kicked Lippitt's gun away.

Tal relaxed his concentration. At the same moment Lippitt jerked spasmodically and just managed to keep himself from falling. He started after the gun.

"Don't!" Tal snapped. "Next time I'll have to hurt you! I assure you that's easier than what I just did."

Lippitt froze, then slowly turned back to face Tal.

"Ronald has never considered selling himself to the highest bidder," Thaag said. "I am only grateful that I was worthy of his trust five years ago. True, he has been invaluable in diplomatic negotiations . . . but he's also helped hundreds of people the same way he helped you, Mr. Lippitt, without their ever knowing. So, you see, the alternative is to remain silent. You know where he is, and you'll constantly be watching him. That's enough. Let him continue his work. Say nothing to anyone."

Lippitt shook his head. "How do I know—how do *you* know—he won't change? How can I know how he'll feel tomorrow . . . or ten years from now? He'll always be a threat."

"Take a *chance*, Lippitt," I heard myself saying. "For God's sake, take a chance!"

"You'll always know where to find me, Lippitt," Tal said as he wiped the blood from his face. "You'll have to trust me . . . as I'll have to trust you. My life is in the hands of the people in this room."

We stood for a long time in silence. Rolfe Thaag found Lippitt's gun, picked it up, and handed it to him. Lippitt snatched the gun, wheeled with lightning speed, and aimed it at Tal's heart. Tal stood calmly, a smile playing around the edges of his mouth. Then Lippitt abruptly shoved the gun into his coat pocket, turned, and looked at me with a question in his eyes.

Suddenly, for the first time, I felt the full, electric impact of the deadly secret we were being asked to share. Lippitt was emotionally separated from Tal, Thaag, and me; both Lippitt and I would be physically separated from each other, and from the other two. Yet there would be an invisible but steel-strong thread binding us all together for the rest of our lives, a thread spun at once of life and death, trust and suspicion. I was intrigued. And I was afraid.

"It's a good deal," I said to Lippitt. "Take it. I don't plan on saying anything. Not ever."

Lippitt turned and walked out of the boathouse. He didn't look back.

I glanced at Tal. "*Will* he keep it a secret?"

Tal smiled thinly, nodded his head. "He intends to at the moment."

"He could change his mind, come after you."

"Well, yes, he could. But I don't think he will." His smile broadened. "Speaking of reading minds: You'd better go get your brother the steak and drinks you offered him before you walked in here. *There's* a man with questions."

Tal put his hand on my shoulder and we walked together out into the smoky sunshine, while Rolfe Thaag melted back into the shadows.

Meet
Mongo...

part genius, part dwarf, part circus acrobat-
turned-New York detective, he's hot on the trail of
his wildest cases ever!

Don't miss these
MONGO MYSTERIES
by George C. Chesbro

☐ **THE BEASTS
OF VALHALLA** 10484-X $3.95
☐ **SHADOW OF
A BROKEN MAN** 17761-8 $3.50

"Raymond Chandler meets Stephen King."
                                        —*Playboy*

"Mongo remains one of the most appealing
creations in the detective world in some
time."   —*Publishers Weekly*

Dell At your local bookstore or use this handy coupon for ordering:

DELL READERS SERVICE, DEPT. DGC1
P.O. Box 5057, Des Plaines, IL. 60017-5057

Please send me the above title(s). I am enclosing $_____. (Please add $1.50 per
order to cover shipping and handling.) Send check or money order—no cash or
C.O.D.s please.

Ms./Mrs./Mr. _____

Address _____

City/State_____ Zip _____
                                                          DGC1-12/87
Prices and availability subject to change without notice. Please allow four to six weeks
for delivery. This offer expires 6/88.

Special Offer
Buy a Dell Book
For only 50¢.

Now you can have Dell's Readers Service Listing filled with hundreds of titles. Plus, take advantage of our unique and exciting bonus book offer which gives you the opportunity to purchase a Dell book for *only 50¢.* Here's how!

Just order any five books at the regular price. Then choose any other single book listed (up to $5.95 value) for just 50¢. Use the coupon below to send for Dell's Readers Service Listing of titles today!

 DELL READERS SERVICE LISTING
P.O. Box 1045, South Holland, IL. 60473

Ms./Mrs./Mr. _____

Address _____

City/State _____ Zip _____

DFCA - 12/87